DECIMATION

NEON
BOOK SIX

ALLYSON LINDT

ACELETTE PRESS

For everyone who keeps asking me "BUT WHAT NEXT?"

"You can't go back and change the beginning, but you can start where you are and change the ending."

- C.S. Lewis

CHAPTER I
NICO

No matter how many centuries I lived, each one held something new and unexpected to discover.

One of the most recent examples being the man—the god—in our sitting room, in front of the fireplace. Despite the fact that he knew people who could summon light in many forms, Bragi insisted on ensuring electricity ran through our home, and that we had electric lights.

The dim bulb flickered over his shoulder, illuminating his book.

It had taken years for me to admit it to him or myself, but I did adore him. He was smart, creative, stubborn, and he cared.

"You make me nervous when you just stare." Bragi didn't look up from his book.

I chuckled to myself. "I do not. You love it when people stare."

He glanced at me with a raised eyebrow. "That I do. However, I prefer it when you're touching, too." He set his book on a nearby end table. "Join me."

I didn't need to be asked twice, and I crossed the room to settle into his lap.

Bragi wrapped his arms around my waist. "You're worried."

"Yes." It had taken me a while to get used to the fact that there were no secrets with him. In some ways it was disconcerting, having him always know what I was feeling. It was also a relief. There was no reason to hide any of it. "Aren't you?"

He pulled me into him. "Yes. I'm working on a solution, though."

"You do not *solution away* a prophecy." I would laugh at the absurdity of the idea, if the details of the prophecy in question weren't terrifying. One of the reasons I'd locked my heart away from Bragi for years after I met him, was because gods tended to be tied to fate.

It was a cycle. The newest pantheons got too big for their britches, they thought they ruled the world, and destiny came along and took them down a notch. Replaced those who were too cocky with updated variations.

"Perhaps not. However, Vidar has a theory that the outcomes can be redirected." Bragi was definitely cocky, though not necessarily about being a god. There were ancient poems about him though. The bard. The fool. The artist who dared to think he could have it all, and would lose every bit of it, including his power, and his lovers.

Me.

The redheaded woman we'd both seen in our visions, who couldn't possibly exist because she was a Valkyrie and there were no more of those.

Not that the ancient words said any of that in so many words. However, if one spent enough time studying the poems, their meanings typically became clear.

Slightly cloudy.

The cycle had started again. Gods and immortals feared for their lives, and—more important to them—the loss of their status.

I'd never taken issue with Vidar. He was a bit abrasive for my taste. However, Bragi had a literal sense for how honest people were, and if he trusted Vidar, I did as well.

That did not mean I trusted that the prophecies could be overcome. Time had taught me that lesson more times than I could remember.

"Where is Vidar this afternoon?" I leaned more of my weight into Bragi. Vidar was our guest for the next month or so, but he was as prone to wander as Bragi.

Bragi kissed my shoulder through my sleeve. "I'm not enough company for you?" he teased.

"You're quite often more than I know what to do with." Which was the reason I didn't want our guest walking in on us.

Bragi let out a heavy and exaggerated sigh. "He left a few hours ago with an idea. *I must talk to Finn, before I forget.*" He spoke in tone two octaves deeper than his own.

"Any hints as to what his idea might be?" My question was more idle curiosity. Vidar's ideas tended to be structured and intricate, but not creative.

"Not the slightest idea. I assume it has something to do with avoiding the prophecies. I truly think he's got a good plan."

Ahh. "He may. I simply don't wish you to get your hopes up."

"I will try not to." He trailed a light touch down my torso, to tease along the top of my trousers. "I may need to get something else up instead, to numb the disappointment."

I grabbed his hand before he reached my cock, and adjusted my position to face him and straddle his legs. "Are you trying to fuck me, to forget your woes?"

"Absolutely not." He broke free and caught my

hand in a single twist of his, then captured my other wrist as well. "I'm trying to fuck you because I like the sounds you make in the throes of passion."

I smirked. "Then by all means, please continue."

Bragi loosened the laces on my trousers, then captured the back of my neck in a tight grip as he crushed his mouth to mine. The intensity of the kiss was magnified by the wisps of passion flowing through our connection.

He could share a tiny fraction of the emotion he felt. It was something he avoided outside of sex, and even then it was rare. Which made the slivers I felt of my affection mingled with his that much more enticing.

I pushed his shirt up, tugging the loose fabric out of the way to kiss along his neck and down his chest. To tease a nipple with my tongue.

He pulled my face up for more kisses, stealing my breath and a gasp from me. There was a power in this sensual dance. A type of allure I'd never felt elsewhere. Bragi trailed his mouth down my jaw to suck on the tender skin where my neck met my shoulder.

Incredible.

With each touch and moan, his or mine, I grew harder. I felt him stiffen underneath me as well. A reverberation of arousal.

Bragi teased my mouth with his, over and over. Kissing and nipping and sucking my lips, while he trailed his fingers down my chest. His touch through fabric sparked along my senses. This was always intoxicating with him.

When he brushed my cock, I jerked against his touch. When he wrapped his fingers around my rigid shaft, I groaned into his mouth. His slow stroke was a drawn-out torture of the most delicious variety. His soft hand moving up and down, occasionally squeezing and always milking.

I rocked against him, grinding against his erection as pressure built inside me. His touch grew more insistent and so did my movements, becoming a steady hump. He stroked harder and faster, and I reacted in kind. A cyclical build of desire, flowing between us. Making me harder. Making my need swell.

I bucked against his touch, and his cock jerked beneath me. My body tensed with the need for release, and my breathing stuttered.

Climax surged through me, and I spilled as Bragi continued to jerk me. I emptied myself into the space between us, and kept rocking. Kept grinding into him.

His touch was too much against my now-hypersensitive skin, but it also felt wonderful. As did the grunting noises coming from his throat. His cry when he came was music to my ears. His explosion of pleasure from his own physical responses as well as my orgasm.

I collapsed against his chest, not caring about the mess between us.

I should tell him not to have this conversation with Vidar, but I didn't have a reason to offer him beyond instinct.

"Ask me," he said.

I couldn't. Despite knowing he felt what I wanted to say. "I won't let my doubt destroy your chances."

"Our chances," Bragi corrected me. Because the prophecy applied to him *and* his loves.

"Exactly." I had no reason to worry about Vidar's plans. What I'd seen with past prophecy was exactly that—in the past. I wouldn't stop Bragi from trying to save us.

That didn't mean I could stop myself from being concerned.

CHAPTER 2
BRAGI

Pubs. Saloons. Taverns. They were among my favorite things. A place where people could imagine themselves as anything, and share those tales with anyone.

I sat across the table from Vidar, in the one down the street from the house I shared with my love, and let the ambiance wash over me. It was its own form of worship and prayer. Patrons giving thanks to the inspirations that kept them hoping.

"You told me another came true last month." I hated to harp on about the subject, however answers were critical to preparing the rest of us for whatever came next.

Vidar sipped an ale, his stoicism not hiding the disquiet that radiated from him. "Cú Chulainn…"

"Ooh." I winced, not needing to hear more. The once-king had succumbed to madness long ago, but that wasn't to be his final fate. The sisters—the dragons who wrote the prophecies eons ago—saw him losing everything. His family, his kingdom, his life, and any chance he had at redemption.

Experience, a good portion of it Nicodemus's, showed that these things happened in cycles. One prophecy came true and then dozens more, like soldiers falling one after another in a brutal battle. I assumed because most of the collections of tales ended in brutal battles themselves.

I didn't believe that it would all happen tomorrow, or in the next decade or two. This was something that would take place over the next couple of centuries; still a blink in time to some immortals.

"Myself and a handful of others are coming together," Vidar said. "We feel like there's not only strength in numbers, but knowledge. We want to diminish the collateral damage."

Which was a polite way of saying Vidar and others he'd spoken with wished to stay alive. The fear he radiated, the worry at the idea of losing who he was, was potent and genuine.

Not that I blamed him or any god. I had a lot left to experience, especially now that I'd discovered love. Especially because the ancient texts about me involved Nico as well. The man I loved. The man I would obliterate reality for.

"What do you want from me?" I was honored to be invited, but I wasn't a fighter. The other gods he'd mentioned were all warriors. Symbols of battles and wars.

"Your survival." He meant the words.

Hints of other feelings lay underneath, marring the sincerity, but that was the case with everyone. Emotions were as complex as those who radiated them. It was rare for an individual to feel one thing and only one at any given time.

When they did, I had no interest in being near them. A feeling so pure it obliterated all other thoughts was as toxic to me as a patch of poison ivy. It could infect me, blister my soul, and leave me incapacitated for hours or days while I tried to shrug off someone else's heart.

"I'll ask again." It warmed me that Vidar valued our friendship enough to include me in this venture, despite the ego that drove him, and most gods, to want to be the sole survivor. There had to be more to his request, though. "What is it I can do?"

"Research. Reading. Your knowledge of what's come before and your ability to draw out the tiniest but most significant pieces of a tale from those around you."

That was something I could do. "Who else has agreed?" When we'd spoken about this on previous occasions, Vidar had given me the names of others he was talking to, but it wasn't a complete list and most of them hadn't agreed at the time.

"Hel. Morganna, Macha, and Finn. Loki—"

"No." That was enough information for me. "Loki is unpredictable."

"Is he? He wants the same thing any of us do. To live long enough to see what comes after Ragnarök."

That wasn't my concern. "Unlike you or me, his methods can be... arbitrary."

"He can be guided. Nudged."

"Does he truly offer anything that we can't find somewhere else?" The way I asked the question, it sounded as if I'd already made up my mind.

I supposed I had, which meant I had a say in who else I worked with.

"He can be quite persuasive when required. Like any of us, he has a lot to offer."

Unlike most of us, he had experience with destroying another god. I did hope that wasn't a consideration.

There was also a prophecy about Loki that said he'd be brought to his knees by some little upstart of a goddess. Fascinating how each person Vidar had recruited stood to lose something big if the prophecies came true.

Then again, why would those with a bright future want to sign up to stop it from happening? "Count me in."

"Excellent." Vidar grinned, and finished his ale in a single swallow. "Welcome to the board."

The conversation shifted to other topics. Which continents Vidar was frequenting for worship.

With what were the other gods busying themselves.

Though Vidar was staying with us, there was something about the pub setting that made swapping stories more fun. Id enjoyed Vidar's company for centuries, and the ability to simply sit and reminisce was one of the biggest reasons why.

I was riding the high of hope when Vidar and I headed back to the house that afternoon. Vidar retired to his room, and I sought out Nico, who was baking.

He wanted to be happy for me. He wanted to share my enthusiasm.

His worry kept him from feeling the smile he gave me, as he kissed me on the cheek. "How did it go?" he asked.

"Wonderfully." This entire plan was going to be amazing. The things that Vidar had planned... "I know you have your doubts, but this will work out for us. Who knows? Perhaps some day in the future, we'll even meet our redheaded Valkyrie."

Nico frowned. "Most of the time I hope we won't."

"Why?" I could feel his reservations, but couldn't place a reason.

"I'd hate to meet someone like that, only to have her snatched away by a bitter fate."

I gave him a reassuring smile, though I didn't feel it. All the Valkyrie's were gone. "You don't have to believe yet. When it works out, you'll see. You'll know."

~

Now

The most effective lies are the ones founded in the truth.

A century ago, I had no idea then that Vidar's plan, Hel's plan, would mutate to include torture. Brainwashing. Manipulation. Murder. And it never occurred to me that after centuries of what I thought was friendship, Vidar had been manipulating my emotions.

Possibly intentionally, though to this day I doubted it. He was just such a raging fucking narcissist, that any concern he felt, any fear or worry, was all genuine because it was all centered on his own life and salvation.

He believed he was saving the world... for himself.

He believed that *by any means necessary* was the only way to keep himself going.

As the years and decades bled away, the little things that nagged at me about TOM became big things. So many times, Nico begged me to stop. I didn't recognize at the time that feeling the anguish of students day after day was gnawing at me. Wearing away my defenses.

Filling me with the kind of negative emotion that bled from me when I was with Nico. It was why he'd started wearing a crystal that kept me from influencing him.

By the time I figured out that TOM had eaten away at my kindness, I was so tired of feeling, so sick of how sick the world was, that it was easier to hurt —me and those around me—than to wallow in the pain, curl up in a ball, and surrender.

Why weren't Nico and Magnus back yet? Had it been that difficult for him to convince her to return?

I headed outside, and called their names.

Nothing.

Where were they?

The longer I searched, the closer I moved to the border that kept us hidden, the more my concern grew. Did they leave?

It was difficult for me to believe they'd both agree to do that without letting me know.

Did Vidar get them?

The fury and concern that surged inside was potent. I called Magnus's phone. When the other end of the line clicked, I fully expected Vidar's voice. I braced myself, as a plan raced through my head. I'd have to call in favors. I'd have to prostrate myself in front of other immortals and beg for help.

I'd need to—

"Hello." Nico's voice was flat.

Thank you. "Where are you?" I kept my question cool. No reason to expose my panic.

Voices echoed in the background of Nico's side of the call. Dahlia? Okay. Magnus was upset, but she'd gone somewhere safe. Good.

"I've recovered my memories," Nico said.

His even, emotionless delivery knocked the air from my lungs. "That's fantastic." I didn't have to fake my enthusiasm. I was happy for him, though the news may not be good for me.

"It's wonderful." He didn't sound like he meant it. "Don't come near us. Either of us. Ever again."

Fat chance of me listening to that command. "Nico—"

My plea was met with dead air as he disconnected.

Fuck it all.

CHAPTER 3
MAGNUS

I was sitting on the bottom mattress of one of several bunk beds.

Rather, I was looking at six-year-old me sitting there.

TOM. I was on The Order of Mistletoe campus. Or looking at myself there.

Except I didn't get here until I was a teenager.

"Hello?" I tried to push the word out, but no sound reached my ears. I stepped closer to me and reached for her. "Hello?" I said again.

She met my gaze, a haunting look in her green eyes, and opened her mouth.

There was still no sound, but I was assaulted by so many emotions. Too many. All at once, until it was louder than any shout and I couldn't distinguish any individual feeling.

I sat up with a gasp, and my eyes flew open. I was in my room, in my apartment, at NEON. Dahlia and Nico sat by my bed, watching me.

"Please be quiet." I muttered the request before either of them could speak, and before my brain caught up to my mouth.

Nico frowned. "We're not saying anything."

Then how— I pressed my palm to my forehead. "But you are." Their every emotion screamed at me; all of it noise and none of it distinguishable. "Where's Bragi?"

They both scowled.

Now I recognized pity. Distrust. Regret.

That last one was Nico, and I tried to focus on seeing him, rather than letting his emotions live in my skull.

"I left Bragi behind," he said.

"Why?"

"I remembered."

Such a simple response, but it was laden with the noise that screamed at me. What I felt wasn't only Nico, it was the people outside in Bangkok. The people through the gate that led to NEON.

I couldn't think about anything else.

I closed my eyes and named each emotion, labeling a mental box, and shoving the thought onto a shelf in the back of my mind. The same way we'd been taught in school.

The task seemed insurmountable as I picked at the edges of the blob. It should have been worse when Nico's and Dahlia's concern surged, but their reactions gave me a starting point.

Breath through your nose. Shrug it off. Name it and banish it.

I didn't know how long it took before I dared look again. The feels weren't gone, but they were quieter.

"Are you all right?" Dahlia asked, then gave a dry laugh. "Obviously not, but you know what I mean."

"No." My reply came out more sharply than I intended. Now she was hurt. I steadied myself. "I need another few minutes of silence. You don't even have to leave the room." Because it wouldn't matter. I'd feel them regardless if they were nearby.

Dahlia nodded, and after a pause, Nico did as well.

I turned inward again. Boxing these things wasn't working. I didn't have room in my psyche to store and ignore them all, which meant no shortcuts. This had to be done properly.

Would that drive me insane? *Properly* meant admitting each feeling was there, naming it, and letting myself feel it for long enough for it to dissipate.

How was I supposed to feel *everything*?

I clawed my way through enough of the chaos to find my own thoughts in the middle of it all. The methodology quieted the bedlam enough for me to open my eyes again.

"Do you remember anything?" Nico's question was kind.

Was it ironic that *he* was asking *me* that, or just a bad coincidence? "I remember needing you and good sex."

His embarrassment surged.

Where was the crystal from Maeve? "Dahlia knows I fuck. She does too. No secrets here."

Dahlia shrugged. "It's true." She was worried about me. Frustrated that the conversation wasn't the one she wanted to be having, but she wasn't fazed by the topic.

"You kissed me. After," Nico said. "You said you wished I could have back what I was missing, and then I did. Your crystal broke. You screamed and passed out. I couldn't bring you back to Bragi, so I called Dahlia."

"Did you wish his memories back?" Dahlia asked. "Can you do that now?" She poked my cheek and lifted my arm and pried my hands open.

"What are you doing?" I meant beyond trying to lighten the mood. It was odd to feel her intentions, but not know her meaning.

Dahlia looked at me. "If you're a Djinn, you have a magic lamp, right? We destroy it and you don't have to go back." One corner of her mouth tugged up with the attempt at humor.

It was enough for me to laugh. Not a big, loud laugh, but more a sound of relief. "I'm not a genie. Not that I know of."

"Thank the gods." She puffed out a sigh. "I always get jealous of how much better you look in pink than I do."

I missed her. Something else about what Nico said was odd. "You got your memory back. Why did you call Dahlia?"

She stuck her tongue out at me, and I poked her nose. "People usually call someone *they* know. I'm glad I'm here," I said.

"I know villagers. None of them could help you." Nico was more embarrassed by that than by me being open about sex. "I cut ties with most of the world when I left Bragi. Besides, I was calling to get you help, not me."

And going to Bragi wasn't an option. Because Nico had remembered their past. If I was struggling with putting the pieces together from an hour or two of missing time, I couldn't imagine how Nico had dealt. I was surprised he was still coherent.

"How did you bring his memories back?" Dahlia asked.

She was going to hate that I'd left her out of what I discovered, but, "I don't know, but I'll tell you what I do know. So much has happened in the last twenty-four hours. I hadn't made it here to tell you yet."

Dahlia was more disappointed and hurt than angry. "Because you were having sex." But she also understood.

I gave her an apologetic look. "*Good* sex."

"Yeah, yeah. That's fair." She'd already forgiven me.

"I don't know how I did the memories thing," I said. "But apparently I'm a conduit? Like, magic can go through me and into other people, and I'm channeling some of what the babies are, and maybe that was part of what did it. There was a crystal that was helping me control it, and I guess it broke?"

Dahlia squeezed my hand. The gesture should be sympathy. That was what lingered at the surface, but I was hit with a wave of complexity. Her adoration for her men. For me. Her distrust for Bragi. Wanting Vidar dead. Wondering if what was happening to me was Nico's fault.

The onslaught was so potent, I might as well be reading her mind. I jerked my hand away, and Dahlia frowned.

"I'm channeling someone else's power," I repeated. "Empathy."

"Oh. *Oh.*" Dahlia's mouth formed a circle.

Realization spread through Nico, too. As if some things suddenly made a lot more sense.

"That sounds awful," Dahlia said.

"You have no idea." If Bragi had asked me a few months ago if I understood what he felt, I would've said *sure. I know what emotions are like.* But I really couldn't have fathomed this. How did he do it for so long? How did it not drive him insane?

Because he gave up on trying to be sympathetic and reveled in the pain instead.

Like that, I almost understood, and I hated myself for it.

"It's so loud in my head," I muttered as much to myself as her.

"What do we do?" Nico asked. "Send me somewhere and I'll go."

He meant it. He wanted to protect me.

He couldn't, but the sentiment was sweet.

"Maeve said I needed a more permanent solution, to meter my power," I said.

Dahlia was surprised again. "Maeve?"

"She's an elf."

Dahlia stared at me with shock. "According to the books, Queen Mab is a fucking fae queen."

Oh. *Oh.* Why didn't I put those pieces together before? How had I missed who she really was? "Not anymore she's not." And now I wanted to hear that story. "I was hoping maybe Tatiana could help."

Tatiana was one of the first women after me to become a Valkyrie. She was descended from a line of voodoo priestesses and she not only knew magic was real, but practiced it. She was easy to explain the entire thing to, and had abilities that extended beyond a Valkyrie's.

"You call her." Dahlia stood. "I'll go grab your stuff from the cabin, so you don't have to deal with Butt-face Bragi, and we'll go from there."

Great. Wonderful. Not that I had any idea what to do next. "I need to get Tatiana here first. Or me to her. Then maybe I can think."

CHAPTER 4
BRAGI

I left the cabin almost immediately after talking to Nico. No reason to stick around if they weren't coming back. I hitched a ride to the airport, which was where I was now.

I gave a warm smile to the young man working the check-in counter, and handed him my boarding pass. Magnus would probably point out I could've checked in on the internet or at the kiosks, but I wanted the interaction.

"Where are you flying today?" His name tag said he was Tad.

"Detroit. To visit an old friend." Rather, I hoped Anubis would not only see me, but talk to me.

When I left TOM, the board had already crumbled. The only reason the campus still existed was because Vidar had the presence and power to maintain control over many of the remaining soldiers. I hadn't cared what he did, as long as I wasn't a part of it, and Magnus was safe.

Tad's fingers flew across his keyboard. "Just checking the one bag?" He worked with practiced efficiency.

"I prefer to travel light." I preferred not to travel this way at all, but if I was going to stuff myself onto a plane, I wasn't dragging along my entire wardrobe. When I left the cabin, Nico's and Magnus's things stayed behind—they were more capable of retrieving them than I was of returning their luggage. Something had prompted me to leave my journals as well.

I didn't need to relive my past through my words. It haunted me regardless.

Magnus should've been safe from TOM. That was what I'd convinced myself of. She made the decision to walk away, and she and her friends were powerful. I didn't know—how had I never seen it—that Vidar had always wanted her specifically. That keeping and controlling her was a priority?

"Hmm... I get that." Tad glanced at my ID for all of half a second, before returning to his typing. "I have you staying over in Atlanta?"

Not by choice. Whose ridiculous idea was it to route a flight from Jackson Hole to Detroit through Atlanta? "That's right." It was still my fastest option.

I needed Vidar dead. Period. That meant finding someone who could help me figure out the puzzle of killing him, and that meant flying to whomever I tried to work with.

Even with my power I wouldn't have been able to destroy Vidar, unless poetry slamming him to death was an option. And I definitely couldn't do it now. Not alone.

I'd burned so many bridges in the last century though. The list of gods and immortals who wouldn't speak to me was far longer than the number who would.

"You're all set." Tad handed me my boarding pass and ID. "Follow the signs to security and then to your gate, and have a safe flight. Next please." He was already looking past me.

Security was next. Whoever invented this process must be a trickster god, and must be far more powerful these days than they let on. The chaos that existed here... It could feed the right god for eons. Perhaps that was how Loki had stayed relevant after all this time. TSA lines at the airport.

I didn't need chaos, though. I needed a god who was familiar with death. Not just the indirect ones. There were more gods of war than almost anything else, besides sex.

But oddly enough, very few who were directly associated with the dead.

The elemental and elder gods and spirits knew a

lot about death. Like Nico, they weren't death themselves but were experienced with it. But it was difficult to explain to a river spirit, who had only ever seen their own banks and shores and rocks, that some god on another continent was worth any of their attention.

There were other gods from other continents. Africa. South America. North America. A number of them didn't care about the prophecies because they didn't feel like Ragnarök involved them. Min cared because of Kirby.

But that could also work to my advantage. At this moment, I didn't give a shit about the prophecies either. Not the overall reach or what happened when they all came to fruition. Magnus and Nico were my only concerns.

And that meant destroying Vidar.

Anubis. As far as I knew, he didn't take issue with me, and he was still part of this world.

The trick would be convincing him I was the reason he should take a side, and hoping Min hadn't warned him away from me.

Twelve hours, and far-too-long layover later, I stepped from a car in the middle of a neighborhood that could best be described as *in transition*. To the unpracticed eye, one might guess the streets were dying. Several buildings had boarded up windows, fences and overgrown grass surrounded others, and still other lots were simply empty. Dirt or broken concrete where a structure no longer stood.

There were hints of life here, though. Not old, vanishing life. New and full of hope, like the first buds of green, on a flowering bush after a hard winter.

One example was the automotive shop I stood in front of. The classic design was still in place—a windowed garage door that slid up, amid a restored cinder block service station. There was a jackal on the sign, and the place boasted that they could bring any car back to life.

Anubis didn't just deal with the dead, he gave a second chance to both people and things that had their potential taken from them too early. This neighborhood for instance.

He still had a space in the basement where he honored the dead and sent them to the next life. The general public didn't know about it—I didn't suspect most people wanted their automotive restoration shop also conducting mortuary-type services—but it wasn't a secret among immortals.

The garage door was open, and I recognized the 1930's Packard he had on a lift in the air, because I'd owned one a lot like it when they were new. With as much rust as, and more pine needles than, paint this one had seen better days.

There was a dark-skinned man about six inches taller than me, pulling a wheel off the car corpse.

The garage lighting glinted off his smooth head, and his overalls hid the kind of strength only a god could maintain without a lot of work.

Anubis spared me the briefest glance before returning to his task. "Afternoon. Are you in the market for something that reminds you of better days?" His accent hinted at a blend of languages and dialects from the various tribes and countries where he was still worshiped, and his voice was deep and smooth, like the slip of silk.

I had no idea if he was talking about cars or being more figurative. "I wouldn't call anything I've seen in the last century or so *better days*."

"Ah. Something new. Refreshed. You want a different outlook on life." He set the last wheel on the ground, and turned his attention to the newly exposed bits of car.

"I really have more of a question."

"Only one?"

"One to start. There may be others depending on how the first goes." As in, I couldn't tell if he was going to be responsive to this conversation. Things were starting politely enough, but I wouldn't call the exchange friendly. I was going to poke and prod a little more, to see if it was safe to broach my real reason for being here.

Anubis handed me a wrench, and pointed to the car. "You can ask, as long as you help. I need another set of hands."

That seemed fair. I stepped closer, watched as he maneuvered around a large bolt, and then held the tool according to his instruction.

I was startled when he pulled out a large mallet and hammered the metal, sending rust flying everywhere. "I should have worn my raincoat." I tried to keep my tone light.

He chuckled. "You should give me your riddle."

"Have you ever had one of these you can't bring back?" I had a hard time believing that the guarantee on the sign out front was possible under normal circumstances. Not *every* car could be saved.

"It depends on how one defines *bring back*. There are times when the only thing remaining in the new is an original hood ornament or a side window." Another few hits with the hammer, and he seemed satisfied. He wiggled something free that looked like a record or a flat donut, with a handful of rust holes in it.

His answer led me to another question. I'd follow it to see if this went anywhere. "If you do that, is it really the same car?"

"Again, it all depends on how you define it. To me, in that case, it's more of a tribute to the original. A reminder of what it once was. To another person, it's the same as having their beloved back in their garage."

This conversation was moving in the wrong direction, but it had my fascination. If all that remained of Vidar was a pocket watch, I'd find that an acceptable outcome. Then again, we were talking about cars, not gods. "What does it take to reach that point, where so little remains?"

"The rot and decay have to eat through the frame, body, seats, mechanics, and everything else, to the point where no pieces can be salvaged."

I could see how applying that to Vidar would work in theory, but not in practice. "What if the parts are constructed of indestructible materials?"

Anubis stopped his work, set down his hammer, and finally gave me his full attention. "Then I assume that sort of decay doesn't happen. Would you like to ask me your questions directly, rather than deriving meaning that isn't there from our existing conversation?"

"I would."

He took the wrench from me and set it with the other tools, then nodded toward the main building. "Let's go inside." He closed the garage door, flipped a switch to turn off the lights, and we headed in.

There was a small kitchen, decorated with the types of antiques that would make any collector swoon, from a still-running, classic refrigerator, to a shelf filled with glasses in a muted rainbow of colors. Anubis grabbed two glasses. "Would you like some water?"

"Please." I took a seat.

He filled both glasses from the sink, set one in

front of me on a coaster, and emptied his in a single swallow before filling it again. He sat across from me.

"I know a lot of you like your vague questions and innuendo, but the dead don't have any time for secrets or hidden meanings," Anubis said. "Tell me what you're looking for, who do you want to destroy, and I'll tell you whether or not I'm willing to help."

Here went nothing. "Vidar."

Anubis's posture changed in a blink, going from neutral and casual to tense, with a scowl on his face. "I don't have your answers, but I will help you find them."

"Like that? Not that I want to dissuade you."

Anubis clenched his jaw. "Too many souls have crossed my doorstep who never had a chance to realize their potential, because of him."

I supposed it was a good thing I was looking to destroy one of the few gods who had made more recent enemies than I had.

"Your countrymen have more experience with this than I do," Anubis said. "Helblindi, for instance. Have you asked him?"

The name took a moment to register. Some gods used Anglicized versions of our names, and others simply picked new ones to match the era. Helblindi —one of Loki's brothers—was one who had changed his moniker with each new age. Or rather, each new incarnation of the woman he loved.

Last I heard, he called himself Blake now, and he'd managed to keep Luci alive this time. He'd surrendered his power to save her life, and to keep Morgana from killing her.

"I'm not on good terms with Blake." I'd been on the *other side* for too long. "However, after he made Morgana impotent, Vidar gleaned all he could from her and the situation. I believe he's patched all those holes. If he hasn't, I'm not privy to the details from either party."

"Therein lies the problem, I assume," Anubis said. "You're not on good terms with most of them?"

Was I supposed to feel bad that he knew that? Most knew that. "Which is why I've come to you."

Deep lines creased Anubis's forehead as he went silent.

I let him think.

"There was Ga-Gorib," Anubis said. "Thought indestructible, but defeated by being attacked from behind."

I'd heard the stories, but didn't have more details than what Anubis provided. "There may be something there, but I'd need to know more."

"It's been centuries, but there are people I can ask. There are other stories about taking someone's power, but I'll need to look into them."

"Thank you." I couldn't express my gratitude enough. "I'll be staying nearby, available to talk again when you know more."

Anubis looked surprised, but simply said, "I'll be in touch."

The prospect of an answer was promising, but it wasn't enough. Every moment I went without a concrete solution was another moment Nico, Magnus, and our children were in danger.

CHAPTER 5
NICO

Before I left Bragi... Before I met him... Before I withdrew from the world, I was a different man.

It wasn't easy to see while I lived it. My outlook shifted with the calendar, with the decades and centuries, a millimeter at a time. From one day to the next, I saw the same man in the mirror.

When my memories rushed back in a single blob, a few hours ago, every moment I'd lived, regardless of its significance, assaulted me at the same time. I had no sense of how old or new a memory was.

Which was where my surge of fear on Magnus's behalf had come from. Bragi being at TOM, being part of the things those students suffered, was as fresh and new in my mind as the first time I was reborn *and* the most recent time.

I was starting to make sense of some of those

memories now. Realizing that anger was older than the good times I'd shared with him. With Magnus.

That month with Magnus in Bragi's house, where neither she nor I knew what he was hiding, it was at the surface too. I grasped onto it because I recognized it. I recognized her and that it was recent.

When Dahlia returned with our things, I let Magnus tell Dahlia most of what had happened since they last saw each other—it was a big list for just a few days—while I processed the jumble in my mind.

"It's safest if you stay here, both of you," Dahlia said when Magnus was done. "Nico, I'm sure Frey wouldn't mind getting you an apartment. Or..."

Magnus was sitting up in bed now. She grabbed my hand before I could think of an answer. "Or, you could stay with me."

This apartment was nearly as big as my house, and her bedroom certainly had enough space for two people. That wasn't the reason I wanted to take her up on her offer though. With everything right there in my mind, I wanted to be closer to her. "I'd like that."

"Do you need anything else?" Dahlia asked.

Magnus shook her head. "A shower. A good night's sleep."

"More answers that we currently have," I added. Like, how did I remember everything in a blink.

What came next? What had I been doing for the last century?

I knew that answer now, however I wasn't satisfied with what I saw in my mind.

"I can leave you alone to get the first two. We'll regroup for the last one?"

Magnus nodded.

Dahlia gave her a quick hug, and offered me a tight smile and a nod, before leaving.

"You shower first," I said to Magnus. "Your hair will need longer to dry."

She gave a tight laugh. "I have a diffuser on my hair dryer. I adore that the world is falling apart around us, and you're thinking about my wet hair. I'm not going to catch a cold."

"No. It can't be comfortable to sleep on, though."

"It's not. I'll be back in a few, I guess."

As Magnus turned toward the bathroom, a thought stood out among the jumble of memories, and I grabbed her wrist.

At her sharp gasp, I let go.

Her, *sorry* was breathless. "Emotion."

"I understand." Something else I was remembering was how Bragi dealt with the same. "I simply want to say, what you told me in the clearing—that you don't know what we have or where we're going?"

Lines creased her forehead. "Yes?"

"I meant what I said. We have time, and it's not

the most important thing to figure out now, regardless."

"I'm glad. Because I still want to." Magnus gave me a stilted wave. "I'll be out soon."

When Magnus emerged from the shower, I took my turn.

Amidst it all, I struggled to sort the snippets of my past into recognizable images. They merged with the time spent with Magnus and Bragi in the cabin over the last week, and with the way Magnus approached life.

After Bragi, but even before, I'd withdrawn from the world. After centuries of losing friends, it was easier to let humanity and gods be, than involve myself with them.

Had that been the right choice?

When I finished my shower, Magnus was just saying *goodbye* to someone on the phone.

"That was Tatiana," she said. "She does tattoos, and she doesn't know if she can help with what I need to control this conduit thing, but she said we should stop by tomorrow, and she'd see what she could find in the meantime."

"I hope she can help."

Immortals healed instantly from most damage, but magically inflicted scars were a possibility. A lot of tattoos contained the kind of magic that insured they would stay on the most damage-resilient beings.

"Me too." Magnus patted the mattress next to her. "May I ask you something?"

"Of course."

"Why are you still here? Don't get me wrong—I'm glad—but you know who you are. You know where you can hide. Your life was fine before Bragi called you to revive me, and ever since..."

Ever since, I'd been enmeshed in chaos. The sort of trouble I had intentionally steered clear of. "It's been a long time since I enjoyed someone's company as much as I do yours."

"It's not just because the sex is good?" she teased.

The talk of sex didn't embarrass me because I was ashamed of it. It had been a long time since I had a physical connection with someone, and I didn't know how I'd ignored that need for decades. "The sex is not the reason, but I do enjoy it."

The twist of her lips made me think she was looking for more of an answer. Or perhaps I simply wanted to give one. "A lot of lives run together when you've been around as long as I have." That sounded cold, rather than reassuring. "You'll understand in a few hundred years." That was dismissive.

Magnus shook her head. "I hope I never understand that."

"Me too." The answer slipped out before I could consider it.

She tugged at the blanket and crawled halfway under. "Keep me company tonight?"

I slipped under the quilt, and she snuggled into my arms the instant I stopped moving. She was warm. Soft. Vulnerable for someone so strong.

I wanted to wrap her up and hide her from the rest of the world. Was this what Bragi felt?

I couldn't excuse his actions, and his name made me miss when I'd had this with him.

He wasn't here now, Magnus was. I would hold her as long as she let me, and I would ignore the whisper in my mind of *the last time I had this...*

I didn't sleep much, even after Magnus drifted off next to me. With the silence around me, I had time to sift through my memories. To grab at some and try to make sense of others. It was a slow process, one I didn't expect I'd ever complete, but putting some order to the pieces was necessary to keep me from losing my mind.

I dozed fitfully, but full consciousness returned early in the morning. It was too easy to lay in bed, holding Magnus, so I did.

When she stirred a few hours later, I couldn't help but watch her wake up. That slow climb toward consciousness where her breathing shifted. She moved, but didn't pull away from me. She stretched and slowly opened her eyes.

"What?" She asked the moment she saw me.

I gave her a smile. "Simply enjoying the view."

She pushed up onto her elbows, and poked my nose playfully. "Watching people sleep is creepy."

"For the person sleeping. For me it was perfectly acceptable," I teased.

"You're right, you are different than before." Magnus sat up and stretched again, elongating her entire torso, and giving me a stunning show when her shirt stretched tightly over her breasts and stomach.

I didn't pull my gaze away, and I didn't try to hide the staring. "In a good way, I assume."

"Dunno yet. We'll find out." At the sound of a knock from the front door, she wrinkled her nose. "Get that?"

"You want me to answer the door in your apartment?"

"It's almost definitely Dahlia. It's not like the folks are dropping by unexpec..." She trailed off with a frown. "Yes, please."

"As you wish, my mistress." I climbed from the bed and gave her a deep bow.

That earned me a tiny smile, and I pocketed the expression as I went to see who was visiting.

The moment I opened the door, Dahlia slipped past me. "Is she still sleeping? *Get up lazy bum*," she shouted.

"She's awake. She wanted a moment to get decent."

"By *get decent* he means pull my hair out of my

face." Magnus emerged from her room wearing the same camisole and shorts she'd slept in, but her wild curls were now restrained. "You're so noisy."

Dahlia stuck her tongue out. "You're so lazy. I want coffee."

"So you should have brought us some." Magnus's tone was still light. The entire exchange could sound crabby under other circumstances, but the women's smiles and lilting tones made me think this was a typical, fun exchange for them.

Dahlia strolled past both of us. "Am I going to see anything I don't want to? Too bad. Should've hidden it." She walked into Magnus's bedroom without pause.

Magnus followed to the doorway, and paused, watching the room.

"Get dressed." Dahlia tossed something, and Magnus caught it without hesitation. Another something followed, and then a third.

Magnus stripped off the top she'd slept in, and pulled on a sport's bra. There was no hesitation on her part. No glance back at me. "Still wondering where the coffee is," she said as she buttoned up the shirt she'd been thrown.

"I'm thinking Seattle." Dahlia emerged from the shadows of the room to join us.

I had seen close friendships before, but this was unfamiliar. How had I gone eons without witnessing a dynamic like this? It was a closeness even most lovers didn't have.

Why didn't you call someone you know? Magnus asked me that last night. A simple question, but it nagged me now.

She dropped her shorts, stepped out of one leg, and used the other leg to kick them into the air and catch them. She tossed her discarded clothes across her room, to land in a hamper against the wall, then shimmied into the jeans Dahlia had provided.

This wasn't the struggling, sad woman I knew from when she was recovering at Bragi's. And the traces of paranoia I'd seen on being reintroduced a few days ago had been tucked away as well.

As with me comparing myself to my past, this was a different Magnus. I liked each aspect of her, but I wanted to know more about this one.

"If we're going to Seattle for coffee, are either of you concerned about being out in public?" I hated to be the disruption in this conversation.

Dahlia looked at me. Stared. Several seconds passed, and she raised her eyebrows.

Magnus glanced over her shoulder. "I assume everyone will stare if you go out like that."

What? I— Right. I climbed out of bed to answer the door, which meant I was in nothing but my boxers. "I should also dress."

Magnus grabbed Dahlia's hand, tugged her out

of the room, and moved both of them out of the doorway. "We'll wait." Magnus said.

"But not long," Dahlia called as I closed the door between us.

"He doesn't know us yet." Magnus's retort was still audible. "He thinks this is weird."

She could feel my emotions. I was used to that from Bragi, but not her. "Not in a bad way." I raised my voice enough to be heard.

Dahlia laughed. "See? Besides, he needs to get used to it. Hurry and get dressed," she called. "I'm hungry."

I saw no reason to argue. In fact, doing so might be dangerous. I quickly pulled on some clothes and rejoined Magnus and Dahlia in the living room.

Magnus hooked one of her arms through mine and the other through Dahlia's, and a blink later, we were in a new location. The protective shield the two kept around us was a faint shimmer barely visible to me.

We stepped into a building that radiated comfort and familiarity, though I'd never been here before. The scents of roasted coffee and fresh pastries rushed around us.

Magnus wore a bright smile as we strode to the counter. She looked at ease. Happy.

When I walked away from Bragi, it was because he'd cut himself off from caring. He'd withdrawn into himself and the pain he felt around him, and I couldn't watch it. I couldn't be with someone who would do that. What I did instead... Was it that much different?

"What are you having?" Magnus and Dahlia asked each other at the same time, and then laughed.

"I don't know." Magnus looked at me. "What are you having?"

"Black coffee."

Dahlia made a rude noise with her lips. "You're such an adult."

I was unsure where the insult was. "As are both of you."

"Nah." Magnus wrinkled her nose. "We're in our early thirties, but we're definitely not adults."

I didn't understand, but she seemed confident in her answer.

There were a lot of things I no longer understood about the world around me, and it hadn't bothered me before. Now, I wanted to learn.

Bragi wasn't the only one who had pulled back from the world. I had too. After seeing so many people come and go in my lifetime, with Bragi being the most recent disappointment.

Unlike what he did, I didn't turn to hurting others in order to punish myself.

No. My inaction cost others their lives though.

"I've got it." Magnus's cheer was a contrast to

my darkening thoughts. "I want the chocolate frap, extra whip, and salted sprinks."

"Ooh." Dahlia continued to study the menu. "That sounds good, but I want cinnamon instead of sprinks. And a cinnamon roll. Or a fruit tart. Or a blueberry muffin. *Fuck.*"

"I could get the tart, and you get the muffin. We'll share," Magnus said.

This was something I knew and enjoyed. Sharing food and mealtime with friends. "The cinnamon roll does look delicious."

"It's decided." Magnus tugged me toward the counter. "And don't worry about the other thing— you can have your black coffee today, but we'll figure out how to undault you."

"How will you know you've succeeded?" I asked as Dahlia ordered.

I handed the cashier money when she gave us the total.

With the last week fresh in my mind, and my entire past near the surface, I couldn't help but examine who I was over the centuries. Magnus explaining Star Wars to me... Watching it with her... My memory of flying a few days ago as if it were for the first time blended with the early days when flight was still an incredible rush.

I missed that appreciation for the world around me. That love of life that I saw in Magnus.

Dahlia pointed toward tables outside. "You'll

know you've been unadulted when you stop worrying about pants when you go out."

"Trousers are important." I wanted to understand. I truly did.

"Who needs pants when you have legs like these?" Dahlia gestured down, past the bottom of her skirt.

I glanced at her and then myself. "I don't have legs like those. I do need pants."

"Don't sell yourself short." Magnus tugged on my waistband, pulling me closer. "I think you have sexy legs."

When Magnus and I were getting to know each other, when we were staying with Bragi, she'd spent more than one night *remembering* Dahlia. She'd told me Dahlia's biological parents were Skuld and Vidar.

I had to imagine that for Vidar, seeing this was what Dahlia became, he must have been so furious.

How wonderful for Dahlia.

The two of them kept up the back and forth while we took our food, and found a table outside in the sun. We set the three different plates of food in the center of the table, so that we could all reach.

Magnus plucked a strawberry from the fruit tart.

"It tastes better if you eat it all together," I said.

"I'm not the one eating it." She pressed the strawberry to my lips.

I was wrong. This would be delicious. I drew the

fruit into my mouth, along with her finger, licking enough to tease before releasing her.

Magnus's giggle was sweeter than the strawberry.

"Hey. Third wheel here." Dahlia smudged frosting onto Magnus's cheek.

Magnus reached for a napkin. "But you love to watch."

"I love to *be* watched. Hugely different," Dahlia said.

I grabbed Magnus's wrist before she could wipe the frosting away, and leaned in to press my mouth to the mess. I licked the sticky sweetness away.

Magnus's sigh was contentment where Dahlia's was frustration.

"You're so pouty." Magnus plucked a crumble and blueberry from the muffin and ground it into Dahlia's nose.

Dahlia's tongue slid between her lips, growing longer and snakelike as she extended it up, to lick the tip of her own nose clean. Then she stuck her shifted tongue out before it vanished into her mouth.

This was ludicrous, and I wanted to experience more of it. I'd ignored this part of life for so long, and I couldn't any longer.

Bragi was right about one thing—Magnus was a bright light in the middle of the bleakness, and she made me want to live again, rather than just existing.

When we were done with breakfast, we headed to New Orleans. The building was similar in size to my house, with wooden shutters open wide. The paint on the shutters was chipped and peeling, as were the layers of stucco, revealing the different colors the shop had been over the decades. The sign over the door proclaimed *Real Voodoo* in neon red letters.

"I thought you were getting a tattoo," I said.

Magnus quirked her mouth in a half-smile. "We are. Tatiana is a woman of many talents."

"Is she someone you went to school with?" I'd known probably longer than these two that the gods at TOM were doing horrific things. Known and turned away. Blamed Bragi for perpetuating it, but ignored it myself. Meeting the people it impacted drove that point home.

Dahlia shook her head and pulled us inside. "No. She's fucked up in her own way."

"Who is?" The woman behind the counter was about the same age as Magnus and Dahlia. She had dark skin, and was nearly as tall as I was. Slender, and statuesque. The shimmer around her was as chaotic as the shop interior.

I ducked under the assortment of masks and other trinkets that hung from the ceiling.

"You are," Magnus said. "Hey, girl."

The woman grinned and stepped from behind a counter covered with corked bottles in various shapes and sizes. "Hey, yourself." She pulled Magnus into a quick hug and then Dahlia.

Tatiana stepped back to take a second look at Magnus. "You're pregnant."

"Fuck me, can everyone tell?" Magnus sounded exasperated.

"I don't know about everyone, but I can see two other faint auras, and *oh my God, congratulations.*" Tatiana finished with a squeal. "Can I say a prayer for them? To protect them?"

Odd request for someone who knew gods were real.

Magnus scowled. "Prayers don't work."

"Agree to disagree," Tatiana said.

Magnus's nostrils flared with her exhale. "This is a matter of whether or not I believe. We all know gods. We know—"

"If you don't believe, then it doesn't hurt you." Tatiana's voice softened. "Let me do it for my own sanity?"

"For the record, I hate that argument," Magnus said. "But you're awesome, so if it will make you feel better okay."

Tatiana hovered her hands over Magnus's stomach, and her mouth moved in silent words. The faintest glow radiated from her hands, vibrant green and soothing. When Tatiana pulled her hands away, she turned to me.

"Who's the pretty boy?"

I extended my hand. "Nicodemus. You can call me Nico."

As she shook my hand, and a blank look settled on her face. She shook it off with a furrowed brow, while studying me. "You've lived a lot of lives."

"You can see that?"

"In a way. Mostly I sense it."

"He's a phoenix," Magnus offered. "Nico, Tatiana is a Valkyrie."

Fascinating.

"Pleasure to meet you, Mister Phoenix," Tatiana said, then turned to Magnus. "You're here for you, though."

Magnus nodded. "Can you do it?"

"It took some digging to find what you were asking for, but yes." Tatiana nodded toward a beaded curtain.

I took in as much of our surroundings as I could as we headed through the shop. The craftwork in figurines and bottles and masks was stunning and unique, and the scents were potent. Chatter drifted in from the street and combined with a music barely audible through hidden speakers.

I'd been hidden away for so long that this was all new to me.

In the next room, Tatiana set Magnus up in a

large chair, and indicated that Dahlia and I could take seats on a bench by the wall.

"These won't stop what you're experiencing with the power surges," Tatiana explained while she arranged her workspace. "They're more like a leaky faucet. I need the right side of your neck exposed."

Magnus undid the first few buttons on her shirt and slipped it down her shoulder, showing off her long, elegant neck. "That's not encouraging."

"I'm looking into something stronger, but this will make a difference for now. You'll still have control over what gets through. It'll keep you from dealing with a non-stop onslaught." Tatiana scooted her chair up to Magnus, and prepped the area for the tattoo. "The glyphs are meant to stop a smaller power, rather than being for someone hosting two other magical entities."

She meant the babies.

Magnus's nostrils flared with the deep breath she took. "Understood. Let's do it."

Tatiana used a pen to draw a series of glyphs onto Magnus's skin, while glancing between her phone screen and her human canvas. I didn't recognize the symbols, but I knew enough about various written languages to see the precision in Tatiana's work.

A pale glow buzzed around her tattoo gun as she began the actual inking. While she worked, we all chatted. Banal conversation at first. How had everyone been? Had anyone seen or read anything good lately? Why was Magnus deciding now to do this?

The longer we talked, the more Tatiana's accent changed. What started as if she'd learned to talk from a Hollywood movie had more of a French or Cajun twang to it.

"...and then Vidar..." Dahlia trailed off with a frown, and Magnus clenched her jaw.

"You need to relax the neck, Boo." Warning slid into Tatiana's voice.

Correction—distinctly Cajun. Something I saw with older immortals was that some adopted the accent or dialect of whatever region they were in, to keep a low profile. However, when they were around friends, they would slide back into their preferred language.

It made me a bit sad for this young woman that she'd learned that lesson so early.

Magnus drew in a few breaths, and the tension visibly faded from her body.

"Anytime y'all talk about homme, y'all be boudein'," Tatiana said. "Co faire? Dahlia tells me. Magnus stops talking so I can work."

Dahlia blew out a noise raspberry. "Short version? He's an asshole god."

"Gonna need a few more details than that." Tatiana was focused on her work again.

"He was one of our teachers in school," Dahlia

said. "He had that kind of air around him that made people flock to him and follow him. He never hesitates to use it. Turns out he's a power-hungry asshole who's willing to roll over anyone and everyone to get more power."

"What's he doing with it?" Tatiana glanced over her shoulder at Dahlia for the briefest moment.

I knew what he'd told Bragi, but wasn't sure if it was reality, or just another story. "He used to say he wanted to turn the world into the paradise it used to be."

Tatiana snorted. "I don't get it. How does a guy like that get so many people to follow him? Not judging y'all, but I also am. How does a zeerah vieux like that convince anyone he's a podna?"

I wasn't familiar with the words she was using, but I could guess her meaning well enough to mostly fill in the blanks. She thought Vidar was bad, and didn't know how he'd tricked people into thinking otherwise.

Dahlia worked her jaw. "It's weird to say now, but he's charismatic. Attractive. Confident..." She didn't sound certain of anything she was saying.

"Still dun buy it," Tatiana said.

It was difficult to explain to someone who hadn't been there, but I was willing to try. "I've known him for a long time. I never called him *friend*, but for centuries, he was good friends with the man I loved."

Magnus flinched.

Because of the reminder of Bragi, or Vidar's influence, or something else?

"Vidar doesn't walk up to anyone and introduce himself by saying *I want to destroy the world you know and you're going to help*," I said. "Not unless he's given up on making an ally of you, and he wants you to think he no longer sees you as a threat."

Tatiana sighed and shook her head. "I still don't get it."

I hadn't either. Not for a long time. I currently had a unique perspective that allowed me to explain Vidar's draw better than I ever wanted to.

CHAPTER 6
MAGNUS

I didn't like talking about Vidar this way, because Tatiana was right—I should've seen it from the start. How manipulative he was. How horrible he was.

But I'd been sucked into the stories he wove about a better world, and how we'd help build it. I wanted so badly for what he described to be real that I was willing to excuse red flags. It was easy to see looking back, but hindsight and all that.

That same knowledge I had now made it hard for me to excuse my actions then.

It also made me wonder... Was I making the same mistake with Bragi? Trusting him again and again?

No. Because I didn't trust him now.

I wanted Nico to explain this in a way that let me

forgive myself for the past, but that didn't seem likely.

"Talking to Vidar when he considers someone necessary is similar to the way we're all talking now," Nico said. "He's warm, friendly, and sympathetic. He's good at reading a person and determining what drives them, and a master at using that for his own gains."

That was all accurate. I could agree.

Nico continued. "As I understand it, you're a Valkyrie because you chose to be."

I'd explained how I got my power when we were staying with Bragi. When I was recovering. When I thought Dahlia was dead.

"Kirby said *you can be this* and you said *yes*. Why?" Nico asked.

Tatiana hesitated from the briefest moment, her gun poised above my skin. She resumed her work. "It's complicated."

"Give me one reason." Nico's tone was coaxing rather than commanding.

Though the rapid-fire jabs from the needle were painful, I welcomed them. They kept my mind off the jumble of emotion around me, and the way it polluted and amplified my own feelings on a complicated subject. If we were sitting around a table having this conversation, I'd be climbing out of my skull from ambient feelings.

"The world is a shitty place." Tatiana lifted the

gun long enough to move to a new spot. "A lot of people make it shittier by only caring about themselves. The more of us who are acting in opposition to that, the better things get."

Nico's mood shifted toward contemplative at the words. He'd been doing that a lot today.

I couldn't agree more with Tatiana.

"Let's say you're working the front counter, and a customer comes in," Nico said.

Tatiana let out a tiny snort. "This Vidar vieux? Old white man in a fancy suit? I'm kicking his ass to the curb before he can say a word."

"No." Nico shook his head. "A woman. She's older than you, but not *old*. Maybe twenty years? She looks like you. She talks like you. Her mannerisms and actions make you think her life has been similar to yours, or that she's from a neighborhood like this one. As she chats with you, her stories are like those of the people around you. She's familiar with their suffering, and the reasons why it's different from other people's."

Tatiana's grip tightened where she was holding me in place by the shoulder, and her emotions surged. She understood the image he was painting, but she was pushing back against it.

I wrapped my hand loosely around her wrist, and tried to focus on reassurance. Was that possible? I wasn't sure, but she relaxed her grip and continued to work.

Nico watched us the whole time, the concern on his face not offering nearly as much insight into his thoughts as the sympathy spilling from him. "She doesn't ask you to give her anything or to join any cause. She's a paying customer, looking for a way to help a friend. Maybe a prayer for grief. A tincture of comfort. *Whatever you recommend*, she says. You sell her the appropriate items, and she goes on her way."

"Where are you going with this?" Tatiana's voice was hard, to mask self-doubt.

Nico held up a finger. "I'm getting there. She comes back a few weeks later. You may not even recognize her at first, because she was simply another customer. She wants to thank you for your help, and says you have a true gift."

"I do."

"She wants to know about it," Nico said. "About you. She's not asking you anything invasive, and never too many questions at once. She becomes a regular customer and gets her answers through casual conversation each time she comes in. You're not doing anything different than you normally would. You're genuine and kind. Most of what you tell her comes back to the fact that you do this job, so you can help people with your gift."

I didn't care for how close to home some of this hit. The setting for Nico's story was different, the details varied, but the idea was too much like what I'd gone through. It reminded me of how I was sucked into the lies at TOM, and why I was willing to let Dahlia go for a short while, to side with Vidar.

"Dahlia was never sucked into his lies." Tatiana's reply was defensive. If Dahlia didn't buy in, Tatiana would know better too.

Dahlia let out a sharp laugh. "He didn't think I was worth using, so he never put that kind of effort into winning me over. He was never cruel to me. It was more of an indifference."

"Which is the way he treated me, as well," Nico said. "For the purposes of this hypothetical, though. Tatiana begins to look forward to this customer's visits. They're random, but friendly. A nice break in the day. Sometimes she buys something for a friend—never for herself—and other times she was just thinking of Tatiana and wanted to say *hello*.

"This goes on for a year. Then two and three. One day, she's not acting like herself when she visits. She's distraught. It takes some work to find out what's going on, because she's reluctant to admit it. She's sick. You want to help, and surprisingly enough, you know the right spell. She refuses—*I'll be fine*. You insist. *I can do this for you. You do so much for others, let me help just this once.*"

As Nico told the tale, his voice shifted an octave higher to indicate other voices. Did he know that Bragi's influence shone in his storytelling?

Tatiana finished her work, and wiped away the excess fluids.

"Am I done?" I could still feel everyone.

She shook her head, and hovered her fingers over the fresh ink. My skin tingled, then heated to scalding in the impacted area, and then the sensation was gone.

So were the emotional voices. "It's so quiet in my head." I didn't mean to say that out loud. Empathy that had overwhelmed me before was a muted background noise now. Like freeway noise from a house several miles from the road.

"That's the point." Tatiana snapped a photo and showed me on her phone. She'd crafted a stunning piece that was mostly runes, but she'd intertwined them into an intricate pattern. "What do you think?"

I reached for the fresh design, but didn't touch it, while I examined the picture of her work. "It looks freaking epic, but I love it more because it's working."

"This time I mean it when I say don't move." For the next few minutes, Tatiana cleaned the fresh art more completely, prepped it, and taped plastic over it.

With the external noise gone, I could hear myself more clearly, including the fact that my stomach was grumbling. Didn't I just have breakfast—I glanced at the clock on the wall—hours ago, apparently. Oops.

"*Now* you're done." Tatiana kicked her rolling stool out of the way, stepped back, and offered me a hand up.

I accepted, bracing myself for the wave of whatever she was feeling. It was a whisper rather than a roar. I could deal with that. "Do you want to go with us to get some lunch?"

"Will Nico finish his story?" she asked.

Nico nodded. "I will."

"Then fuck yes. I'm gonna introduce y'all to real Jambalaya. What happens with the regular customer who forces me to drag the truth out of her about being sick?" Tatiana turned to watch us while she walked backwards out of the room. "I'll navigate, while pretty boy tells us what happens next with my selfless, sick customer."

Nico raised his brows, but fell into step with Dahlia and me.

"Despite her protests, you insist you want to help. You tell her she does so much for others. She should let you help her, just this once," Nico said.

"I'll be back after lunch." Tatiana waved to another woman behind the register, never looking behind her, but not hitting anything as she continued to walk backwards out of the shop. "I'm not falling for a manipulation like that. She's not getting me to drag that information out of her."

Nico shrugged. "Aren't you? After three years of this woman being nothing but friendly? You're not looking at it from the perspective of hindsight. You're telling me you can't think of a single customer right now who meets this description, who you'd help if they needed it?"

Tatiana twisted her mouth. "I'd rather not."

"They're not all like that. Most of them never will be." Dahlia spoke with a kind of certainty that was reassuring. When did she get comfortable with not all people being assholes? "It's not on you for liking them. For trusting them. They deserve it. This is on the one person who takes advantage of you for it."

She made it sound so simple, but she knew as well as I did, it wasn't that straightforward. The guilt was always there, looming in the background. *Why didn't I see it? Why didn't I know better? With Vidar. With Johnny. With Bragi...*

He was different.

Is he?

This wasn't supposed to be my introspection. I shook aside questions I didn't have answers to, and followed Tatiana and the others into a restaurant that was mostly a long counter with a line of people crowded inside. Tatiana knew a lot of the people behind the glass divider, and waved at them while she shouted out, "Four plates. Four Cokes."

The order echoed through the kitchen as one person called it back, another repeated it, and then another. We moved forward with the line, when we reached the end, the woman at the register pushed four takeout boxes and four styrofoam cups toward us.

"Let me." Nico pulled out his wallet, and no one protested. The three of us women had learned many times—never complain when someone with more than a century under their belt wanted to grab the tab.

Each of us grabbed a box and a drink, and we found an empty table out on the sidewalk. The plastic fixture wasn't meant for this many people, and we balanced our food on our knees as much as on the tabletop.

"Dig in," Tatiana said.

We all did. That first bite of food hit my tongue, and the combination of flavor from spices and meat and vegetables made my stomach growl for more. "Fuck me, this is good." I shouldn't have said that with my mouth full, but I was too busy shoving another forkful in to care.

"And you'll never want it from anywhere else again." Tatiana looked smug. She ate more slowly, like a normal, not-starving person. "I assume this woman in the story eventually lets me heal her. That's the point, isn't it? Then what? She asks for favors again and again?"

Nico washed down his food with a sip of drink. "Possibly, but most likely not. You heal whatever it is that's contaminating her. You remove what you think is a tumor. Maybe you think that's all you've done. Perhaps you figure out that instead of curing her, you've removed the seal that someone put in place to keep her manifesting her full power."

Tatiana started coughing. She shoved her food fully onto the table, hacking until she took several swallows of soda. As the fit calmed, she cleared her throat several times. "No. I couldn't have."

"That's how Vidar works." Nico's tone was somber. "If you realize and kick him out, he got from you what he wanted. If you don't figure out the truth, he'll be back. He's still your friend. He can afford to play the long game. It's been a few thousands of years, and he's patient. He will drag out a *friendship* like that for centuries. Though, when it comes to working with younger people, students for example who are psychologically and physically tortured on a regular basis, it's easy for him to play what I believe you call *good cop*."

Tatiana looked at me. "I'm sorry you went through that."

Seeing Vidar's behavior pulled apart this way didn't make me feel any better about having fallen for it. "It doesn't matter. Now that I—we—see him for what he is, we're going to destroy him." Speaking of... My fingers drifted to the new marks on my neck. "I don't suppose you can teach me to do this with him, but with the snap of my fingers?" Muting Vidar's power would be a huge plus.

"It doesn't work that way. I'm sorry," Tatiana said.

"Hold on a moment." Nico frowned. "You're not going to fight Vidar in your condition."

I scoffed in disbelief. "Say what? *My condition?* I'm not suddenly incapacitated."

"You are pregnant though," Tatiana said.

Unbelievable. She was taking his side? "And you *blessed* me."

"They have a point." Dahlia sounded apologetic.

I looked at each of them with a scowl. "I'm not letting this go another eight months. He's a threat *now*. He's coming after us *now*."

No one had a comeback for me. The painful silence that settled around us as they all shoved food in their mouths was as loud as any shout.

"Are you kidding me with this?" I wasn't letting the topic die.

"We can hide. We can keep you safe." Nico made it sound as if his suggestion was perfectly reasonable.

Fuck me. "*No*, we can't. He always finds us. He's actively looking for either me or Dahlia right now, and at this point I'm not sure which, but it doesn't matter. Besides..." I shouldn't say this, but I was going to anyway. "I'm at my strongest right now."

"No." Tatiana clipped off the word. "You can't draw on power that way. That's like eating yourself from the inside out."

I didn't appreciate the visual. "It's not. What's the alternative? Give me a real solution other than this."

More silence, and I pushed back from the table in frustration.

The air shifted. I wouldn't have felt it if I weren't focused on the lack of input from my friends.

My brain didn't explain what I was feeling until Vidar placed a hand on the small of my back. My lunch surged up my throat and I swallowed it back.

"Here you are." His voice was smooth and calm.

CHAPTER 7

MAGNUS

My skin was going to crawl off my body and slither away. Vidar kept me between my friends and him, and his hand hovered over my lower abdomen. Power radiated from his palm, not hurting me—yet—but potent enough I didn't have any trouble identifying the threat, even through the fresh marks on my neck.

This was a fear like I'd never known. I couldn't lose Dahlia again, and if he took my children away...

I was ready to do whatever he asked, but I swallowed my plea. All my questions. I wouldn't offer what he wasn't looking for.

"How did you find us?" Nico asked.

I hid my wince. It was a simple question, and one I wanted the answer to, but it meant giving him something. Our curiosity. Our attention.

There was no reason to wait around for the

answer. I met Dahlia's gaze, and she fiddled with the pendant around her neck. It was something we learned as an assassin team. An unspoken language of agreement that was as much instinct from working together as anything.

She was ready.

I bit my bottom lip and grasped at Nico and Tatiana. She would be doing the same. In a blink we'd be back at NEON.

But there was something keeping us here. An invisible bubble outside of ours.

"Don't do that." Vidar's tone remained conversational. "I simply wish to talk. You never want to talk."

"Maybe because you keep trying to kill us." Dahlia looked like she was in a casual posture, but I saw the tension coiling through her. The way her eyes slid from place to place, looking for an out. I was doing the same.

Vidar made a *tsk* sound. "It's not me hunting you, it's the prophecies. You know that."

"But it's not." Dahlia said. "I know exactly the opposite."

Because as a dragon, she had the visions too. The same mental images that her aunts had, so long ago, that told them what the future held.

However, unlike them, Dahlia had proven the visions weren't always real. Our futures weren't written in stone, and the prophecies could be defied.

"I won't hurt anyone—not all of you, not the children, and not any innocent bystanders—if you hear me out." Vidar actually meant that? Bullshit. "To answer Nicodemus's question, your shields work wonders, Dahlia. Skuld would be proud of you."

Dahlia scowled. "Fuck you, Daddy."

Vidar grunted, and I felt the slightest whisper of displeasure.

Thank anyone listening that I couldn't feel more of him.

"The shields create a void wherever you are. So if one knows where to look..." Vidar trailed off. "To be honest, it took you longer to show up here than I calculated."

"Look at us, we're talking." I didn't want to hear him yammer on. Not ever again. The only thing Vidar loved more than power was the sound of his own voice. If he was talking, we had time to think. Not that we'd ever come up with a good plan before, but this was a better option than surrendering immediately. "We're listening even."

He pressed into my back. "Come with me, Magnus."

Gross. "I don't do that anymore."

"I get so *sick* of your fucking sarcasm." When he emphasized a word, he came down hard on the syllable, making me jump involuntarily. "Both of you. Why the *fuck* can't you take—" Vidar cut himself off with a sigh.

I kept my gaze locked on Dahlia. I needed the focus. I needed to not see Nico's concern or how badly Tatiana was taking this. And if one of us had an idea, I'd see it on her face or she'd see it on mine.

Vidar trailed light fingers over the plastic covering my new tattoo. "Does this skillful design mean you know who you are? What you can do?"

He *did* know I was a conduit. How long? Was his discovery recent, or had he kept it from me when I was younger?

"I can't do anything more than your basic Valkyrie." As I responded, inspiration struck, and I shot Dahlia a *be ready* look. Could I tug on Vidar's power? I'd seen Bragi's. Touched it. Could I do the same here?

I focused on his presence. On feeling the energy that slipped from him, rather than on his touch. "Haven't you heard?" Keeping up my half of the conversation was important so he didn't know I was up to something. "I'm the least useful of any of us." I didn't need to fake the bitterness in my voice, as the words attached to a very real insecurity.

Vidar's hot breath hit my skin, and I swallowed a retch. He dragged his nose up the side of my neck. "Oh, but you're so much more than that. Would you like to hear a story?"

"Not really." Dahlia slipped her foot closer to

Tatiana and her hand was closer to Nico's than before, but her movements looked incidental rather than intentional. "It's a little late in my life for you to try to win me over with bedtime fairy tales."

I swore I felt Vidar's smirk.

"Good. Because I'm so excited to share."

Honestly, their antagonistic relationship—Vidar and Dahlia's—was the least dysfunctional thing about our interactions with him.

"Once upon a time, there was a god," Vidar said. "He—"

"*Holy fuck.* Are you really going to open that way?" I let the exclamation slip out to hide that I was reaching for power from Dahlia. From Nico and Tatiana. Not a lot. Enough to bolster me. To mix with Vidar's and maybe break the hold he had around us.

"He'd come from a beautiful world." The only indication Vidar heard me was a flicker of surging power from his hand.

I grasped those threads too.

"Magic lived everywhere," Vidar said. "In everything. You have no idea how stunning it was. Modern life, *the grind,* didn't exist. It was a literal paradise. A utopia."

"The problem with a utopia is it's soiled when shitty people live there," Tatiana spoke up.

I wanted to hug her for the blatant dig.

Vidar let out another, longer, sigh. "That *was* the problem. As the world evolved, more and more of those beautiful, magical things faded. This god saw too many go who shouldn't have. He mourned their loss for so long. Until the day he realized the kind of beauty he wanted, the kind of paradise they used to have, required sacrifice."

"So everything you're doing is for the greater good?" There was no reason for me to dig deep for the meaning of his story, but I didn't buy it.

He let out a grunt of confirmation. "You of all people should appreciate that."

"Not the way you're implying." It didn't matter that I didn't have details. I'd seen enough of Vidar's destruction that I could guess his definition of *sacrifice* required more than I was willing to take from the world.

"No?" He didn't sound surprised. "When I told you as a child that I was the only one who could help you save the world, it was true."

My answer was a barking laugh. I had so much power wrapped around me now, it should be enough, and the sooner I could get rid of this dirty, grimy, corrupt slime that was Vidar's magic, the happier I'd be.

"Maybe next time you'll come to me, after you've had a chance to think about what I just said." Vidar rested his fingers on my neck again.

I shook my head. An answer to his offer, and a signal to Dahlia. "Don't hold your breath. Or do. I don't care." I tugged hard at all the magic, and Dahlia tensed.

Vidar clucked. "Naughty girl." He pressed his fingers to the fresh tattoo and his power surged inside me. My skin crackled along the fresh marks, the sensation a thousand times more intense than when Tatiana activated them.

And then the world's emotions rushed in, making me stumble.

"Now that we have that out of the way, you and I can take this somewhere else," Vidar said.

I tensed, ready to act, and Nico rushed between Vidar and me so fast he was a blur.

I wouldn't let Nico die for me again, and I grabbed at his arm.

The magic of flame rushed into me, mingling with slime and life and death and infinite possibility. It was coming from everywhere. My friends. The people around us. Vidar.

It took the last of my focus to shape it all into something that felt offensive and weapon-like, and shove it back at Vidar.

He grunted and let go of me.

The instant I felt his grip release, I spun and put space between us, summoning my Valkyrie wings and armor.

Tatiana did the same, and what looked like a blurred wall appeared around us, cutting us off from the people on the street. Dahlia had separated us from the crowd, to protect innocent bystanders.

Nico flew past me in a blur of flame, and a fist clenched around my heart.

"We already did this." Vidar knocked Nico back with a flick of his wrist.

Tatiana and I were already darting in from different directions, swords drawn. Out of the corner of my eye, I saw Nico land on his feet, and slid into an attack stance.

Dahlia appeared from nowhere behind Vidar, and gripped his shoulder. Blue energy crackled around him, sparking and sizzling.

I felt it. Her. Him. Their power still surged into me.

Vibrant fuchsia, like water made of flame, circled Tatiana. It was her magic mixed with her Valkyrie power.

Vidar grabbed her wrist and flung her away in a similar fashion to Nico, right as my sword struck him.

He doubled over with another *oof*.

The street vanished, and so did Vidar.

We were back in a clearing near the cabin. Just outside of Dahlia's wards.

The entire exchange felt like an eternity but took less than five seconds.

All the power I'd drawn into me was still there. Vidar. All of it. It clawed at my mind and filled my thoughts with darkness and sunshine and flowers and death. It stole the strength in my legs, and dragged me to the ground.

"Magnus?"

I didn't know if that was Dahlia or Nico. Both?

They were both in my head. Not them. Their worry. Their rage. Everyone's.

It all tore from my throat in a scream that threatened my eardrums. I let it all out, pushing away everything that wasn't me. Roaring into the sky until it was all gone and my throat ached and my heart ached and everything ached.

I felt Dahlia again. Nico.

Which also meant Vidar hadn't hurt my children. Thank fuck.

With the internal chaos gone, the external bled in. My phone was ringing.

Nico pushed me toward the house. "We should get inside the wards."

"Where's Tatiana?" Dahlia asked.

The noise was all tangible. Something I could confront and deal with. I followed Nico and Dahlia as I pulled my phone from my bag. Tatiana's name was on the screen. "Found her." I hit *Answer*. "Hey." I couldn't hide the strain in my voice.

"Oh Gods, you're all right. You are all right, aren't you, Boo? All of you?"

"Yes." I was sure. A glance at Dahlia and Nico

confirmed they looked okay. "Where are you? Are you safe?"

"I'm safe in my shop," Tatiana said. "I appeared here, and y'all were gone. Do you want to come back? He burned the tattoos off."

I reached for my neck, but stopped short of touching the damage. "Not today. It was fun though. Thank you."

"Yeah." Tatiana's laugh wasn't amused. "Oh. Hang on."

Silence met me. And then stretched out.

"Everything all right?" I nudged when there was nothing from her for a moment.

"He took my charm."

"What charm?"

"It was from Mamere. I had it around my wrist, and now it's gone." Distress filtered into Tatiana's voice.

Why would he do that? "What did it do?"

"Nothing? Luck. Safety. But it wasn't a big magical talisman or anything."

"I'm sorry." In the grand scheme of things, it wasn't anywhere near the worst that had happened to someone because of me, but it was still due to her helping me. "I'll get it back."

"No. Stay safe, Boo. I'm here if you need," Tatiana said.

I hung up and turned back to Dahlia and Nico. "So, she's home, and did one of us bring us here?"

Dahlia shook her head. "I would've taken us back to NEON."

"I would've dropped us inside the wards," I said.

Dahlia looked skeptical. "So Vidar sent us here?"

"I think you actually did damage to him, Magnus." Nico spoke up.

That was hard for me to believe. Wait. "Why did he send us *here*? Why not drop us in front of NEON?"

"He doesn't know you've gone back to NEON?" Nico suggested.

Oh. *Oh.* That felt like it had to be useful somehow. We just had to figure out how. Along with why Vidar sought us out there.

But I knew that—it wasn't just to talk to me. He said he was waiting for me to visit her. He wanted to get both of us at the same time. Intimidate me, and take the charm from her. That had to be it. Vidar seemed random, but he planned everything to the letter.

"We have to stop him. We have to—"

"Stop." Nico grasped my hands, his voice calm. "What you have to do is stop and think this through. Not here."

"He's right. Reacting never gets us anywhere," Dahlia said. "If we leave from inside the wards, Vidar will think you're still here. We'll go back to NEON. We'll talk this out."

I hated the waiting. There was so much waiting. No plans. No action. They were right, though, as much as I didn't want to pause anything. "I yield. Let's regroup."

We appeared in the apartment Dahlia lived in with Frey and Fen. "I want my laptop for this," Dahlia said. "I'll make notes."

She also had access to a digital archive of magical books that she'd been building—we both did. We'd already been through dozens of them before, but maybe we missed something.

"Make notes about what?" Fen's voice came from behind us, where he'd just emerged from the kitchen.

He moved like liquid stealth, especially for such a large man. Probably had something to do with the fact that he was a wolf god.

"We ran into Vidar." Dahlia pulled her computer from a shelf under the coffee table, set it on top, and opened the device.

Fen crossed the room in a blur, kneeling on the floor next to her and looking her in the eye. "You're not going out there alone again. Neither of you."

I scoffed, and Dahlia's disbelief surged in to mingle with mine. Hers was tempered with affection, though.

"I'm sorry. Who the fuck do you think you are?" She raised her brows and stared down Fen.

His features shifted, so his nose was sharper and his fangs were more distinct. "The man who's not going to let you get hurt." The growl in his voice was unmistakable.

She growled back. "So you're going to lock me—us—up?"

He was worried. I understood that. I was more than a little jealous. He had to know by this point that Dahlia did what Dahlia wanted to do.

"I'm going to tell you that whatever you're doing, you're not doing it without me." Fen's voice was hard.

The low rumble of a dragon echoed from Dahlia's chest.

Despite the outward appearance, I felt the love flowing between them. The protection. The possessiveness. And the sweetness.

Nico's chuckle disrupted the staring match.

Fen scowled at him.

"Is it odd that I missed this part of the world?" Nico asked.

"The growly asshole part?" Dahlia countered.

Fen reinforced her question with another deep, threatening sound.

She stuck her tongue out at him.

He gripped the back of her neck and kissed her hard.

I gasped when Dahlia did, as a surge of desire washed through me. It wasn't as intense as being part of the kiss myself, but the sensation bordered on overwhelming. There was no way I could do this for another eight months—especially if whatever I was given to mute the emotional noise kept breaking.

"I miss being part of the family you protect at all costs." Nico's comment brought me out of my head.

He was right. It might ache to see what Dahlia had with her guys, but she also had me.

"It's worth holding onto, and something tells me you're more a part of it than you realize," Fen said.

Nico fixed a gaze on me, and I felt the currents of affection. "I wouldn't mind that at all." His voice softened.

Feeling that wasn't bad.

I needed control over this empathy, regardless. There had to be another way. It didn't matter how much training I had, this was different. Did centuries of living really give Bragi the ability to function on a regular basis, with so many other voices in his head?

There had to be more to what he was doing.

Dahlia and Nico filled Fen in on the rest of our day, including Vidar's bizarre Thanos-style story, that he'd taken Tatiana's charm, and that it was possible I'd hurt him, but we weren't sure, and I didn't know if I could do it again on command.

I wanted to be more a part of the conversation, but every time someone had a surge of feeling, so did I. It was like watching my favorite TV show, but with the volume screwed up, and in my head instead of external.

Through it all, I kept coming back to two thoughts.

I couldn't keep this up for another eight months, and Bragi might be the only person who could help me.

"Hey." Dahlia's soft voice drilled through my thoughts. "Earth to Magnus."

I blinked away the chatter and looked around. "Where did Nico and Fen go?"

"Fen is showing off his weapon collection—that's not even a euphemism. Where did *you* go?"

I didn't want to tell her, but if I did, she'd point out all the ways I was wrong. She'd remind me of every reason I couldn't trust Bragi, and I'd be able to move on to a new solution. "It's stupid."

"I doubt that." Dahlia perched on the arm of the chair I sat in. "Tell me."

Spit it out. Just say the same things you're thinking. "A few days ago, Bragi told me something."

Dahlia tensed, and it was as if she was getting pre-angry. Prepping to be furious. "What's that?"

"He said you and your guys would burn down the world for each other. And that sometimes, not everyone good can be saved."

Dahlia let out a strained chuckle. "Never tell him I said this, but he's right."

Oh. "But what he did, the way he lied to me about you, that wasn't. What he did at TOM, that wasn't right either."

"No." Dahlia's pre-anger was ebbing, replaced with a kind of sad acceptance. "But what we did at TOM wasn't right either."

"We thought it was."

Dahlia nodded. "Because we bought into what we were told. I'm not defending him, but when we were all fighting Minato, when you and Fen wouldn't wake up? I would've done an awful lot of questionable things to bring you back. It wouldn't have mattered if they were things you wouldn't forgive me for, as long as you were still here. What's going on in your head?"

Besides feeling how serious and sincere she was? Besides knowing she didn't judge me even for a moment for bringing up Bragi? "I need to learn some sort of control on my own. Of my emotions, of everyone else's, and probably of anything that flows through me. I think he can help me."

"Okay." Dahlia was fine with it. Not completely. She didn't trust him, but she agreed with my decision.

This wasn't what I wanted. She was supposed to deter me. Stop me. "It's a mistake, isn't it? For me to trust him, especially with this? I've trusted him before, and I was wrong. I trusted other people... Vidar..."

Dahlia bit her bottom lip. "Bragi is not Vidar. It's easy to see the similarities, but Vidar manipulated us. Used our pain to control us. Still hunts us and taunts us and is doing so many fucked up things not only to you and me, but to the solders he still controls. For all we know, to the world. And Bragi walked away from it all, the same way we did. I hate him for teaching me that it was wrong to let my feelings show, but the ways that saved all of us?"

"You're saying I should do this?"

"I'm saying if it feels right, you have to listen to your gut," Dahlia said. "Our instinct steers us all wrong sometimes, but if we stop trusting ourselves, that's when we're fucked."

Then that was that. "I don't suppose you can tell me where to find him."

Dahlia had inherited that gift from Vidar—the ability to feel anyone in the world and where they were, as long as they were out in the open.

"Yes. It's not as if he's hiding," she said.

"I guess he's not in danger if I'm not there."

"Or Bragi's willing to risk Vidar's wrath if it means distracting him from you."

"You really sound like you're defending him." I could say *no* regardless of what Dahlia thought. I didn't have to do this.

But I wanted to.

"I'm saying if I had lost my power and the men I love and you, and the only way to keep them safe was to take on one of the most powerful gods in existence, I wouldn't hesitate. And the last thought on my mind would be collateral damage."

I could argue that was a hypothetical, and she didn't know that for sure, but Dahlia had basically done exactly that at least once. True, she had her power, but it hadn't been enough to defeat him, so it was the same as going in unarmed.

"I'm going to see Bragi." Saying it aloud made it real, and cemented in my mind that I wanted to. "Don't tell Nico?"

For the first time since we started this thread, Dahlia didn't like what I was saying. "Don't lie to him."

"I won't. I'll tell him, but I need to figure out how."

Dahlia nodded. "I have your back. Always. Are you going now?"

It was barely nightfall and there was no way I was sleeping anytime soon. This was an action I could take *now*. "Yes."

Dahlia gave me an address and a room number. I wasn't surprised to see it was the most expensive hotel in town, but I was shocked that the town in question was Detroit.

I should be grateful he wasn't across the street from NEON anymore.

In a blink, I was standing in front of the room in question. I knocked.

Bragi answered, staring at me wide-eyed.

It wasn't easy to force out the words. "I need your help. Please."

CHAPTER 8
BRAGI

I couldn't believe she was here. Standing in front of me, strength and softness, beauty and justice.

Creation, I wanted to hold her.

She was asking *me* for help. I had no idea what I could offer in my current state, but I wasn't going to turn her down. "Anything."

"You can't promise me anything." The purse of her lips was alluring rather than deterring me.

"It doesn't matter, I promise it anyway." I stepped aside and opened the door wider. "What do you need?"

She moved into my room, but lingered as I closed the door behind her. "You want to ask where he is."

I hadn't even vocalized the thought to myself, but she was right—the desire was there. The worry was there. Stories told throughout history implied that reading thoughts was a skill unto itself, as if people spoke in full sentences in their minds the way they did out loud. As if looking in someone's head was the same as opening a book.

None of that meant anything if one couldn't read the emotion that went with disconnected splashes of thought. Context was everything, and empathy wielded correctly offered more mind-reading power than telepathy ever could.

Magnus was adjusting to this power so quickly.

"You're feeling again. Where's the crystal Maeve gave you?"

"Shattered. Same for these." Magnus pulled back the collar of her shirt to expose a series of small scars on her neck. "That's why I'm here."

"You'll have to be more specific." I still couldn't guess what I could offer.

"Ask me first. Get it out of the way."

I wasn't asking her about Nico, because I didn't want this conversation to be about anything but Magnus and me. I did want answers, though. "Where's Nico? How is he?"

"He's safe at NEON."

Two of the best words I could've heard. I was relieved not only that he was staying hidden, but that Magnus was willing to give me a location.

I moved further into the room, giving her the space to follow. The suite had a sitting area, with multiple spots to pick from, and the bedroom was behind a door. If I had to be here for a while, and had no home to go back to, I was going to appreciate the comforts I could.

"Where did the fresh scars come from?" As long as I was voicing my concerns, I might as well get to the other one as well.

The way Magnus hesitated was telling. "I had tattoos done by a friend. Vidar showed up almost instantly. Removed them. Stole a bracelet from her that had been passed down from mother to daughter for generations. Taunted us. Left." Her voice hitched on *left*.

"If I ask you for more details, will you give them to me?"

Magnus shook her head.

Because she was here for help, but didn't trust me.

I'd earn that. "What can I do for you?" I asked directly.

Magnus hesitated near the doorway, then moved further in.

I wasn't going to watch her hover at the edge of the rug, pretending she didn't want to fidget. I took a seat, hoping it would prompt her to do the same.

She settled in the furthest chair from me, perching on the edge. "Teach me how to not feel all of *this*." She gestured at the air around her.

"I taught you that in school." Rather, I taught them what I could.

Magnus shook her head. "No. You taught us to hide our emotions from others and ourselves, and that only goes so far. Especially when I sense everything that everyone around me is feeling. I want to know how *you* handled it. Whatever you did for you was more than willpower. Something you didn't think we could or should learn."

She was right.

"There is a way to use magic to shield your mind. There was no reason to teach any of you that if you couldn't use it."

"Some of them—us—could have."

Because every student there had the potential for magic—it was why we'd recruited them. It was true, I could've determined who was capable of learning the deeper skills. Originally I opted not to because *I* still needed to be able to read my students.

By the time Magnus's class came along, I'd convinced myself I was doing it the only way.

"We all made mistakes at TOM," was the best answer I could give her.

She clenched her jaw, but didn't answer.

"I can only teach you the theory, and tell you what worked for me," I said. "Without magic of my own, I can't do more, but I promise you everything I have."

"How long will it take?"

It had taken me centuries. I needed to figure out the details though, since no one was teaching me.

"We won't be done this evening, if that's what you're asking. I'll explain the theories to you, and walk you through as much work as we can do. Like any exercise, it's tiring. You'll need to break, process what you've tried and learned, and come back to it multiple times."

Magnus didn't look happy about that, but she gave a terse nod. "Thank you."

I ached to close the distance between us, and she had to know as much. Parts of this were better done with as little contact as possible.

"There's magic in everything." I was best off diving into the lesson. "Most of it is insignificant. Wisps at best, but if you can identify it, you can weave it into something more."

"I think I saw some of that earlier, when we were facing—" She snapped her jaw shut.

"Facing whom?" I already knew the answer, and the fact that I hadn't been there—couldn't be there—filled me with rage.

She gave a tight shake of her head. "No one. That's not why I'm here."

It was a large part of why she was here.

I wanted to push, and it wouldn't do either of us any good, so I continued. "The trick is, recognizing what mutes things, and that includes portions of your own empathic power."

• • •

"Is that it?" Magnus sounded skeptical.

I half expected her to get up and walk out. "That's the theory. Do you want me to teach you how to use it in practice?"

The twist of her mouth, the almost-audible whirring of gears in her head, was endearing. "Yes," she finally said.

"Step one is sorting through the emotion. All of it. You may think you know which is yours, but I guarantee, none of us ever get there completely. As you practice identifying your own, you'll see the differences in the others, too. Each person will have a unique taste or sound. Each energy that seems to be attached to an individual but isn't will compliment or sour their flavor."

Magnus made a face. "In other words, I'm mentally licking people?"

"I hadn't thought of it that way, but I suppose."

"Gross." She shuddered.

"That's why you focus on... licking yourself." That sounded both wrong and enticing to watch.

Her scowl deepened. "Double gross." Her tone went flat.

I shrugged. "You don't like it, then learn to feel yourself and not me."

"*Ugh*. God, I wish you could feel my disgust right now."

For a moment, I was certain I could, as potent as

any emotion I'd detected before I lost my power. Like the empathic version of a ghost limb.

"All right. Focus on finding me." Magnus screwed up her face and squeezed her eyes shut. Seconds ticked away, turning to a minute, and then two.

She let out a loud huff and pried one eye open to look at me. "Any more details about how to do that? Also, if you could *want* a little quieter, that would be swell."

"I'm doing what I can to mute it." And I was. I would spend eons telling Magnus all the ways I was drawn to her, but forcing a mental onslaught on her was different. "You remember what I told you at Maeve's? To look for the lines of magic? It's similar to that. I wish I could describe it better." I thought for a moment. "Say you walk into a pitch-black room, filled with blankets, towels, and pillows. Soft things. Fuzzy things."

The look Magnus gave me was pure disbelief. "Nap time?"

"Pay attention." My snap was intentional. I recognized her joking was a way to hide her frustration, but this needed at least a level of seriousness. "Your job is to find the velour pillow. You can run your fingers over everything, and some you'll instantly know aren't right. There will be others that feel too similar. A quick touch won't tell you which one you're looking for. You need to pause. Consider.

Examine. And you need to be okay with the fact that sometimes you'll get it wrong."

The last bit of my statement made her scowl come back. "All right, let's do this."

We spent the next three hours with her delving inward again and again. At some point, the quips faded, then vanished. When the only words out of her mouth were filled with frustration, we'd hit a wall.

"You need to stop for the night," I said.

"I don't have it yet." The edge in her voice sliced the air.

"I told you at the beginning, this takes time and practice. If you do it while you're drained, you run the risk of injuring yourself or getting it wrong more and more, even if you know what you're doing."

Magnus closed her eyes. "Just one more try."

"No." I forced the command into both my voice and my emotion.

"I can't walk out of here without anything, and I can't come back for a few days."

"You don't have *nothing*. What you learned today is going to help, even if you're not all the way there."

She sank back into her seat, and her entire body seemed to melt into the cushions. "How did you do this for so long?"

"The same way you do anything—you push through because you don't have a choice." I could mention the fact that I gave up. That it broke me eventually. That wouldn't help her right now.

Magnus gave a tired chuckle. "Yeah. Why are you in Detroit?"

"I'm looking for a way to defeat Vidar."

"And you didn't think to loop me in?"

I raised my eyebrows. "As you might say—are you serious right now?"

Magnus shrugged.

I'd go through the reasons. It was a short list. "Would you have taken my call? In addition, there's no way I'm putting you in Vidar's path."

"In my condition?"

"Yes."

She clenched her teeth and a growl escaped.

There was that whisper of emotion again. Almost as if it was pushed into me. The frustration. The impotence.

I was familiar enough with my own to know this feeling wasn't mine, but that didn't mean it was anything other than a ghost of the past. "I'm not being unreasonable, looking out for you, and neither are your friends." It was easy enough to guess I wasn't the only person who wanted her to be more cautious than normal because of her pregnancy.

"Is it as reasonable as you deciding to fight possibly the most powerful god there is, without any power?" She countered.

"That's different. What I choose to do only impacts me."

"It's a fucking death sentence," Magnus said. "If you wanted to die, I could've left you to Johnny."

"I have to do anything I can to save you and Nico." I had to try. There was no other option.

"Then it doesn't only impact you."

I gave her a tight-lipped smile. Her argument wasn't perfect, but it was a decent counter.

This visit had to end soon. As much as I wanted to keep her here, it wasn't safe. As much as I wanted to spend the entire night talking, in a way we'd rarely had a chance. Perhaps have her go get Nico. Take the time to just be us.

Because I couldn't have that, I slipped a thumb under a leather cord that hung around my neck, and removed the crystal. I crossed the room and held it out for her.

"Oh." Magnus's gasp was one of recognition. "But no. No more trinkets or external objects to silence the noise."

"As far as I know, this won't work on you. It never impacted me when I wore it. It simply kept me from influencing others. You left it behind after the three of us..." I frowned, unsure how to finish the thought.

"After we found out you lied."

I wouldn't argue with her, especially about that. "I never claimed otherwise."

She took the leather cord from me and held it so the crystal was at her eye-level. "If it's not to help me block things, why give it to me?"

I wasn't sure. "Nico gave it to you to protect you from me. It doesn't need to do that anymore, but sometimes gifts like that become more. I still want you safe. If you don't want it, you can return it to him."

She was quiet for a moment, as she let the crystal fall into her open palm. "He's going to wonder how I got it."

Wasn't that an interesting revelation? All this talk about lies, and, "He doesn't know you're here."

"I'll tell him." Magnus sounded more like she was reminding herself than assuring me. "But he's more angry with you than I am. Who knew that was possible?"

Was it about the same thing he originally left me over? I suspected as much. That I'd been part of TOM. That I'd meddled in so many lives. I could assume his anger had surged again because the memories were as fresh as if they were new, but I didn't want to do that. I'd rather talk to him.

Not that I could take back what I'd done—no more than I could with Magnus—but I could do things differently moving forward. Overall I didn't know how I felt about any bit of the information.

"Me neither," Magnus said in response to words I hadn't spoken. "And thank you for not judging me for keeping the secret." She took a deep breath, and slipped the necklace over her head. "No secrets. Take me with you."

I gave her a puzzled look. "To...?"

"Whatever has you here, looking for information to defeat Vidar. Let me help."

"Anubis has me here."

Magnus stared me down. "You think that means *no*, but it sounds like a good reason for me to join you."

"All right." Regardless of what I wanted, what I or anyone else told her, she was going to do what she wanted.

"Like that?"

"You'll go see him without me, you'll do all of this regardless... This way, if you're with me as my guest, things are more likely to go smoothly." Unless I found out Magnus had some sort of ties to Anubis I didn't know about. He interred her grandfather, or built her grandma's hotrod or something. "I'm waiting for him to get back to me, but when he does, I'll let you know."

She stood, and it took every ounce of my willpower to not step closer. To not wrap my arms around her and steal a kiss.

Magnus held up a finger and pushed me back, only a few inches. "You gotta stop with that."

"Not likely." Not because I was cruel, but because I couldn't help but want her.

"Was this how you felt in the garden, when you were helping me get my Valkyrie powers back?"

"No." It was true, I'd felt every single pulse of desire that came from her. The difference was, *I'd* wanted to act on the urge, and she wasn't interested in that from me.

"Never assume," she said softly. "I do need to go. Thank you." She vanished from the room.

I hated the empty spot she left in the room. Hated knowing that it may be another century before I saw Nico again. Hated that I had to involve her in what I was learning, to have any chance of keeping her safe.

I couldn't stop her from going after Vidar, any more than she could me. This might buy me the time I needed to figure out how to keep her safe in any fight that happened.

Because I was going to save Magnus. And Nico. It didn't matter what it took. I'd make sure Vidar was destroyed and they could live the lives they wanted.

CHAPTER 9

NICO

When Fen and I returned to their living room, only Dahlia remained.

"Magnus needed to step out. Deal with all the feels," she said.

I wasn't surprised. Bragi used to do the same thing.

That memory was as fresh as all the others, and it twinged inside me with longing. It couldn't have been easy to deal with that, and seeing Magnus share struggles Bragi had drove the point home.

"You're welcome to join us in the bar." Fen spoke up. "Drink. Watch the dancers. Or not."

"I think I'll follow a bit of Magnus's lead." I had never been much of a pub person. Even though I was working at one when I met Bragi, I'd been a cook, tucked in back, away from the patrons.

Neither Dahlia nor Fen seemed offended by my answer, and they wished me a good evening.

In Magnus's place, I felt a bit lost. I'd spent decades sitting home and reading, yet this moment of respite was foreign amidst the bedlam of the last few days. Her apartment was as sparsely decorated as my home, which made me feel like she existed here, rather than *living*.

In a way though, she was like me before I'd remembered my past. Not that she was able to forget hers, but until recently she'd been lost. In places she didn't recognize as hers. That was a portion of what drew me to her at Bragi's, when she was injured. She didn't seem sure of her place in the world, and I knew the feeling.

My gaze drifted to Magnus's room, where my suitcase sat. Each time I looked around the apartment, my attention fell back there. I still had Bragi's journals.

That was the last thing I wanted to waste my time on. I didn't need the nudge anymore, now that my memories had returned.

Reading his words, his unfiltered observations about the world, meant seeing his motivations.

I didn't want that.

Yet, I was drawn to the leather-bound books. Within a few moments, I was sitting in a chair in the living room, starting from Page One. I wanted to read the entirety through an unclouded mind.

His words drew me in, like they had a few days ago. Even when Bragi was speaking to a page, there was a cadence to his stories that was compelling.

There were stories in here about more than me. An archive of others he knew.

There was a tale about him and Loki causing mischief. Another about an encounter with Finn and Gwydion, and a disagreement between them.

While trickster gods weren't as prolific as gods of war or fertility, there was at least one in every pantheon. The gods like Bragi, who represented specific elements of a culture, were the ones who tended to be the most diverse.

There were a couple of stories about a woman named Skye, a mortal witch who had a mechanical creativity that Bragi seemed to adore. *She sees a beauty in the ugliness of metal that most men can't comprehend. She's working on a device she says can build utopia, and it's a vision I wish could be brought to life.*

When he talked about Macha, a Celtic goddess, his language was similar. *As brutal as she is loving, she can drive men to destroy kingdoms with their swords one day, and rebuild them the next by sheathing their weapons in good women.*

The paragraphs about me were the hardest to read. I let my gaze drift over flowery language and metaphor, and tried not to hear his voice whispering the words in my ear, as he had once upon a time.

I was absorbed in his past to the point that I was startled when Magnus said, "Hey."

My head shot up to find her in front of me, a few feet away. Dark circles lingered under her eyes, and exhaustion radiated from her.

"Are you all right?" I hated seeing her in any sort of discomfort, especially like this.

"Tired. Overloaded. Need sleep."

I'd take that all away from her if I could. Wrap her in comfort and be her peace for the night.

As the sentiment spilled through me, she almost smiled. "I'd love to have you join me, for cuddles, when you're done with that." She nodded at the journal I held.

Bragi's musings could wait. I set the book aside, joined her in the bedroom, and stripped down as she did.

This thing that we'd never done before now —sharing this intimate space, sharing a bed— was comfortable and familiar. How was that possible?

It didn't matter.

We climbed into bed, and I held her as she pressed her back into my chest.

This had to be wreaking havoc on her mind, and the best thing I could do for her was be an island of calm. At least I could do that, though.

This couldn't continue. This running and chasing and never having answers and always looking over our shoulders. I couldn't do this, and neither could she.

I was tired of hiding from the world. It would be easy to blame my withdrawal on Vidar. On Bragi.

It had been my choice from the start, and it was time for me to stop. I had to figure out how to help Magnus and her friends and myself in some way other than being a cuddle buddy.

How?

AS MAGNUS CLIMBED out of bed in the morning, I couldn't help but recline and enjoy the sight. It didn't matter if she was tired or alert or angry or happy, she was stunning. Always.

She stretched and I drank in her elongated form. The way her strength and softness blended into a statuesque frame. Was she starting to show signs of the pregnancy? That barely there bump?

My gaze landed on a leather cord around her neck, and I frowned. Was she wearing that yesterday? Not when we were at Tatiana's.

"I thought you'd discarded the remnants of the crystal Maeve gave you." As I spoke, my mind processed the worn strap—so dark brown it was nearly black. It looks familiar, but most cords like that looked the same from a distance.

She looked down, and her hand flew to her chest,

covering a portion of the necklace but not all of it. "I did."

"Is that something you picked up last night while you were out?" I didn't need to interrogate her about her jewelry choices. I wouldn't do the same if she wore a shirt I'd never seen before.

This piece was different. Why did I know it?

She moved her hand and slipped her thumb under the cord, pulling the attached crystal free. "Yes. I picked it up last night."

It was mine. Rather, it had been. I used it to keep him from influencing me, and I'd given it to her to use for the same purpose.

She'd left it behind when she and I walked away from him the first time.

If Magnus had it, unless she'd gone back to Bragi's house and searched the ashes for it, she'd gotten it from him.

I didn't know why she would go out of her way to dig it up if he couldn't influence her anymore, and it didn't look like it had survived a weather-worn, war-torn house.

She'd gone to see Bragi. She'd kept it from me.

Which realization upset me more?

"Why?" I asked.

Magnus kept her distance from me, fiddling with the crystal. "I need his help controlling the flow of emotion. I didn't know if I could tell you."

Yet, she'd let herself be caught in the deception.

I'd seen how badly this could fuck with him—feeling what others felt—and he was familiar with it. I understood why she thought working with him would be helpful. But, "You can't see him again."

"Excuse me?" The apology vanished from her voice and posture, and she straightened. "Did you just... I *can't?*"

"No. You don't know who he is or what he is."

"I have a decent fucking idea. I've spent more time with him in the last few decades than you have. I know what he's capable of."

"You don't." Did I? My memories were beginning to slot themselves into an order. The rage I had at him when he gave up, that wasn't fresh anymore, but it was still potent. I still recalled watching him slide into apathy. "Lying to you about Dahlia was only a hint of what he'll do for himself."

"He did it to keep us sa—." As the words passed Magnus's lips, she snapped her jaw shut and her eyes grew wide. "This isn't about him, it's about the fact that you just gave me an order—one you question yourself, by the way—and who the fuck are you to tell me what to do?"

I didn't question my resolve. I didn't doubt my inability to trust Bragi. Reading his journal last night hadn't filled me with sympathy or reminded me of the man he was before the world beat him down and the weight of their worries became too much for him to bear.

"If an experienced driver says *these conditions aren't good for high speed, don't go fast*, if a skilled swordsman says *this blade is dull, don't use it*, then you listen. I am telling you, this man is going to hurt you again. Don't go back to him."

Magnus scowled. "First of all, if anyone tells me *don't*, then I probably *do*. There's a difference between an order and *here's my knowledge and my recommendation, do with it what you will*. All of that aside, *you* are not an expert on the people around you. I have my own opinions and life experiences, oh, and right now, I can *feel* how honest he's being with me. How much of the truth you're telling me. I don't fucking want to, but I can. And he's not the only one hiding things from himself."

I wanted to argue, but she wasn't in the right frame of mind to hear me.

Magnus's nostrils flared. "Fuck you. I'm going to take a shower." She stormed from the room.

Unbelievable. I flopped back into bed, and let anger and frustration fill me. How was I supposed to make her understand?

What if she was right? That doubting part of my mind that she'd called out was ready to take her side.

Right about what? Bragi was dangerous. I left him because of what he became.

What if he'd changed?

People didn't change.

He had. Decades had passed like minutes, and one day...

When he started working with Vidar... Hel... Morganna... Loki... The others... He was the man I loved. His empathy meant he found joy in bringing joy to others. He bought into Vidar's sales pitch, because it was one of a utopia, similar to the picture Vidar tried to paint for us yesterday.

As Bragi was at that fucking school, day after day, feeling the results of the training, it gnawed at him. He wasn't silent about it. He argued with Hel and Vidar. Pointed out that their methods were the cruelest sort of indoctrination.

I watched it all devour him. As with so much of my past, this fresh hindsight provided a perspective I didn't have when I lived it. Back then what I saw was a man who was angrier than I remembered. Meaner.

And at some point, I'd realized he'd stopped caring.

No. Worse. he delighted in the suffering of those around him.

That was when I'd left. When I woke up one day and realized that it wasn't joy that kept him going anymore, it was agony. Dining on the pain he was fed on a non-stop basis.

I couldn't let that happen to Magnus. I couldn't watch a slow decline into that form of madness. Bragi should've taken steps back then to stop Vidar, but I could do so now. I could help her. I could stop wallowing.

I was lost in the reverie long enough that I didn't hear the water shut off. When Magnus emerged from the bathroom, wrapped in a towel, she still wore a frown that etched deep lines in her forehead.

"It's a little late for retrospection, and you're still wrong." Her anger hadn't faded. She grabbed some clothes from drawers, and vanished into the little room again.

When she came out again a few minutes later, this time dressed, she didn't so much as glance at me as she left the room.

Was it possible to give her space with her able to feel everything I did? Wondering that didn't stop the questions from bouncing in my head as I got ready for the day as well.

I joined her in the kitchen a short while later. She had made coffee, and was leaning against a far counter sipping from a mug with a cartoon unicorn, who appeared to have a rainbow coming from its rear.

I didn't realize Magnus had been to those parties.

She glanced at me, and put several meters of distance between herself and the coffee maker.

Were we going to not talk now? That was unacceptable. "I—"

"Stop." She bit off the word. "You're not sorry—

why the fuck are men never sorry?—and I already know the rest. I don't want to listen to you work your way through it out loud."

While I understood what she meant, it wasn't a good approach. "That's going to make it difficult to resolve this."

"There's nothing to resolve. You don't get to tell me what to do or who to speak with, and I don't listen when you try."

My frustration was back.

"Good." She huffed.

There was a knock, and Dahlia called out, "Are you decent?"

Magnus and I weren't done. "No," I shouted.

At the same time Magnus said, "Yes."

Dahlia pushed into the apartment. "Magnus wins." She paused in the entryway and looked between us. "What did you do, Nico?"

"Why would I have done anything?" I understood next to nothing about their language.

"He tried to tell me what to do," Magnus offered.

Dahlia rolled her eyes. "Asshole."

This felt similar to the argument she had with Fen last night, but without the playfulness.

"Fight later?" Dahlia crossed the room to the island that separated the kitchen from the rest of the room, and set her laptop on the counter and opened the lid. "You have to see this."

"Gladly." Magnus joined her.

I let my frustration flow, along with the spite that told me to do so, and observed from where I stood.

I listened to a woman talk about what a server farm was. This seemed like an odd topic for Dahlia to be worked up over. I understood she and Magnus were tech savvy, but—

"One has gone missing—" the woman on the computer said.

What? I moved closer, to see the screen. The argument with Magnus evaporated from my thoughts, as the person with the news said that a large block of UWS computers—Ubiquity Web Services—had vanished into thin air. As in, hundreds of acres were just... gone.

Even with the explanation, I barely understood the technology aspect, but I recognized that this was a bad thing.

"Is she fucking serious?" Magnus sounded stunned.

Dahlia gave a bark of a laugh. "Yes. I went there the instant I heard"—She held up a finger when Magnus opened her mouth—"for about two seconds. Long enough to confirm for myself. It's not hidden. It's not there but in a different realm. It's gone."

"Fuck." Magnus sank onto a stool next to Dahlia.

I needed to understand more. "What kind of impact does this have?"

The unfocused look Magnus gave me was far from the irritation that had been there moments ago. "It causes chaos. It draws a huge amount of attention to the fact that people can do this. It has the potential to send thousands of companies and people into a tailspin as they scramble to recover archives and restore online business portals."

"It was the series of servers where we had our magical book repository," Dahlia added. "I had been working on identifying which old texts were based on the originals, and archiving them. I have backups, but my most recent work is gone."

"More important is what it *could* do." Magnus picked up the story. "One of Dahlia's strengths is the ability to blend magic with tech, and she's created a system that finds."

"Finds what?" I asked.

Dahlia spun to face me. "People. Things. Whatever I tweak the code to make it do. The only reason Vidar gave a shit who I was before my dragon woke up. He can do that magically, but the software magnifies it. It reaches out and... touches things, for lack of a better word.

"We believe this is Vidar who did this?"

"Not any other gods making gestures like this these days." Magnus was pale.

I wanted to be able to wrap my brain around the magnitude of this event, but the women's reactions filled in what my knowledge couldn't. "We need to find out why he did this, unless one of you knows."

"We can guess, but no. This is... No." Magnus gave a rough shake of her head, and the glazed-over look she wore vanished. "You're right. We need answers."

"Frey is talking to Aya. To see what thoughts she has." Dahlia sounded as though she'd reset too.

Magnus stood on the bottom rung of her stool, to reach across the counter and grab her phone. "I'll call Min."

I would stand back and watch.

Several gods had adapted to technology, but any that I'd learned to use had been reluctantly.

This was ridiculous. I was an ancient and powerful being, and I was cooling my heels while the people around me worked to keep their lives and their world from crumbling. I needed to do something. Train with them. Fight with them. Bring my own skills back up to snuff.

Keep Magnus—all of them—from falling prey to Vidar. I hadn't stopped Bragi. I'd pushed him away rather than helping him, and couldn't make that right. This was a place I could make a difference, though.

Frey walked into the apartment while Magnus was still on the phone. Dahlia offered him a tight smile and he kissed her on the forehead.

"Nico." He gave me a nod. "I may know something, but not much," he said quietly.

A moment later, Magnus said, "Okay. That sounds good. Thank you. Yeah, we'll keep you posted." She set her phone down and gave us her attention. "You first," she said to Frey.

The way Frey rested his hand on Dahlia's leg, and she leaned into him was so natural. Sweet. "Aya didn't know much. She agreed it was probably Vidar. There are others who might do something like this, but she doesn't think they have the power to vanish an entire building full of hardware. She doesn't have any better guess to what Vidar would be up to than *Dahlia's tech*, but she did say there was someone who might."

"Who?" I asked.

Frey frowned and shook his head. "She's only heard rumors that there's someone out there who deals in magical tech, but she's never been able to find out more."

"Min gave me a name." Magnus leaned in. "Most of what he said was the same, but he added a bit more. He can see that there are pieces of his domain that were relocated magically before this happened. Someone went out of their way to make sure his websites didn't go offline."

"What kind of websites does Min have?" I couldn't fathom what a fertility god was doing with an internet presence.

Magnus smirked. "Porn."

Oh. Perhaps I should have guessed as much.

"Which backs up his theory that Vindres was involved," Magnus said.

Frey let out a sigh-growl at the name. "I suppose that would make sense."

Dahlia screwed up her face. "Is that the— No. Really?"

"According to Min, that's him," Magnus confirmed.

This time I understood the conversation. Vindres was an incubus. He ran a club that some compared to NEON, and it was certainly a den of iniquity and a haven for immortals and supernatural beings. But Vindres tended to focus more on debauchery and less on consent.

He was also heavily involved in concepts a lot of magical beings preferred not to deal with themselves. The digital world was on that list. "Bragi knows him. Reluctant friends." I couldn't believe I was bringing him up.

"I can talk to him," Magnus said.

No one else seemed bothered by this suggestion. In fact, Dahlia was nodding.

"Why you?" I wanted to know.

Her scowl was back as she stared me down. "It was what I specialized in at TOM. We called it *honey pot interrogation*."

"You?" I was familiar with the concept. One of Bragi's.

"You're surprised I have skills?" The edge slid into Magnus's voice.

I didn't want to fight. Not about this. Not about her staying away from Bragi. "I know you have skill, but I don't know what they all are. I'd like to learn that about you. In this case, it doesn't matter if you're the best."

"Why not?" Dahlia asked.

"Vindres is paranoid. Rather, he was two centuries ago, and I doubt that's diminished. He won't talk to anyone without an introduction, including a gorgeous redheaded Valkyrie. Do you know him, Frey?"

Frey shook his head. "By reputation. Never had an interest in meeting him."

"I can't imagine him seeing Magnus. You can try."

She clenched her jaw. "No. There's no try here. If I don't get in the first time, I don't suspect I get a second chance."

"Then we need to find another place for information." Dahlia sounded defeated.

It wasn't the next step any of us wanted, but at least it was a next step.

CHAPTER 10

MAGNUS

I was still furious at Nico for believing he had the right to tell me where I could and couldn't go, and that was amplified by the fact that he wasn't sure he was still upset at Bragi.

As if he was punishing me for his indecision.

But I planned to forgive him as soon as he realized he was wrong, and there were more important things to focus on right now. For instance, who could help us figure out why Vidar took an entire data storage warehouse.

"I can make some more calls," Frey said. "Fen and I have a few names we can reach out to, and Aya said she would do the same."

I wanted to talk to this incubus Nico and Frey mentioned. If that meant approaching him with Bragi, so be it. The only reason I wasn't pursuing that now, was because I didn't want to shut down any options, and if I walked out right now to talk to Bragi, I might not discover what our other choices were.

Dahlia and Nico were right before—this was too important to jump into without thought, and Vidar was too dangerous to ignore any possibilities.

I had an idea, though it wasn't one I wanted to pursue. When I met Maeve, we'd talked about a lot of things in the hours while Bragi recovered. Including the fact that she'd given Vidar a great deal of information over the decades.

She'd assured me quickly that she did so before she realized what he was, and I understood, because I'd fallen for his bullshit too.

Why couldn't we afford Bragi the same?

Because that situation was more complicated. Bragi's sins weren't his collaboration.

The problem asking Maeve for information about Vidar was that she hadn't been forthcoming the first time we touched on the subject. She said she'd helped him, that she regretted it, and that she continued to refuse help each time he asked.

She had repeatedly changed the subject when I tried to go back to the topic of him, though. Asking her again seemed unlikely to yield any new answers, and if it pissed her off, we may not be able to turn to her in the future.

Which meant risking pissing off Maeve. If we didn't stop Vidar, there was a chance none of us would live long enough to need her help again anyway. What a shitty, sobering thought.

"I may know someone with answers," I said. "Maeve."

Frey raised his brows. He knew the name?

"Are you going to follow the same ritual Bragi did?" Nico stumbled on the name, but his hesitation was mostly emotional. He was conflicted.

Then again, so was I on the matter of Bragi. The longer I lived in this condition, the more I under-stood— "I'd rather not spend that much time on it. I will go alone, though."

Nico opened his mouth, and I stared him down, daring him to object. He wanted to. He was strug-gling with the impulse. "We need to talk before you go."

About the disagreement. About Bragi. "No."

"You can't go during the day." Frey wasn't trying to stop me. I felt that he was being reasonable about this.

"Why not?" I had to admit, sometimes this empathy thing came in handy. If I couldn't tell that Frey was being reasonable where Nico was being controlling, I would've snapped at both of them.

I'd forgotten more of my training than I realized. Or maybe I'd clung more tightly to the negative bits of my upbringing—like the inability to trust and take things at face value.

"The magic that keeps Maeve's realm hidden is

similar to what I use on NEON," Frey said. "The wards bind multiple places into a seemingly single space. But for her, the connection doesn't exist in the daylight. If you go out there now, you'll only find Montana."

Dahlia studied him, leaking curiosity. "How do you know that?"

"I know Maeve." Frey made it sound like the most natural and casual of statements.

Dahlia jutted her lower lip out so far the pout was comical. "How come everyone knows Queen Mab but me?"

"I'll introduce you when this is all over." Or I would as long as Maeve was still speaking to me after tonight.

Frey *tsk*ed and shook his head. "Promise me you won't call her that to her face."

"Fine." Dahlia's huff was exaggerated.

Not fine. I understood Frey's explanation, but, "What am I supposed to do until tonight?"

Nico opened his mouth.

"Practice what you did with Vidar." Dahlia talked over him.

Thank fuck for Dahlia. "I don't know how I did it," I said.

Frey squeezed Dahlia's knee and stood. "Was it an accident? Did it just happen?" His questions were curious, looking for answers rather than accusing.

"No but yes? I intentionally looked for his power

to draw on, but I don't know what happened after that. I doubt his interference helped." Looking back was uncomfortable. Everyone else's powers and emotions were memories, but mine were more tangible and real, still living near the surface—

Oh. Was this what Bragi had been trying to get me to see?

I tucked the thought aside to examine it later.

"If that's what you have, that's where you start." Frey gave Dahlia a quick kiss. "I'm going to make more calls and see what Aya found. Sparring room is open." He squeezed my hand. "Be careful. You two get stupid when you're angry. Don't get stupid."

I didn't appreciate the advice, but the affection underneath softened his words. Besides, it was possible he was right.

Frey left.

"Do you want to change?" Dahlia asked.

Part of our training growing up was learning to fight in any type of clothing, so we were prepared regardless of where we were. If I was allowed to choose though, I'd always choose comfortable clothes for working out—regardless of whether it was physical or magical training. "Yeah. Meet you next door?"

Frey had a doorway in their apartment that opened into an amazing training gym. There were mats for grappling, training dummies that could stand up to various magics, and a massive outdoor space for workouts that required more room.

"Five minutes." Dahlia hopped from her stool. "We can start small, and you can add in what Bragi taught you last night."

Nico's frustration pulsed.

I should probably talk to him. "Fifteen minutes," I said to Dahlia.

She gave me a half-smile, and I felt the *good luck* in her heart, before she followed Frey out the door.

I turned to Nico. "I should have told you where I was going, but I don't regret that I went, and you can't stop me from going back."

"I know. I don't like it, but I won't do that again."

It wasn't an apology, but I'd settle for an understanding. I'd rather that than him pretend things were okay when they weren't, to make me happy. "Okay."

"May I join the two of you? In the gym?"

I knew he could fight—I'd seen him do so against Vidar—but I got the impression he didn't. "Why?"

"This isn't the kind of battle that you go into unprepared, and once upon a time, I was capable of far more than I let on. I'm going to fight Vidar with you, and that means I need to be familiar with how you all fight."

"You're not going to tell me I can't fight him,

because of my condition, or because you won't allow it?"

Nico wanted to. He wanted very much to roll me in bubble wrap and hide me from the world for the next several months. "We just had that conversation. That's not an option, so I'm going to be smart about the reality."

Good answer.

I texted Dahlia to see if one of her guys had sweats Nico could borrow, and she sent me back a string of laugh-crying emojis.

He assured me he was fine in what he had.

A short while later, I was changed, and Dahlia, Nico, and I were walking into a room with a small entryway, and a large parquet floor spanning out in front of us. We could put down mats, but Dahlia had already blinked across the room to the training dummies against the far wall.

She relocated one to the middle of the room as quickly as she had moved to it. "There's your target," she called as she walked toward us again.

"What am I supposed to do with it?" I could think of several options. Shooting it was easy, but she and I tended to steer clear of firearms these days. I could summon a spear as part of my Valkyrie armor. It was the least efficient weapon I had access to, since we weren't part of a phalanx or fighting people on horseback.

"You're a conduit, right? That's the big new revelation?" Dahlia reached us. "When Vidar found us, you felt me?"

That was an understatement. "I feel all of you. All the time."

"Not just our emotions?" Dahlia placed her hand under mine, our palms touching, and sparks tingled over my skin.

They didn't bounce off, though. Instead, the energy slid into me, mingling with my own power. "Yes," I said.

"You have two powerful beings next to you. Practice borrowing from us and directing that somewhere else. I don't know if you can focus it like a projectile, or if it's more ambient, but you hurt Vidar somehow." Dahlia squeezed my hand.

She made it sound easy.

I doubted it would be, but here went nothing. I grabbed snatches of what Bragi taught me last night, about distinguishing me from what was around me. The edges were still fuzzy. Nico and Dahlia and the world bled into what I recognized as me, but out here it was easy to focus on just the three of us. Which made it easier to eliminate them.

Once I had a good sense of *me*, where I began and ended, I could slip along the connections to each of them. Two different kinds of flame. Dahlia's was icy and relentless, and Nico's was white hot and focused.

With Vidar, he hadn't burned off Talia's control

tattoos yet. I'd had a filter to sense everything through. I'd also been pulling as hard as I could, because there was no holding back with Vidar.

Here, Dahlia and Nico were walls of power surging around me. There was no restraint or filter, but I needed to be cautious with what I borrowed.

Could I take a little wisp? Snatch a sliver?

I tugged, but stopped myself with only a snippet from each of them. Now, to focus it on the dummy. As I wrapped the threads of magic in a ball in my mind, the shape swelled. The power grew until it was throbbing in my skull.

It was too much. It escaped in a rush, and the entire building rattled around us. Instinct kicked in and I put up a Valkyrie shield to stop debris from hitting us.

Not that it did. Frey and Dahlia had done a solid job of reinforcing this place against the kind of destruction most of their magics could cause.

Giddiness surged inside me. "Did you see that? I did something. I almost had it."

"Yay." Dahlia squealed and gave me a quick hug. "Do it again."

Definitely.

I repeated the same steps, but this time when I had the magic in my head, I focused on not letting it grow or get away from me. It needed to stay small. I didn't need to add to it.

The surge happened again. I recognized it as the

mental ball of energy swelled, and I couldn't stop it as it burst out of me.

The building rattled again, and several of the lights above our head shattered, showering us with glass and plastic that bounced off the invisible shield I still had in place.

"You shouldn't be able to do that." Dahlia was stunned. "No one should if it's not an all-out fight."

I was aware. "I'll be more careful. I almost have it."

But I didn't. For the next few hours, various things rattled and shook and exploded around us with each of my attempts. Sometimes I pushed out a little more energy and sometimes a hint less, but there was never a moment where I could control how much escaped.

As a tenth training dummy was destroyed, this one engulfed in flames that both froze and burned, my frustration was higher than it had been since school. "Why can't I get it?"

"Why do you have to keep blowing up targets?" Dahlia was annoyed, and it was bleeding into what I felt, magnifying it, and reverberating in my skull.

"We're done for the day." Nico wasn't quite as annoyed, but he was close.

Did he have any idea how much he sounded like Bragi right now? "You were going to stop telling me what to do."

"Magnus." His voice was hard, but affection lay underneath.

Fuck him. I didn't want to feel that right now. *"What?"*

He cupped my face in his hands, and forced himself to be calm. The emotion carried into me, and clashed with my wanting to stay annoyed.

Nico crushed his mouth to mine with an intensity that stole my breath. The intensity of his passion and desire threatened to overwhelm me. It was intoxicating and distracting and overwhelming. He pulled away before I could break the kiss, and he dropped his hands.

I wanted his touch back. I wanted to lose myself in it. Just another thing I couldn't control.

"This mood in the air? That's you." Nico's voice was firm but kind. "Bragi used to do the same thing."

"I'm not doing anything." Except suppressing the desire to cry and scream and laugh maniacally...

Nico was forcing himself to be soothing. "Not on purpose, and no one is blaming you, but I'm telling you so that you're aware. What you're feeling right now is so strong that you're pushing it out."

I wanted to argue, but what he was saying made too much sense. I nodded. "We should go."

Dahlia invited us down to the club before it opened, to get some lunch and if we wanted, stick around while she practiced her show. Her mood was still sour, and I didn't blame her. Today's

training was a big ol' pile of shit-filled disappointment.

There was a diner next door to the club, and the
three of us ordered food and ate our lunch in sulky,
dejected silence.

Nico tried to remain a calming force, but he was
getting tired.

The three of us trooped back into NEON, Dahlia
had Frey cue up some music, and she hopped on
stage to work through her dance for tonight. She was
the club's headlining burlesque dancer.

I'd say *benefit of fucking the owners*, but Dahlia
was *really* good. That wasn't just me being biased,
either.

As a heavy beat filled the room, Dahlia moved on
stage, matching the rhythm. She kick-turn-stepped
toward the left edge, and a loud screech echoed from
the speakers. She scowled, and kept going.

Another few twirls, nothing fancy. She was
getting a feel for the beat and putting herself in the
right frame of mind. When she stepped toward the
right side of the raised platform, there was another
screech—audio feedback.

"You have to tone down the power display near
the sound system." Frey's voice came over the speakers, chiding.

Dahlia's scowl deepened, and she pushed more
energy into the dance. As she neared a hidden
speaker again, the squeal reached ear-splitting, and

a shower of sparks accompanied a small explosion near a few meters from her head.

"I thought the sound system was shielded," Dahlia shouted.

Frey's sigh caused an odd sort of doppler sound all around us. "They are, but there are limits to everything, even the strongest shield."

Like we'd seen in the gym.

If I was causing this, I needed to be anywhere but here. I pushed back from the table. "I'm going to go." I walked quickly from the room before anyone could stop me.

As soon as I was done with Maeve, as soon as Bragi would see me again, I was going back to him for more training.

CHAPTER 11
MAGNUS

I couldn't block people out, they couldn't block me out…

Was this what Vidar wanted me for? My chaotic lack of control?

To the casual observer, Vidar's actions might look random and reactionary. Taking an entire data storage center? Why would someone do that?

He calculated it all, though. Not intricate, complex plans, but there was a reason for all of it. For instance, he hadn't sought us out in New Orleans *just* to taunt us. I was certain it was nice bonus for him, because *fuck* the man loved to hear himself talk. But he'd been waiting for me to go. Waiting for an excuse to get to Tatiana.

Could he have snatched her charm without the whole show? Without a doubt. He wanted us to know, though.

He wanted us to know he was the one who destroyed Bragi's house--but what was in it? There had to be something there. What was in the data center he'd taken? Why the fuck did he seem to want me? Or was that a lie? Was he really trying to get to Dahlia, since he hadn't been able to destroy her?

I told myself I wouldn't do this. Second-guessing Vidar got us in trouble.

Until I could go see Maeve, I was best served practicing what Bragi had taught me so far.

Nico was sympathetic. He'd seen this before, and recognized what I needed.

When it was dark in Montana, I left to see Maeve.

I appeared near the same spot where I'd encountered Bragi fighting Johnny. Where I'd first met her. According to what Bragi told me and what I'd seen last time I was here, I could follow a path and her house would be only a few clicks away.

Blinking directly there wouldn't work, because her wards prevented anyone but her from doing that. This got me a lot closer than the couple of hour drive Bragi had to take, though.

"I afforded you a certain amount of leeway, because of the history I have with your family." Maeve's voice came from behind me. "This is simply rude, though. Your mothers would be disappointed with your lack of respect."

She was an emotional void. No feelings radiated from her.

So. Nice.

I didn't appreciate the guilt, though. "You'll need to try another tactic if you want to make me feel bad. You told me to come back to you or someone else."

"I have to enforce the rules for everyone." She touched my arm and we vanished from the nothingness and reappeared in her cabin. "If I make exceptions..."

Yeah, yeah. "I notice you reacted to me being there all but instantly. That means you could've done the same the other day with Bragi and Johnny fighting on your borders."

"I could have. I chose not to."

"Great. We both know how to exercise our ability to make choices." I studied her. "I do want to be polite. You deserve that. I'm on a tight timeframe though."

Maeve shook her head and turned away, to walk into her kitchen. "Nothing is that time critical, I promise you."

"Keeping my mothers away from Hel and Vidar was."

Her footsteps faltered, and her shoulders rose and fell. She resumed walking again, putting the kettle on to boil.

"Maybe in the grand scheme of things, the individual doesn't matter," I said. "But in the moment, to the people living it, we very much matter. Is immortality worth anything if we can't appreciate the people that make every single moment unique?"

"Did you come here to lecture me? You and your three whole decades of life experience?" Maeve faced me and crossed her arms.

I shook my head. "No. I did come for a favor, and I did bring offerings." I set the bag of snacks that Frey had provided on the table.

"I don't want the food," Maeve said. "It's symbolic. You know that."

Dealing with ancient beings could be touchy—they expected deference simply for having existed for a few centuries—but I also respected her. She had experience, she helped me before, and I was asking for a lot and offering nothing in return.

"Then a true exchange. Please. Whatever you ask of me is yours." I meant it.

Maeve turned away again, to pull a teapot and cups from one cupboard, and a wooden container with tea from another. "You know what I want from you."

To keep my children safe. To keep myself safe. "I can't do that without some help. Yours, or some-one's." I could pause and wait for her retort, but the words were pushing to be heard. "Vidar wants something from either me or my sister. I don't know what. Or maybe he wants my children. It may not matter to you—those are insignificant details in the grand scheme of things—but if he takes me, or her, or them... someone ends up destroyed. And we can't keep that from happening if we can't figure out how to stop him."

"I still don't know." She poured the hot water into the teapot, and steam escaped, vanishing in the air. "My answer hasn't changed."

"But you can tell me what you've told him in the past. What kind of things you taught him. Gave him."

She placed everything on a tray, and it floated to the table as she walked behind it. The silver platter settled as neatly as if she'd placed it with care. "Sit." She gestured to a chair, and took the one across from it. "Tell me what happened to the crystal I gave you."

"It shattered. I think I overloaded it." I took a butter cookie from the plate she nudged in my direction, and I nibbled at the crumbly sugar. "I got tattoos like you suggested—Vidar burned them off." Tilting my head sideways, I exposed the scars.

"You overloaded..." Her voice was quiet, and the frown already etched on her face grew more stern. "I never gave Vidar more than theory. The type of power he wanted... It didn't seem possible at the time. I can tell you which books I recommended. Which texts. I can't offer more than that, because I don't have more."

It could take hours or years to sift through a bunch of books. I'd still take the list, but even if it was short, we'd have to know what Vidar was looking at and how he interpreted or mutilated the information contained within. "Thank you."

Maeve poured each of us a cup of tea, and I added four sugar cubes to mine. As I stirred them in, I watched them slowly dissolve. Eaten away by scalding liquid.

There was probably a metaphor for my life in there, but I wasn't going to dig for it.

The two of us sipped our tea in silence for a moment.

"What of your friend?" Maeve said. "The one with the missing memories? Do you have the salve ingredients for the stream?"

How did I forget we were doing that? "He got his memory back. It just returned."

"I see. I'm glad for him."

Inspiration struck. I was about to push my luck, and asking for this was a bad idea, but it was the lesser of two evils.

If Bragi was actually evil at all.

"Are you still willing to make one of the salves?" I asked. "For Bragi?"

When Maeve set her cup in its saucer, it was with a loud clatter, and tea splashed up the edges, nearly spilling. "You're pushing your luck, child."

"My offer of a favor still stands." Why was I doing this?

Because he would help in the fight against Vidar.

No other reason. None at all. Nope. Not one that I would admit.

"Bragi is dangerous." Maeve's voice turned stern. "Why would you help him?"

"He can help me."

Maeve reached across the table and gripped my wrist. The longer she squeezed, the more the tendons ached. "The real reason. Tell me why."

I didn't know. I couldn't say. I— "I'm starting to understand." The words were too real as they spilled past my lips. "What changed him. What made him what he became." With the constant assault of other's feelings, all day and night, it was easy to imagine that becoming something bitter and twisted.

Especially if those feelings came from an entire campus of emotionally tortured students.

Maeve let go of me, and the blood flowed into my hand again, tingling under my skin.

"You have the list still? Of ingredients?"

I nodded.

"I'll do it, and in return you listen to what I have to say. Truly listen."

"I will," I said. "I'm listening."

Maeve pushed her teacup aside, and drew in a deep breath. "Bragi thinks the spring doesn't work. He thinks the story is false. A little more than thirty years ago, he wanted his old self back."

I knew all of this, but I kept my mouth shut. I'd promised to listen.

"It works, but not ever in the way one expects. Bragi came to me, and I gave him what he wanted. Two months later, your mothers came to me, to tell me they were finally pregnant."

Nope. There was no way she was implying— *No.* "I was *not* born to save Bragi."

"I'm telling you what happened," Maeve said. "If you choose to proceed, I'll make what you're asking for."

I wasn't...

I couldn't be...

It was a coincidence. Kirby didn't believe in those, but the world was chaotic. Sometimes things just happened. Every once in a while—more often than most liked to admit—things just fell in line in a fucked-up way. "I need to go." As in, somewhere that I could process this and-or freak out.

"I understand." Maeve rose as I did. She held up two fingers and a piece of paper appeared between them. "This is the list of the information I've given Vidar over the centuries." She pulled me into an awkward hug. "Stay safe. I'd love to meet your children."

My mind had moved on from this, and was stuck on in a loop of *I was not born just to heal Bragi.* I nodded though, and when I took the list from her, I was at the edge of her territory instead of in her house.

This wasn't true. It couldn't be. I was more than—

I was a fucking Valkyrie. I'd saved people. I had a life and a family and...

I was more than a creature created for wish fulfillment.

The list from Maeve got tucked away in a safe space, and I sent two identical text messages—one to Dahlia and one to Bragi.

I need to talk to you.

The former, because she would keep me from spiraling and the latter...

Would Bragi assure me it wasn't true? Tell me he didn't know? Reinforce that I *had* saved him, and ask if that was really such a bad thing?

Blinking myself back to NEON, I walked in through the back door. Dahlia was waiting near the staircase that went to the upstairs apartment. She wore a silky robe, which meant she'd finished dancing, but hadn't changed into *normal* clothes yet. "What's wrong?" she asked.

"I can't even..." I let out a heavy sigh when the words didn't come.

She wrapped an arm around me and steered me upstairs. "Frey and Fen are working, so we'll have privacy. I'll make sure we have privacy." She guided me into their apartment and sat me on the couch. "Don't go anywhere."

I was too lost in the revelation to make a joke about *where would I go?*

Dahlia was back a moment later, shoving a pint of ice cream and a spoon into my hand. "Now. Eat at least two bites, and then talk."

"Yes ma'am." I almost smiled at the concern.

With a medicinal dose of brownie-batter cherry-chunk in me, I repeated what Maeve told me.

Her expression stayed sympathetic, but she couldn't hide the tainted disbelief that spilled from her.

"This was a bad idea. I'm not ready to talk about this." I stood.

Dahlia grabbed my wrist and pulled me on the couch again. "Sit down. Shut your mouth. Admit that my initial reaction is reasonable and give me a moment to process."

I scowled at her, but obeyed. "How am I going to tell Nico?" Of all the things I could be worried about...

"First you figure out how you feel about it. The rest will wait." Dahlia was already becoming okay with the news—more so than I was—and wanting to reassure me.

"If I was born because Bragi wished to be healed, am I anything more than a doll?" I clamped my mouth shut. Time to stop feeling, and just let her talk, like I promised.

"You are so much more." Sincerity and belief spilled out with Dahlia's reply. "Be analytical about this for a moment. Life is never as simple as a story makes it sound, and when it comes to prophecy and fate... You've seen the results of taking those at face value."

"But—"

"Not done yet. Eat more ice cream." Dahlia shoved my spoon into the pint and pushed the container toward me. "We've both seen this first-hand so many times. We've both lived it over and over. When I have a vision, it's not straightforward. I'm the one seeing it, and I can still misinterpret it. I was destined to become a dragon. To form this bond with Frey and Fen. Do I think that fate created me solely for that purpose? No. I refuse to believe that about me or you or Kirby or Brit or anyone."

"What do you believe then?" I asked through a mouth full of ice cream.

She took the spoon from me and took a bite for herself, before returning the utensil. "The one thing they taught us at TOM that I think was real is when they called us potentials. Everyone has potential, ours was to become something magical. Not everyone there realized it. Not everyone they tracked became more.

"My visions aren't fixed. The outcomes aren't set

in stone. I've proven that. I exist because I exist, and maybe the universe nudges me one way or another, but I choose whether or not to follow that path."

"In other words, I would've existed regardless, and I just happened to wind up in Bragi's way." It sounded too simple, like I was missing something or brushing off the truth.

Dahlia nodded. "Most likely. It's also likely that you weren't the only one who could've done it. I'm not saying you're not special—you're one of the most important people in the universe, in my opinion—but Bragi wanted to go back to himself. He made that wish. He was looking for a way to make it happen."

There was a deeper meaning in that, but I couldn't hold onto the thought.

"Yes, if a butterfly flaps its wings on the other side of the world, maybe a hurricane happens in Florida," Dahlia said. "A hurricane happens in Florida regardless. On the other hand, if you order a mocha tomorrow morning instead of a caramel latte, you don't change the likelihood of a coup happening in Texas."

"I'm not sure the analogy works." I was beginning to wrap my brain around it though.

Dahlia took another spoonful of my ice cream, and chewed thoughtfully. She was trying to organize her thoughts to change my mind.

I'd have to stop being stubborn for that to happen.

Fuck.

"We always have a choice," Dahlia said. "*Always.* We don't live our lives because the prophecies tell us to, and we don't ignore things we want, just to spite fate. You are who you are because you choose to be that person. *That's* why you've made an impact on so many lives, and that's why Bragi loves you."

I swore my heart stopped beating at the word *love.* When did she land on his side?

But she wasn't. She was stating a fact. A series of observations...

Dahlia took the ice cream from me, set it on the coffee table, and gripped my fingers, drawing my attention. "If fate chooses to take advantage of who you are, if some stupid fucking magic stream abuses the opportunity, that doesn't make you any less you. It doesn't reduce your importance to yourself or any of us. You are who you are because you choose to be," she repeated.

"When did you get so smart?"

Dahlia pressed her forehead to mine. "I stopped trying to fight my potential. It's mine, gods damn it, and I'm the one who gets to own the Hel out of it."

I loved everything about what she was saying.

I just needed to convince myself to believe it.

CHAPTER 12

BRAGI

Over the centuries, I'd written dozens of complex tales. Interwoven narratives and sublimely subtle plot points.

None of them held a candle to the convoluted mess that Vidar seemed to have constructed. He wanted certain people dead. He wanted them alive. He'd stolen a bracelet from a witch. A fucking charm.

It was easy to assume all the power grabs over the centuries had poisoned his mind, and this was nothing more than lunacy. I was afraid the truth was far more dangerous. As long as I'd known the god, he'd been a master of making the simple look complex.

People made assumptions based on their life and experiences. I'd done the same when it came to Vidar. Assumed that *the truth* was *the truth* when he told me things and showed no sign of lying.

And right now, I felt like the entire picture had been laid out before us, but we couldn't see the forest for the trees.

I was trying to break things down. For example, why take the other Valkyrie's family jewelry?

As I strolled through the streets of Detroit, the question nagged me.

Vidar liked working with existing gifts. They were easy to imbue with potent magic.

It's been passed down from mother to daughter for generations.

I stopped in the middle of the sidewalk as Magnus's words clicked. A protective talisman owned by a family of witches, where it was gifted again and again? That charm could be more potent than a dragon's claw. Particularly in a loving family.

"Are you all right?" A woman next to me asked.

Instinct made me brace myself for the concern—and possibly disdain—coming off her as she brushed my arm. Of course, there was nothing.

I gave her a warm smile. "I'm fine. Simply distracted. Thank you." I started walking again.

There was a *Take It & Leave* convenience store a few blocks from my hotel, and that was my destination.

Most of the TOM soldiers, especially those who were smart enough to leave, assumed that we—the gods—impacted their lives, but they made no difference in ours.

They'd all been raised on a strict nutritional regimen. Balanced proteins. Fibers. Calorie counts. We were creating physical specimens after all.

One of the side effects was that almost every one of them saw sweets as a forbidden sin. Sure, sex was a weapon. A tool. They could fuck whoever they wanted.

But prepackaged chocolate cupcakes?

Those were the ultimate indulgence.

For me, knowing the hearts of everyone around me for so long, I'd learned to appreciate the same. Some emotions were easier to spread than others—obsession and hate sat near the top of the list. At this moment, I hated that I was obsessed with the idea of visiting the nearest gas station for plastic-wrapped cakes.

As I stepped through the front doors, my mind continued to return to the charm from Magnus's Valkyrie sister. It was tickling something in my mind that flitted away whenever I reached for it. I needed the mental equivalent of watching it out of the corner of my eye.

It was easy to find what I was looking for, and I grabbed a package of the local favorite.

If I'd acquired this preference while I was with Nico, would he insist on making it for me instead? The idea warmed me, and made me miss both of them—Magnus and Nico—more than I cared for.

As I took my prize to the cashier, the small

screen behind the register caught my attention. It was some sort of internet news, from what I could see.

I let the young man scan my purchase, and handed him money.

"...reactions are mixed. Some are sympathetic and want to know why governments are hiding..."

I blocked out the sound from the video. Same shit, different century.

"It's wild, right?" The man behind the counter jerked his head at the screen. "Do you think it's real?"

A great many things were real that mortals couldn't wrap their brains around, but I didn't mind a little conversation. "What is it?"

"Ah, man, you haven't heard? So this lady—she's like a diplomat's wife or something—she and her husband are in a bakery in Portugal. She walks into what she thinks is the bathroom. Next thing he knows, she's calling him from Tibet."

"Are you serious?" I stared closer at the screen. At the images flashing by, of two locations I was familiar with, because both sat on the intersections of leylines.

"I mean, that's what they're saying. The governments are going to try to cover it up, but I think it's real."

I would think it was a coincidence—someone got careless with a door that led from one place to another—except that both of those places... Vidar had...

Had what?

"It is real," I said.

The cashier held up his hand for a high-five. "Yeah. Another believer. Right on."

I slapped his palm, still staring at the screen. This was important, and I couldn't figure out— couldn't remember—why.

I needed to go. "Keep the change." I walked out of the store, heading toward my hotel.

"You forgot your cupcake." The cashier's voice faded as the door swung shut between us.

I'd get another one. There was something about Skuld. She had...

What?

A bracelet.

No, that was what I was thinking about before. But it was something with power. Why couldn't I remember?

There was a relic. Skuld used it to bolster something in the FU base in Barbados. I remembered that without an issue, but what was the relic for before that?

By itself, it's just a piece to reinforce the wards.

By itself? As opposed to...?

It didn't matter how hard I pushed for the memory, I couldn't find anything.

Vidar had someone block a portion of my memories from me. Whatever that relic was originally for, he'd hidden it away. I suspected I could remember the FU information because it wasn't directly associated with whatever he wanted me to forget.

Was the piece still there in Barbados? The base had been abandoned when Skuld was destroyed, but did that stay behind?

I couldn't grasp why this was important, but the fact that Vidar had specifically hidden my memories associated with it told me that it was.

I needed to get to the former base in Barbados.

Even if my passport weren't expired, flying would take too long.

My phone buzzed, and it took me a moment to climb from the rambling thoughts before I recognized the sound. I grabbed the device and stared at Magnus's text message. I imagined I could hear her voice saying those same words. *I need to talk to you.*

An ache spread through my chest. I needed the same—to talk to her. To see her. To see Nico.

I needed this answer first. In my current state, she was safer with Dahlia than me. Additionally, if I called Magnus, I would tell her what I found, and then she'd want to go with me.

In theory I was walking into an abandoned training facility, but I couldn't risk her or him. Answering her would need to wait.

How could I get to Barbados now?

Ronan.

Like Maeve, he was an elf. A fae cast out for falling in love with a human, though his *sin* was more recent.

In retaliation for his banishment, he helped others escape—fae, immortals, or anyone threatened by magic. He relocated them to places where they would be safe, and helped them start new lives.

I set Magnus's message aside, and called Ronan. After the appropriate greetings and obligatory pleasantries, I made my request. A door—similar to the one in the news story—that would take me to Barbados.

Fortunately for me, there was one not too far from Anubis's shop. It wasn't a coincidence. Apparently one of Anubis's customers worked for Ronan.

I was surprised and grateful he was willing to help me now, and I changed direction to head for the address he gave me.

Years ago, twenty-five or more, I'd done a favor for Ronan. His daughter, Mia, was struggling with nightmares like so many young children did. Hers were founded in genetic memories, though. As she described them, they were monsters from a realm she would probably never see.

Mia was Ronan's life and joy. He would do anything for her, and he'd talked to so many people about how to stop her dreams. When he called me, he was desperate. I could have anything, he said.

I'd asked for a favor, to be called in at a later time. Really, I was interested in helping the girl.

I'd talked to her enough to get a sense for what scared her about the dreams. Feelings she couldn't put into words, but that radiated from her. She didn't have any of her father's power, she was completely human like her mother, so there was no telling how the images had moved into her mind, but I was there to stop them, regardless.

I introduced her to comic books.

It was true, I teased Magnus about her poor taste in films, but stories like the ones she loved, the ones in comics, kept faith alive—the belief in both something greater than ourselves and in survival. Both important things to all creatures.

Though I didn't read the comics myself, I appreciated the stories for what they were. I'd given Mia a stack of X-men comics and told her that any time she encountered monsters, either in real life or in her dreams, she should pick a hero to call on.

She liked Jean Grey. *She's pretty*, Mia said.

I was fond of a phoenix myself, so I didn't argue.

The single favor Ronan owed me was the reason I hadn't called him for transportation before now. I'd been banking this for a while, and once I cashed it in, it was gone.

But if there was ever a time to use it, it was now, to get to a difficult to reach place, to hopefully find a clue, to help us destroy an impossible to destroy god.

Ronan met me at the door he'd indicated. "Why aren't you able to do this yourself?" he asked.

"Because I can't." I'd rather not offer details.

Ronan simply nodded. I assumed the less he knew, the less he had to hide if asked.

"There's an existing door in the facility," I explained. Vidar had gifted different people different ways to travel. While some could blink from one place to another, others had to walk through doors, so he kept one on site.

In the past it would've been guarded, but it would be clear today.

We stepped into a door in Detroit, and out of one in an underground facility in the middle of the ocean. It should be impossible for this building to exist in this place, but Skuld—Lance at the time— used magics to make it work. I wasn't an engineer, and couldn't explain the mechanics, I simply knew we were here.

"I'll be back in twenty minutes," I said. "If you're threatened, if there's trouble, if I don't return, leave."

Ronan nodded.

I followed the halls toward the center of the building. The hallways were mostly dark, but not as much as I expected. Red emergency LEDs were illu-minated in rows along the floor. Why were these still on?

The question cranked my tension and put my every sense on high alert.

This location had been used to train soldiers for the Followers of Urd, which Skuld had founded using her sister's name, as a means of misdirection when it came to the prophecies. Through FU, Skuld had convinced many gods, like those Kirby loved, that this was the way to save people and allow the prophecies to do what they would.

As a counter, Vidar had formed TOM, where we fought against the same prophecies.

Only to discover a few years ago that the two of them—Vidar and Skuld, had pitted everyone against each other. There were no right sides, because the sides had been fabricated.

When Skuld was destroyed, Vidar shut this location down.

I reached the large gym without encountering trouble, and slipped quietly through a door, letting it swing shut softly behind me. It made me leery that I needed to walk to the middle of the room, with no cover, to reach my destination. This was a wide-open space, larger than a football field.

The more quickly I got this over with, the more quickly we could leave. I strode to the exact center of the entire building—it needed to be in order for the protections to work. There was a book mosaic in the concrete, a representation of a book of prophecies.

When I saw that the trap door in the middle was open, and the compartment inside empty, my gut sank.

Whatever had been in there was no more. Vidar had it. Why couldn't I remember the significance?

"Who's in here?" A barking voice bounced off concrete and made my heart slam into my ribs.

Running wasn't an option in this space, but they hadn't shot me yet. That meant their orders required them to wait.

Odd.

"Identify yourself." A soldier stood in a doorway, assault rifle leveled at me.

I shouldn't have to fear a gun, but it was likely he had god-killing bullets. The ammo worked best on gods who refused to admit who they were.

Given my current situation, I couldn't think of a better way to describe myself.

Odds were high that once I told them who I was, I was dead. Holding back didn't improve those numbers. I raised my hands above my head as I straightened up, and took a step toward him.

"At ease, soldier." Was there any chance they didn't know I was persona non grata?

A light hit me in the face, bright and blinding.

A woman laughed. "No shit. Vidar will love this." That was a second soldier.

"Who's with you?" the man asked.

"It's only me." I moved toward them.

The woman leveled her weapon at me and held it steady. "Don't move while we call this in."

The man stepped from the room.

With the light out of my eyes, I tried to be subtle about looking around. There was no way I could see to run. If I could get to Ronan... If he was still here.

The man returned. "Come with us, Sir." He and his partner fell to opposing sides of the doorway and indicated I should pass between them and in front of them.

It seemed they weren't worried about me blinking from one place to the next, but they did keep a few meters between me and them as they led me down the hallway.

Why were there guards here, but only two?

The structure had changed. There were features here that hadn't been before. Structures. Walls. Why would Vidar be moving things in?

None of this made sense.

I tuned out those questions to focus on getting away. I wasn't combat trained like my peers, but I'd watched students long enough that there were concepts I understood. Basic evasion, for instance.

Our path took us closer to where I'd left Ronan. There was cover in the doorways, if I could reach it. We turned a corner, and I sprinted away.

The wall next to me exploded in a shower of concrete shrapnel, and I kept running. Dodging. Avoiding.

These are long fucking halls, and using the narrow doorways to hide behind wasn't idea, but in the dark, it made me a difficult target.

I was surprised to turn another corner and see that Ronan waited.

More gunshots sounded behind me, steady but rapid.

"*Go,*" I shouted at him. I didn't know what these bullets would do to elves and fae, and today wasn't the day to find out.

He reached out a hand for me instead, grasped mine, and yanked.

We fell through the door, and into an alley in Detroit.

Ronan stood and brushed concrete from his suit as he smoothed the fabric. "What was that?"

"I got caught."

"I heard the gunshots. Disgusting weapons."

"Thank you," I said. "I owe you." I meant that literally. His favor to me had been redeemed, and now I owned him one in return.

"I will collect in the future," Ronan said. "Have a good day." He stepped through the door again, which would take him to whichever exit he wished.

Did Vidar care enough to come for me? He wasn't here yet, so I assumed not.

What did I just see? Was he returning to the base in Barbados? If so, why remove the protective seal?

What was he up to?

CHAPTER 13
NICO

Seeing Magnus today—feeling what she was pushing out—reminded me intensely of Bragi in his early days of working with the students at TOM. I wouldn't watch this happen again.

I doubted that the journals I had from Bragi would give me any insight, but I had to look. If I could combine his thoughts with my experiences from the outside, maybe I could help her in a way I wasn't able to help him.

What if you could still help him?

I didn't have an answer to my own question.

Instead, while Magnus was isolating herself, I searched her shelves for something to read. What little she had that was physical was on a small shelf in her bedroom. She'd pointed it out when she was giving me a brief tour of her apartment.

When she left TOM, she didn't get to take much with her, and among her belongings had been a couple of books she'd read over and over on missions. It was easy to see which those were—the worn and tattered paperbacks at one end of the row.

The books were thick for modern publications. Each with a party of people on the cover, and a dragon in the background. I'd love to lose myself in either one, but didn't dare, for fear of them falling apart in my hands.

Most of the remainder of the books were also the smaller trade paperbacks that had been popular for several decades now. Once upon a time, books like this would've been Bragi's favorites. Wistful stories full of hopes and dreams and fantasies—both magical and not.

Magnus had told me a lot of these were from Brit, but a few were gifts from others. The artwork varied widely. There were scenic beach scenes, and some with objects like ties, and bedposts, and what might be the back of a leather bench. There was even one with a man wearing no shirt, and a wolf next to him.

What were modern stories like? I could pick one at random. The bare-chested man with the pet wolf perhaps.

As I reached for it, something at the other end of the shelf drew my attention. It didn't look like a book at first, or at least not like the others. It was larger, thinner, and flat.

The cover was leather, with thin strips tying one edge together. Bragi used to have several of these as well. Usually bound by the author. The leather was patchy, unevenly cut, and stamped by someone unskilled in leather working.

The entire book radiated the love of either the creator or someone close to them.

With the bindings, I didn't have the same concern about pages falling out of this one as the others Magnus had, and something about this called to me. I brought it into the living room, made sure the coffee table was clean, and set the book reverently on top.

The lettering on the cover had looked random in the dim lighting of her room, but out here, I could see the words, written in a language I hadn't seen in centuries. The book wasn't that old, but the words were ancient.

They didn't hold any deep meaning. They simply said this was *The Story*.

As I opened the cover, I was greeted with stunning artwork. Ink on heavy parchment, which laid out a visual story. Correction—turning from one page to the next, it was clear this was multiple stories. Each only lasted a few pages, before the characters and their clothing styles changed.

I was three tales in, when a familiar representation caught my eye. The stylized images shouldn't look like anyone specific, but they did. I was looking at a drawing of Bragi, with Vidar next to him.

Their clothing wasn't modern, however it was close. Linens on their way to refinement. As many buttons as ties. An electric lightbulb illuminating one scene, and a woman I didn't know, working on a machine.

At least, what would be a machine back then. Metal and gears and unwieldy components.

Why did Magnus have this?

It wasn't important enough to interrupt her isolation. Unlike so many of the things we were dealing with, this wasn't life-threatening.

I flipped through more of the book.

The scene with me, fighting Vidar and destroying myself to buy Magnus time to escape, nearly stopped my heart. Why was this here? What in the world was I looking at?

Anxious energy bled through me, and I found myself bundling the book up, walking to the apartment next door, and knocking, before I registered my own actions.

Dahlia answered, and gave me a tired smile. "Hey. Everything all right?"

I showed her the book. "I found this on Magnus's shelves."

"Ah. The old-fashioned comic. Trippy, right?"

"Quite a bit." Should I be relieved that she knew

what I was talking about and wasn't concerned. "What is it?"

"We found it in an old house of Skuld's. Apparently one of her children drew it, based on the images in their head." She opened the door wider. "Come in."

I'd been looking at dragon prophecies? "All of the events in it have come to pass?" I stepped into the apartment to find Fen in the living room as well.

He gave me a curt nod, but his posture remained unthreatened.

Dahlia walked next to me, as we moved into the living room. "I assume. We lived the last quarter or so of the book, which I'm guessing you saw."

"I did." Knowing the prophecies were real was a different experience from seeing that someone more than a hundred years ago, who I never knew, had drawn one of my deaths so accurately. This wasn't a vague poem that could be interpreted in different ways.

Dahlia had given me the explanation I needed, but it wasn't enough. "Will you take a look at another of the older stories with me? There's something about it that's nagging at me."

"Sure."

I set the book on their coffee table, and opened it delicately to the page that had caught my attention.

Dahlia and Fen leaned closer, gazes on the book.

"Oh, yeah." Dahlia's voice sparked with recognition. "That one was weird. But we figured since it was in the past, it wasn't a priority. Plus, it's Vidar and Bragi—who Magnus was done talking to—so it wasn't as if we could ask them about it."

"Who's the woman?" I asked.

Fen glanced at me. "You don't know her?"

"I didn't know everyone he did."

Fen leaned closer. "This would be around the time you were with him."

I realized as much.

"The explosion in the last panel is kind of pretty and scary." Dahlia turned the page. "Don't suppose you remember anything like that happening?"

"No. But I wasn't everywhere." The thing that concerned me though was I would have been there. The images, the setting, this was when I was with Bragi. "And all of these things happened?" I gestured to the book in general.

Dahlia shook her head. "I've never been able to confirm, but the ones we found information about did, so I assume. We could ask Bragi."

Fen let out a sigh-growl.

Well said. If it was the only way to get ans—

"What is that?" Dahlia pointed at the page, never making contact.

"You're the mechanical wizard," Fen said affectionately. "You tell us."

She squinted and frowned and twisted her head

one way then the other. "I don't know, but I think... I've seen that in... *Oh.*" Her frown deepened.

"Where? Does the machine still exist?" How could it, if it had exploded?

Dahlia bit her bottom lip. "Not the whole thing, but this bit of it right here." She pointed to a tiny but ornate amulet attached to the machine. "It's on display in *The Dragon's Hoarde.*"

I'd been there. Stories had been my one guaranteed companion through time. "Artura's. You can ask her about it."

The *tsk* sound Dahlia made, along her grimace, was unexpected. "She and I aren't really on speaking terms. And..." She sighed. "It's because she's really bad at answering my questions."

"Artura tends to be evasive and removed." Fen's explanation was kinder, but both sounded appropriate from what I remembered of dragons. Which was a lot more than before this life.

In my experience, the elder dragons weren't difficult on purpose, they simply saw life in a different light than the people living it.

I understood where they were coming from, though it pained me to admit it to myself. I'd adopted a similar perspective for a long time. "Perhaps if I speak to her."

Dahlia puffed out her cheeks and they deflated as she exhaled. "You're welcome to try. If she kicks us out on sight, though... Not much I can do about that."

Fair point. "Shall we pay her a visit?"

Dahlia took our hands, and their apartment was replaced with a narrow street, lined by stone buildings. The one in front of us was *The Dragon's Hoarde.*

When we walked inside, I couldn't help but inhale the scent of books. The rows that spanned in front of us whispered my name. I could imagine spending hours here with Magnus. Bragi.

No. Not him.

The woman behind the counter looked the same as she had when I last saw her, more decades ago than I cared to count. She was petite, with white hair pulled into a braid, and violet eyes that studied us. Though her expression was reserved, the downward tug of her mouth was as close as I'd ever seen her get to scowling.

When she turned to me, her expression shifted to curiosity. Not warmth. Elder dragons weren't known for their warmth.

Seeing her helped me slot more memories into place that had been fragments up to this point. Something told me she didn't remember the same things I did, though I couldn't say why I believed that.

"Verdandy." I bowed. While Dahlia called her Artura, I felt it was appropriate to address her by the name I'd always used with her.

The dragon's smile didn't reach her eyes. "Nicodemus. It's been so long."

"Longer than I care for."

Artura gave a brief nod. "Are you here for a recommendation?"

"I am. I'm also here on behalf of friends." I gestured to Dahlia and Fen.

Artura wrinkled her nose. She'd become expressive over the years. "They've drawn you in, have they?"

"They have." In so many wonderful ways.

Dahlia coughed and I glanced at her to see Fen rest a hand on her shoulder. Tension coiled through both of them.

I didn't imagine this type of formality was in Fen's comfort zone.

"How are you enjoying their antics?" Artura asked.

I smiled. "I was unsure at first. However, they've helped me adjust my outlook on the world."

"What a shame."

"Just because you're a—" Dahlia clamped her lips shut and her nostrils flared.

"Yes, child?" Artura said.

Dahlia made a low growl, and the tightest shake of her head.

Fen stepped between the women. He didn't appear to be protecting Dahlia so much as confronting Artura.

The older dragon looked him over, then turned back to me.

"I don't mind at all." It was true. The more time I spent with Magnus and her friends, the more I enjoyed it. "I understand why it's not for all."

"How?" Artura asked.

Her question didn't line up with what I had said. "I don't understand."

"How do you tolerate the chaos?"

Dahlia moved forward again. "The chaos exists everywhere, regardless of whether or not you acknowledge me."

I understood Artura's question now. Though she was asking about chaos, there was a deeper meaning, and it was one I'd been confronting when it came to Magnus. By *chaos*, Artura meant how did I deal with being part of the world. I was setting myself up to lose people. To see those I loved slip away.

"I don't know how I'll deal with it when the loss happens," I said. "What I know is that the experiences are ones I wouldn't surrender, regardless of whether or not it brings me pain in the future."

"Something for you to consider, ancient one." Fen's voice was cool.

Artura sighed. "I think about it more than you might believe. What actually brings you to my shop, Nicodemus?"

I glanced at Dahlia again, to let her answer.

She looked like she was preparing herself for battle, with her posture rigid when she moved toward a glass display case to her left. She reached for an amulet that hung around the neck of a stone bust. As her fingers brushed it, there was a spark and Dahlia yelped and jerked back.

"Only the person it was gifted to, the owner, can touch that," Artura said.

Dahlia twisted her mouth. "Can you tell us more about it?"

Artura's expression went blank when she turned to the bust. "Oh. That." Her tone was flat, but not with disdain. All emotion had vanished.

Odd. "Can you tell us about it?" I asked.

"No. Before you fly into a snit, Dahlia, it's not because I'm being difficult. I don't remember anything about it, aside from the fact that it came from Skuld."

"Oh." Dahlia deflated.

Artura pulled the necklace from the bust, and held it in the air by the leather cord. She studied it. "Skuld would've been so disappointed in you."

I assumed she was talking to Dahlia, rather than the amulet.

Fen growled.

Lines creased Dahlia's forehead.

This conversation was declining rapidly.

"Never believe that's a bad thing. My sister made

terrible decisions based on our visions." Artura handed Dahlia the necklace.

Dahlia didn't reach for the gift.

"I think we may all have done so," Artura said softly. She slipped the necklace over Dahlia's head, and let it hang around her neck. "If you don't mind, I'm closing up early this evening. You'll need to see yourselves out."

That was too easy, but arguing felt like the best way to jinx us.

Dahlia and Fen were as quiet as me, as we wandered onto the street. The door locked behind us, and the store went dark.

A chill raced over me, clashing with my fire.

Dahlia pressed her palm to the amulet. "That was weir—" A gurgle spluttered from her throat as a spear if ice pierced it.

The necklace clattered to the ground, and she dropped to one knee with a gasp, the wound already closing.

Fen was already a wolf, lunging at our attacker.

Screams filled the air, and the people around us backed away, as chaos erupted on the street.

"What the fuck, Johnny?" Dahlia was on her feet again, and seemed to recognize our attacker.

Johnny summoned a wall of ice, like a large shield, and used it to stop Fen's lunge, throwing him into a nearby wall.

Fen rebounded without pause and charged again.

"Get us out of here," I barked at Dahlia.

A magical wall went up around us. "I can't leave him here, and I don't know what taking him with us will do." She grabbed the amulet from the ground and pocketed it.

Then we would fight here. I flung a wall of flame into Johnny's ice, and his defensive weapon evaporated before Fen reached him.

Johnny speared Fen through the shoulder, which pierced the wolf but didn't slow him down.

"I'm a god, baby jotunn." Fen's voice was in our heads, as he communicated in wolf form. *"Do you think I haven't faced thousands stronger than you?"*

Johnny was cautious to keep his throat protected, and he rolled aside, throwing Fen off.

"Jotunn. No shit." Dahlia didn't sound impressed. "What do you want, dickhead?"

I wrapped him in a ball of flame, restricting his movement, but leaving enough of him exposed to give Fen access to attack him.

"I need the amulet," Johnny said.

I knew what happened inside was too easy. "Why?"

"To win back..." He stopped. Stopped fighting. Stopped everything. "Give it to me, or I'll take it."

"You know this man, Dahlia?" Fen asked.

She rolled her eyes. She was still in human form,

and looked unconcerned about the threat. "We went to school with him. He was obsessed with Magnus."

"Who? Yes. Her. Wait. Who? I need to get her back." Johnny lunged for Dahlia, and Fen knocked him on his ass.

"My hero." Dahlia swooned.

I circled Johnny in flames, where he had landed.

He tried to extinguish the flame with ice, but his youth and human half meant that he wasn't powerful enough.

I had no sympathy for him. "Obsessed with Magnus," I repeated.

"Who?" Johnny asked.

Dahlia looked disgusted. "Yes. With her and a few other girls. He was an ass about it, too. I got hurt on a mission and was in the infirmary. His solution to Magnus was that if she sucked him off, she'd feel better."

Fen's growl was deep and threatening, like death lurking around the corner.

"Is her story accurate?" I asked Johnny.

"Yes. No. Who? I need to find her. She's mine."

I didn't understand his confusion, but my fury surged that he would try to claim Magnus. "She's not."

"Even after she told him a billion times to leave her alone, well, obviously he's here now."

I wanted to crush him. Wrap him in a ball of flame, and squeeze it until he was snuffed out. As the thought filtered through my mind, I squeezed my hand into a fist, and my circle of fire tightened as well.

"Dinner?" Fen asked.

Dahlia twisted her mouth. "Gross. Not if you plan on kissing me after."

I had a better idea for his fate. "There's a portion of the fae realm where some jotunn live." How did I know that? I shouldn't remember, but I did. "If you reach out, can you feel it?" I asked Dahlia.

She closed her eyes, and after a moment said, "yes."

"Send him there. He can meet the other half of his family."

The entire fight only took a few minutes, and when Johnny was gone, we were surrounded by a shield blocking the world out.

So much for this being easy.

"We should make sure no one is hurt, and then go." It would be great if one of us had the power to fuzz the memories of the crowd, and make them question what they'd seen.

Fen was human again. "Agreed."

Dahlia dropped her shields. The street was still engulfed in chaos, people were asking what had happened, and others had their phones out.

Emergency vehicles were arriving on the scene. We didn't see any real injuries, and our being here would only add to the bedlam. We headed home.

We studied the amulet from Artura for a bit, comparing it to the comic. The longer I looked, the more it tied to memories, but they were ones that were still out of order. I couldn't piece it all together.

Eventually, I left Fen and Dahlia, and returned to Magnus's apartment, to stare some more at the art book.

I was engrossed to the point where I didn't hear Magnus when she returned. At the sound of the door shutting, I looked up to see that her face was drawn and her posture could best be described as *limp*.

Without hesitation, I set the journal aside and met her halfway across the living room. She leaned some of her weight into me as we walked back to the couch.

"How did things go?" I didn't want to assume, but her demeanor didn't look promising.

She let out a tired laugh. "I got both far less and much more than I expected from Maeve." She nodded at the book on the coffee table. "I see you found one of my prizes."

"I did. And Dahlia explained it to me."

"Why are you looking at the past?"

"Because I don't think it ever happened." It felt natural to pull Magnus into my lap.

She fell into me easily, with a soft, "huh."

I shared with her the brief story of visiting Artura. How simple and straightforward the conversation was.

"Huh." Magnus managed to make the second grunt sound more surprised. "So something bad happened after."

I was amused that she would assume as much. "We ran into a man Dahlia called *Johnny*."

"Ugh. Seriously? What did he want?"

"As far as I can tell, he thought the amulet would help him find you. He seemed to have a hard time remembering you though."

With a soft huff, Magnus shook her head. "He was the reason Bragi called. The night we saw Maeve. She sent Johnny away and told him he'd never find me again."

Fae magic was potent and with varied consequences. "I don't know why he thought the amulet would help. We're trying to figure out what it does, besides go in this machine. I don't suspect Johnny's answer is the right one."

"No." Magnus shook her head. "Or if it is, the three of you picked up the most useless piece ever, because you all already have me."

Though it wasn't an answer to the relic question, I did like the sound of it. I wrapped my arms around her and held her close, enjoying the comfortable silence.

"Is it true that you have a picture of me that Bragi painted ages ago?" she asked.

The one I'd found when I didn't remember who I was. "No."

"You asked him about it before you got your memories back," she said.

"I do have a picture, and it's of a woman who looks like you. She was a vision and a two-dimensional fantasy from a long time ago who only existed in our heads."

"But how do you know she's not me?"

There must be more to these questions, but I would answer before I prodded for details. "Because when that vision was in my mind, if you had asked me back then to describe that woman, I would've said she was pretty. She must be strong because she was a Valkyrie. I assumed she would make me happy. Someone with a smile like that..."

"If someone were to ask me to describe you, that's not what I would tell them," I said. "I would say that Magnus is fiercely loyal. Smart. Funny. She knows a lot about sand orphans."

Magnus made a sound that was almost a laugh.

"I'd say that nothing stands in your way. That you're brilliant and driven and that when you walk into a room, you're the only person I want to look at. That I'm so happy I know you, and that I want to learn everything I can about you. And that's how I know you're real, and the woman in the painting never was."

"I'm glad I know you, too." Magnus rested her weight against me, and a warmth spread through me that chased any shadows away. She let out a long sigh. "And to spoil the mood... I left a message with Bragi. I'm going back to him for more help, and I'm going to ask him to introduce me to Vindres."

I didn't like that for so many reasons.

Magnus stiffened in my arms. "I'm not asking your permission. I'm letting you know rather than hiding it."

"I understand." Was I that concerned about her seeing Bragi again?

Not as much as I wanted to be. *I'd like to go with you* flitted to the tip of my tongue, but I wasn't ready for that. Additionally, this next step was hers. "I'll be here when you come back." I pressed my lips to the top of her head. "You had better come back."

CHAPTER 14
MAGNUS

I wasn't keeping the information that Maeve gave me, about Bragi's experience with the magical spring, a secret from Nico. But after what Dahlia had to say, and what Nico said about the woman in the picture, it didn't matter if Maeve believed I was the result of a wish made in a magical spring.

I didn't believe I only existed because some god wanted to be better.

What I did think mattered was that Bragi knew. He saw he wasn't himself.

He also wasn't here right now, and I wanted to focus on the man holding me. It felt incredible to be wrapped in Nico's arms. Pressed close. With him wanting nothing more at this moment than to reassure me and keep me safe.

If I couldn't feel his emotions, this would go

differently. Maybe the sex could go back to being because I liked him and wanted to be with him, rather than because I was desperate to escape my world.

The way my brain was right now, the lack of control I had, that much connection would short-circuit me. My feeling so much of him would hurt both of us.

For tonight, I'd enjoy that he was here and didn't want to leave.

IN THE MORNING, Dahlia brought the coffee with her when she came to see if we wanted to spar, as well as more appropriate clothing for Nico to work out in. She warned us Fen would be joining us too.

We opted for an outdoor arena, to accommodate anyone wanting to shift or fly. This was much better than me trying to channel energy from Dahlia and Nico and toss it at dummies. She and I knew each other's rhythms, and she was familiar with Fen's.

Adding Nico to the mix should make things that much more interesting.

"We need to agree right now to no use of what would be considered deadly force, or attacks meant to cause injury," Nico said.

Fen's growl was one of dissent. "We'll all heal."

"Injuries cause resentment." I was with Nico on

this. I also wasn't in the mood for that level of pain, regardless of how quickly it would vanish.

"Besides, the point is to fight better together. We already know what happens when we fight each other." Dahlia was trying to keep her tone light, but a lingering guilt lay underneath.

When she was learning to control her dragon, she'd been trapped in a dream and the result was her fighting against us. The memory was frightening, and I was grateful we didn't have to do that again.

"We'll play tag-slash-flag-football." The idea came to me suddenly. "Someone has a *flag* and the rest of us try to claim it. When we succeed, the next person gets the flag."

Fen sighed, but his disappointment was teasing. Our *play* was likely to get rough regardless of the rules, because of who we were and how we fought, and he'd enjoy it.

"Smart," Nico said. "Give us all a chance to see what we can do together and how we react when we're on the defensive."

I knew it was a good idea, but I liked his praise.

"Who's first?" Dahlia asked.

"You." Fen ripped a sleeve from Nico's shirt and shoved it in her back pocket.

Dahlia glanced behind her. "Are you burying treasure?"

Fen smacked her ass lightly. "If it's sticking out, there's no challenge."

"One other rule." As soon as I said it, Fen scowled. "No changing forms to hide the flag. Half forms are fine, as long as you're still clothed."

Dahlia grew wings and floated up to hover a few meters above the ground. "You three better plan quick."

"I can teleport." I ran through the options in my head as I took all of our skills into account. "Can you fly if you're not a full bird, Nico?"

He shrugged. "We'll find out. I can summon flames though."

"No attacks that cause serious injury." Despite Fen's previous grumbles, and our target, he was instantly protective of Dahlia.

It was sweet, and unnecessary for multiple reasons, and his assumption was a good reminder he didn't fly. "The flame isn't to strike her, it's to fuck with the air currents around her."

"I can hear you," Dahlia called.

Fen glanced at her. "It doesn't mean you can avoid us."

"I bet I can."

I bet she couldn't. I blinked out of sight, appeared behind Dahlia, and grabbed the sleeve from her back pocket, then returned to the guys before she could react.

"That's not teamwork." Dahlia settled to the ground with a pout.

"It's the kind of teamwork we used against Johnny," Nico said. "Fen and I fought him, and you distracted him." He meant it in a playful way, rather than an accusing one.

I liked seeing him slide into our dynamic so easily, similar to when he'd gone to breakfast with Dahlia and me in Seattle.

"We did make a good team." Dahlia joined us.

I wished I'd been there, so I could've kicked his ass.

The current situation deserved my attention, though. The other three had a plan, even without speaking. Fen and Dahlia knew how to move together, but Nico seemed to have an instinct for what he needed to do as well.

They thought they were all being clever and hiding it.

"We haven't started the next round," I warned.

Fen bared his teeth. "There are no timeouts in war."

"This isn't war," I said.

Nico slipped an arm around my waist. It was sweet and so very deceptive.

I stepped out of his grasp before he could snatch the flag. Dahlia vanished from her spot, and I blinked out of sight before she could appear behind me. I landed where she had been.

The instant I appeared, Fen swept my legs from under me, knocking me on my ass, and Dahlia was back, stealing the flag from me.

She tossed it to Nico.

I could be pissed, but I was too busy picking myself up and laughing. "I knew you were going to do that. I let you win."

"Liar, liar pants on fire." Dahlia sang the words.

In a flash, Nico was engulfed in flame, ala Johnny Storm. "Like this?" he asked.

"No taking a shape—"

"That hides the flag," Nico finished for her. "I understand." His pants were still visible, with the shirt sleeve tucked into the front pocket. There was simply a layer of flame between us and it.

It also technically wasn't an attack.

"I say it's legal," I voted. If the stakes were higher, I wouldn't. This was silly though. No pressure to come out on top. At TOM, there always had to be a winner, and I hated it. I was more of a team-work person.

Was it possible to get past what Nico was doing without getting burned though? I had to know, and the question sparked my instinct. "Summon a flame," I said to Dahlia.

She held out her palm, and a ball of violet fire appeared.

I swiped my hand through it, and it wrapped around me like a glove. I blinked closer to Nico, grabbed the flag from his front pocket, and hopped back to Dahlia as the flame-glove evaporated.

"How...?" Nico studied me, awe and adoration radiating from him.

"I don't know. I just did it." How exciting.

Dahlia produced another ball of flame. "Do it again."

But I couldn't. I tried over and over, but now that I was thinking about it, I couldn't make it work. Either her flame burned me, or it swelled inside me until I had to release it into the sky to keep from hurting anyone.

"This is going to end like it did the other day," Fen warned. "We should get back to playing."

I wanted to keep trying. To figure out what I was doing, but he was right.

Mostly. I couldn't help but try similar things a few more times as the game went on. I couldn't reproduce the original result, though.

The longer we played, the easier it was to fall into reading each other's intentions. Fen would leap into the air, as Nico sprung off his back, to distract either Dahlia or me, and push us into each other, mid-teleport.

Once we caught on, their tactics had to change. All of our techniques shifted and adjusted to the combination of combatants we faced and the skills they used.

And most of it happened without words. This was what I remembered about working with Dahlia. About fighting side-by-side with her, whether that fight was physical, or recon. Even without the ability to sense her feelings, we'd always been able to read each other.

With Fen, it wasn't quite as easy, but it was close. He had hundreds of years of additional experience, but he'd also adapted to what we knew.

Nico, who should've been the unknown, slid into the open spot perfectly.

This was who I was when I wasn't broken from grief or hatred. This was the warrior I could be. I knew my own strengths and what my allies were capable of, and I liked this version of me. I liked that Nico brought it out in me, and I wanted to be this Magnus more and more.

An unwelcome thought slid in. Or was it okay to wonder if I could be like this with Bragi, too?

I know Johnny wouldn't have appreciated it—he never did. Vidar only wanted me like this when I was doing his dirty work. The rest of the time, he relied on the shattered Magnus he'd tried to keep crushed for years.

I was tired of being that wilted, watered down version of me. I was sick of being lost in sadness.

It was time to fight.

We took a break to hydrate and cool down. It was true that instant healing meant none of us really suffered from such a basic workout, but the icy sweet liquid still felt good sliding down my throat as

I chugged one of the drinks from the cooler we brought with us.

While we discussed if we wanted to kick things up a notch, I glanced at my phone.

There was one missed call, and a single text, both from the same person.

Bragi: *I'm around. Call me when you're ready to talk.*

Like that, everything else faded to the back of my mind, replaced with a fog of uncertainty.

No, that wasn't right. I was certain, I just didn't like it. I wanted to answer immediately. See him *now*.

"Whatcha doin'?" Dahlia draped her arms over my shoulders from behind, startling me. "Oh."

I felt the shift in her mood the instant she saw my screen.

She backed up. "I think we should call it a day. We did good, got good things done."

"All right." Fen was curious, but he knew the two of us well enough that he understood he'd get answers later.

"Is something wrong?" Nico asked.

I shook my head. "No. Not in the way you think."

"We'll catch you guys on the other side of the door," Dahlia said.

Fen hefted the cooler over his shoulder like it was a roll of paper towels, and followed her to the exit.

When I couldn't feel them anymore, I knew we'd

been left alone in a field in the middle of nowhere. I showed Nico my phone. It was easier than figuring out what to say.

"Ah." Nico's grunt wasn't as friendly as Dahlia's had been, and there was definitely more jealousy.

Are you going to drop everything because some sexy, angsty god messaged you? Are you that desperate for approval? For the wrong kind of attention?

I doubted Nico was thinking any of that. Those words were all from my own brain.

Though I was almost certain part of Nico wanted to go with me, to see Bragi. This would be a lot easier if Nico would admit that to himself as well as me, but my pushing the issue would make him break rather than bend.

"Bragi can help me," I said.

"I know. There's more to it than that." He was right.

I dragged in a deep breath.

Nico pressed his lips to my forehead; that was rapidly becoming a favorite sensation. "Go," he said. "I told you I'd be here when you got back, and I will."

Nico followed Fen and Dahlia out, and I called Bragi back.

"Hello." His voice had always sent pleasant shivers through me.

That didn't mean I'd forgiven him, but I was willing to admit the draw was still there. Last time I saw him, feeling the way he wanted me, that he still loved Nico, didn't do anything to dissuade me from being attracted to him. "Hey. I got your messages."

"And I got yours."

"Can I come over?" I felt like a silly little girl. Playing games. Sending *wyd* texts. I wasn't doing any of those things.

"I'm here."

Was I better off staying where I was? Listening to his voice, but existing in a realm where I couldn't feel anyone? "I'm going to ask you another favor."

"I'm going to give you whatever you want," Bragi said. "See you in a few minutes?"

I couldn't go over there sweaty from a day of working out. I should, and pretend I didn't care, but I couldn't. "An hour."

We disconnected, and I headed back to the apartments like the others had. I forced myself to not hurry through the shower, but to also not make a big deal out of shaving and scrubbing everything.

Why was I putting so much thought into this?

No makeup. My hair could go in a ponytail, and it was fine for me to wear my comfiest oversized sweatshirt, and leggings. I wasn't trying to impress anyone.

Then I was standing in front of Bragi's hotel room, knocking.

CHAPTER 15
MAGNUS

Bragi's smile when he answered was genuine, and the desire that spilled into me was raw, filthy, and desperate. He didn't care how I looked. The only thing keeping him from pinning me to the closest wall, ripping off my leggings, and making me come over and over, was that he wanted me to beg for it.

He needed to know I wanted the same.

I mentally cleared my throat, and returned his smile.

"Come on in." He stepped aside, and closed the door behind me.

I didn't hesitate to move further into the room this time. I was done being terrified of who I was and what I could become. "Thank you for calling me back." When I sent that message to him last night, I was ready to break.

Not anymore.

"As if there was any question I would." Bragi didn't try to hold back his emotion the way Nico was. I could say maybe Bragi wasn't used to it, but he knew what he was doing. "You wanted a favor?"

We could get that out of the way first. "I'd like to meet Vindres. I'm told you can introduce me."

Bragi's shock, feeling it as I saw it spread across his face, made this empathy thing worth it, if only for a brief moment. He slid from surprised to concerned to ready to tell me *no*, no matter the cost. "Absolutely not."

"What happened to giving me anything?"

Bragi was about to be vindictive, to prove a point. He would push me, and I knew it before he turned a snake-like smile on me. He wanted me to know it was coming.

"Don't play this game with me, little girl." Bragi stalked toward me.

"What game?"

"Don't taunt me with what I feel for you like it's your ace in the hole." Bragi stopped when his toes met mine. Like this, it was clear he was taller than me. Broader in the shoulders. Could be really fucking imposing when he wanted to be. "I will take off the gloves, and you don't want that."

"Don't I?" What was I doing?

Not backing down. I was tired of cowering.

"The last time you were here, you couldn't push just me out of your head." He raised a hand and reached to cup my cheek, but never made contact. Instead, his palm hovered near enough to my face for me to feel the heat from his skin. "It doesn't matter how strong you are. You're losing your mind after a week of this. If you walk into Vindres's, it will break you. If that's what you want—if you're looking to be destroyed—I'm happy to do that for you, without you ever going near him."

The emotions that rushed over me were a thousand times more potent than anything I'd experienced when I kissed Nico. Bragi wasn't just feeling, he was doing it with a level of intent that was terrifying. There was lust and longing and hunger and violence.

What he radiated was so intense, he might as well be dragging his touch over my bare skin. It was almost as if he was forcing himself inside me.

He wanted me to think he wasn't holding anything back.

But he was. Hidden behind all the electrifying and uncontrolled passion, was the thing he didn't want me to see. Unlike Vidar or Johnny, Bragi didn't see me as a trophy. He didn't want me in pieces. He would let the world burn to have me, but he wouldn't take me if it meant I shattered.

"You won't break me," I said.

"I already did once." *Regret.*

I shook my head. "If you had, I'd still be serving Vidar."

"I'm not introducing you to Vindres."

Even if it meant I hated Bragi again, he was serious.

"I'm not asking because this is some sort of game for me," I said. "I didn't learn who he was and think *oh, that sounds like a deliciously torturous time. Who can help me live that?*"

Bragi wasn't amused, but he kept his mouth shut.

"Vidar stole a data center. There are rumors, information from Min and Aya, that makes us think Vindres may be able to tell us more."

"How do you think this works? I introduce you, and you ask him *what's up with Vidar, yo?*"

I twisted my mouth and gave him a look of disbelief. "You insult me. I think what happens is that you and I use everything you taught me about interrogation, we have a lovely conversation with him, and at the end of it, we walk out and he has no idea."

Bragi wanted to argue, but knew I was capable. "None of that changes the fact that you're not in any condition to walk into his club. And I don't mean your pregnancy. I can sit here and watch you practice, but that's the only thing that's going to help you. Practicing."

"I'll have had the babies before I figure things

out at the rate I'm going. There has to be more to getting this right." Some of my frustration slipped out without my permission.

"Have you had dinner yet?"

I stared at him, and opened my senses up for a hint of what he was doing. Nothing. There was no deception in his question ."What?"

"Have you eaten yet? Would you like to have dinner with me? We'll order room service and sit and chat. Like going out, but we'll stay in." He was asking me on a date.

I didn't understand. It was a ridiculous tangent. "Why?"

"Why do most people eat together? Because we're hungry and feel the company is better than eating alone."

I couldn't feel any deception in his request. The lust he'd forced at me earlier lingered, but it was always there in some form. Since I was both hungry and not leaving until I got the answer I wanted, there was only one response to give him. "Dinner sounds nice."

"Sit." Bragi directed me to the couch. He grabbed a thin, leather-bound booklet from the table near the phone, and opened it as he handed it to me. "What would you like?"

There were no prices. I'd spent enough of my early adult life in hotels to know that even low-end room service was expensive, and if this was the kind of place where cost was of no concern, this food had to be outrageously priced.

Sure, it was easy enough to say I didn't care how much any immortal spent on me, but this relationship was complicated.

"I'm not trying to buy you," Bragi said. "It's dinner. You don't owe me anything."

I might not believe him if I couldn't feel his sincerity. *Fuck*, life had jaded me. I picked a burger that was probably more than a week's worth of groceries, and a soda to go with it. Bragi called room service to place our order, then settled on the couch next to me.

There was enough space between us that the position felt casual and natural. Did I want him closer?

What were we supposed to talk about? We'd rehashed all the disagreements again and again. I kind of—okay I *really* wanted to just have a conversation.

"I won't apologize for doing what I thought was best to keep you safe, when you came to me after the fight with Vidar," Bragi said.

Not a great lead-in, and I clamped my mouth shut to keep from falling into the same old argument.

"But what happened to you, to all of you at TOM..." Bragi paused.

He was sorry for that. So much regret. He blamed

himself in almost as many types of guilt as I kept stashed away.

"It happened to you too." I felt it. I was living that same decline into *all I feel is pain, and if I keep caring, it will kill me.* But my decline was more rapid.

His sigh was heavy. I wasn't the only one wanting to skip this rehash.

"I woke up your laptop, at the cabin." The way Bragi changed the subject was so abrupt it nearly gave me whiplash. "I didn't mean to—I bumped the table it was on. Were you introducing Nico to Star Wars?"

That memory was better. Softer and warmer. "It's important that he have an appreciation for the classics." My choice of words would make Bragi cringe.

Knowing that didn't make me any less entertained when it happened.

"You do know how to hurt me. A knife to the heart would be less painful." He was being melodramatic.

I was tired of analyzing everything he said. Could we just talk? "You called me Little Girl. You didn't think that would hurt?"

"I thought it would piss you off. Or turn you on. I forget which."

"Liar." I was playful.

Holy shit, was I being playful with Bragi?

We'd done this. Before either of us left TOM. In

those rare moments when we were allowed to be ourselves. I'd shoved that bit of my past aside in favor of hating him, but it was one of the reasons I ever trusted him.

He leaned forward, resting his hands on the cushion between us. "It's true. I already know the secret to turning you on. Wear crappy, unwieldy robes, and carry a magic glowing sword." He meant a Jedi outfit.

I wrinkled my nose. "Wrong." I tilted in and placed my mouth near his ear. "You need to put on a fur suit and growl."

Bragi pulled away, and made a sound that probably should have been, but was nothing like, a Wookie roar.

I adored that he was trying.

A knock interrupted, and he went to let the room service waiter in. The man wheeled a cart into the room, set a series of covered trays on the table where Bragi told him to, and wished us a nice evening.

Watching Bragi arrange everything once the man was gone, including pouring my drink into a pretty cup filled with ice, was a sweet combination of bizarre and painfully normal.

As in, this was what normal people did, and I would never be that.

I used to wish I could be, but even with everything going on, I wouldn't want a regular, boring life in place of this one.

Bragi settled into his seat again. "Dig in."

I did. The burger looked incredible, and it didn't disappoint. The hand cut fries were yummy, too. "If this were a real date, how would you woo me?" I asked after a few bites.

"This is a real date."

"Really?" News to me, but had I ever actually been on a *date* date?

"Aren't you wooed?" He was still playful, but sincere at the same time. "Or do you want flowers? Candy perhaps? I'd bring you your enemy's head on a platter, but I think you'd rather do the honors there."

I would. "Flowers die. I can buy myself candy."

"What would you like? Anything."

"You say that so often—*anything*—and I don't believe you understand the scope of the word."

Bragi gave me a look of disbelief. He made a show of wiping his mouth and fingers on his cloth napkin, then knelt at my feet and grasped one of my hands in his.

A shock of emotion raced through me, but not as potent as similar feelings had been. I was focused on my own heart—what I was enjoying about the moment—and I kept that at the front of my mind.

"If you asked me for a star from the farthest galaxy, I would find a way to bring it to you." His voice was firm and clear and seductive.

I loved the sentiment, but the practicality of his

offer… "Where would I put a star? It's not going to fit in my coat closet. Besides, if you start that big, there's nowhere else to go."

One corner of his mouth tugged up, and amusement trickled from him. "If you asked me for the most delicious cherry, from the rarest tree, in the deepest heart of Japan, I'd bring it to you."

"But then I either eat that, or it goes to waste, and once I've had the best, all others will disappoint." I wasn't trying to be difficult. I was having fun, and he was too.

He stood and pulled me to my feet. "If you tell me that the only thing you want is to live a long life, surrounded by family and friends and discovery, and to never lose your appreciation for the small things, I'll do everything in my power to give you that. I'll crush kingdoms of gods. I'll banish anyone who threatens you to another realm. I'll bribe the kid mixing paint at the hardware store to make sure the dusty rose you want for an accent wall doesn't have too much *dust* in it. Anything."

That was actually pretty swoon-worthy. But I only wanted one other thing from Bragi. "Swear to me you'll never lie to me again."

He hesitated. He was weighing the decision.

If he'd answered quickly, I wouldn't have believed him.

He looked me in the eye. "I swear it." He meant it.

As Bragi let go of my hands, I gripped his fingers tight. What was I doing? Why?

His sigh was quiet. If I couldn't feel him, I'd think it was resignation, but it was appreciation.

"There is one other thing I can show you, about control," he said.

The swell of desire that came with his words was a hint at what *it* was, and I didn't want to know that. I didn't want to be drawn into the temptation. "I thought you said there was nothing else."

"This isn't a new thing. It's the same thing you already know, but it takes the practice to the next level."

I could guess, and I'd be right, but I wanted to hear him say it. "Tell me."

"We should finish our food first."

"I'm not interested. I'll eat later." I needed to hear him say it.

Bragi gripped my hand again. "Follow me." He led me to the bedroom.

My heart hammered against my ribs. Over sex. I didn't get this kind of worked-up about fucking.

Would I be able to handle the emotional onslaught?

Bragi stood me in the middle of the room, rather than guiding me to the bed.

"There's a time and place for sensory deprivation," he said. "But this is the opposite. This is learning to focus on what's external, to keep you out of your head and heart."

Old news. "I know this one."

Bragi let go of my hand, to trail a finger up my arm, until my sleeve stopped it. "This isn't about school and what you learned there. This isn't about detaching or doing a job. The point is to enjoy it."

His touch was so light it was barely there, and I realized I was holding my breath, waiting for the next brush of his hand.

"Concentrate on the sensations and enjoying all of your senses." Bragi moved to my neck, my jaw, and along the edge of my ear, before trailing back down.

"All of them?" *Gods* this was basic, but incredible. I was fully dressed, and if he kissed or nibbled the right spots, I might come from the release of anticipation.

Maybe not, but...

Bragi traced along my bottom lip and slipped two fingers into my mouth. "All of them."

I sucked and licked and groaned in disappointment when he pulled away from me.

He pushed the bottom of my sweatshirt up, up, up to expose my stomach, and glided his fingers under my waistband. "Tell me you want this." His voice was pure command.

"I want it so much." I was supposed to enjoy it. That was the point—to lose myself in the physical.

Fuck yes.

I felt his smile through his touch. Self-satisfaction, and more of the same need that filled me.

"Because I'm going to strip you down a piece of clothing at a time." He pulled my sweatshirt over my head, leaving me in a lacy bra—red, to contrast with my skin. "I'm going to explore every inch of you. I'm going to taste you and discover which buttons make which sounds and when you think you can't take anymore, I'm going to fuck you until you scream so loudly that the people across the street complain."

Yes, please. "That's a big promise."

"I'm a big man."

The playful retort was the perfect sprinkle of levity, and I grinned. "I remember."

He tilted his head closer, the way I had with him in the other room. His breath was hot on my neck. "Such a good, dirty little girl." The purr in his words sent a rush through me. "I hope you didn't plan on wearing these home." He ripped the seam of my leggings, exposing panties the same color red as the bra.

The instant he slipped his fingers between my legs, he'd find out I was already wet.

Fuck, this might just wreck me, and at the moment that sounded like the most incredible thing in the world.

CHAPTER 16

BRAGI

The anticipation I felt, stripping Magnus down and covering her body with kisses, was like no experience in my past.

I'd had sex with countless people over the centuries, and I'd even loved a few of them.

Nico was the most recent, and before Magnus, the only one who left enough of an impression that I still dreamed of him.

I'd been with Magnus before as well. This was more... real. As in, there were no masks here. No fakeness or playing pretend.

We each knew who the other was, and she accepted me despite that.

Or maybe it was because the more time went on, the more she could relate.

Creation I hoped she never completely understood, but I knew on some level she did.

I told her to be present during this, to stay outside her head, and she deserved the same from me. I used my full body to nudge her toward the bed. As we walked backwards, she fiddled with the buttons on my shirt.

"What are you doing?" I asked playfully, covering her hands but not stopping her.

"I'm supposed to be feeling the physical, aren't I?" There was a laugh in her question. "I like the feeling of undressing you, and I'd really like the feeling of your skin against mine."

There was no way I could turn her down with a reply like that. I let her finish unbuttoning my shirt, as I teased my hands up her sides and down to her hips again.

She pushed my shirt off my shoulders, and danced her fingertips over my chest, sending tremors of need shuddering through me.

With a bump, I knocked her off balance and sent her tumbling onto the bed to land on her ass.

Her laugh was incredible.

I should feel the joy that came with that sound. It should ping in my chest the way it did hers, and buoy my mood more.

That was another thing that was different about this—the lack of her emotion in my head. I was trying to teach her how to focus on only the physical, and for the first time in my life, I was having sex and didn't have a choice but to not know what my partner was feeling.

The sensation—or lack of sensation—was both incredible and suffocating.

I crawled up Magnus's body, pushing her to the mattress in the process, while I kissed along her neck. Her chest. Her shoulders.

I covered her entire body in kisses, then came back for another round, tugging her bra down to tease and suck on her breasts.

This was incredible. Hearing her sigh, feeling her squirm underneath me... I could do this for hours. Each gasp she made tugged harder at my desire and my cock.

She hooked a finger in my belt and tugged my waist closer,

I planted a knee between her legs to catch my balance, and she shifted her weight, pressing into my thigh. Her heat radiated through fabric, her core tempting me further.

For the most part, the centuries had taught me patience. All of that knowledge evaporated now, with her underneath me, yielding and playful. Giving herself to the moment and to me.

I wrapped my lips around one of her nipples, to suck and nibble, and she jerked against my leg.

The longer I licked, the harder she ground into my leg. She was so wet, I felt it against my skin, through her panties and my slacks.

Her breath came in delicious pants, and her body heaved from the attention.

I pinched and rolled one of her nipples between my fingers, as I moved my mouth up her body. I nipped at her neck. Her earlobe. "Come for me, gorgeous." My voice was gravel. "You want it. You deserve it."

Magnus worked her hips harder, faster, humping my leg. Pressing her pussy into me, while I pressed back. Her entire body shuddered as a series of whimpers tore from her throat.

For a heartbeat, the entire world froze when she tensed. And she fell back against the mattress with a happy sigh.

I claimed her mouth. Kissed her with dozens of tiny pecks, and ignored the whisper of a nag in the back of my mind.

"What's wrong?" Magnus asked, picking up on something I didn't want to acknowledge.

"Nothing. I love the sound you make when you come. How incredible you look. The universe revolves around you when you're turned on."

Her smile twisted into a question. "But...?"

Me keeping the words tucked away apparently wouldn't stop her from recognizing them. "But I've never not felt it before."

Magnus brushed her fingers over my cheek, and a spark of emotion flamed to life inside me.

I had an idea what she'd done, I used to do

something similar with Nico. This was different though. This wasn't her just sharing what she was feeling, but it was me. This was my power, flowing through me.

Muted, but familiar. Enticing.

"How's that?" Magnus asked.

"Incredible." I pulled her hand up to nip at her fingertips.

Her magical, delicious, sexy fingertips.

She wrapped her legs around my waist, and reclaimed her hand to fumble with my pants. She undid my belt, then the button and zipper, and pushed the remaining clothing down my legs with her feet.

Her need spilled into me, mingling with mine. So did the fun she was having. The joy.

Fuck this was...

I didn't dare vocalize it and ruin the moment. Instead, I leaned in to crush my mouth to hers, in a long, hungry, messy, sloppy kiss. A feedback loop of lust and desire.

Somehow in the middle of all of that, I finished kicking off my trousers, and she managed to wrap her fingers around my cock. Her fingers were softer than a soldier's should be, and her grip was warm. She stroked, knowing she was teasing.

I groaned and lost myself in her touch.

This was good. This was incredible. I needed more.

Again, I glided my body up hers, and she wrapped her legs around me, trying to coax me inside her.

"I don't want this to end," I said.

"It won't be the last time."

Simple words that meant so much more than it sounded like. She meant every implication.

I penetrated her with a long groan. She was so tight and slick as she sheathed and gripped my cock.

Pushing one of her knees to her chest, I angled my body to one side and gripped her fingers. I kissed her palm, then bit enough to make her yelp, and moved her hand lower, between her legs.

"Make yourself come," I said.

She stroked her fingers over her own clit, and I felt her jerk and clench around me.

Fuck me.

No. Really.

I barely moved inside her, but stayed buried deep as she fingered herself. The way her chest heaved as she neared climax again, the look on her face as she reached that peak of orgasm, it was all amazing.

When she was spasming around my cock, crying out at the height of orgasm, I stopped holding back.

I slammed inside her, hard and fast. Frantic. Pinning both of her knees to her chest and pounding at a steady, insistent pace.

She was still riding her climax, I felt it inside me as I neared my own. The circle of her need built on me, drew out hers, heightened mine, again and again.

I came hard, spilling inside her, and continuing to fuck like a frantic beast until the high ebbed.

We slowed to a stop, and I rested inside her a bit longer, before rolling aside and pulling her into me.

Until now, I'd convinced myself that I didn't miss the empathy. That I was glad it was gone, and I'd be fine if it never came back.

But in that brief moment, I was whole. Which left me desperately wanting to feel that way again all the time.

For now, I could enjoy what I had. Magnus, in my bed and in my arms. I held her close to me, and kissed lightly along her shoulder and back.

"You think this was a mistake." Her voice was soft.

"You misunderstand."

"Oh?"

"Now that I've had you, I can't give you up."

Magnus's laugh was light and clear. Sweet. Perfect.

"Besides, you're not focusing on what I feel, you're still focused on the physical," I said.

She pressed her back closer to me. "For training?"

"For sanity."

We lay quietly for a moment, until Magnus pulled away to roll onto her side. She propped herself up on one elbow to meet my gaze, and brushed her fingers along my shoulder. "Where did the scars come from?"

"Failures." It was tempting to leave the answer there, but I felt compelled to finish the thought. "Most of them are early attempts to learn about the technique I used on you. I suppose a few are incidental, from other battles fought over the centuries, but most..."

"Yeah. I get it."

"I didn't mind at the time." I told myself it was all in the name of making sure that when I lost my power, I could get it back. Fat lot of good that did me. "I was drowning in the agony that was TOM, and this was a way to punish myself."

So much for post-coital bliss and whispering sweet nothings.

Though, that wouldn't be us, would it?

"How did Nico get his memories back?" I asked.

Magnus dragged in a deep breath and her nostrils flared. "I kissed him. I wanted him to remember."

"The same way you did with me a few minutes ago." When my empathy came back.

Unlike with Nico, mine didn't stay.

"I guess in a way," Magnus said. "It wasn't a conscious thing either time. Tonight it was more like... you wanted the experience back and I wanted to share it. That was all I was thinking."

Why did Nico keep what he lost, and I didn't? Was that part of her unconscious doing? Could she do it again, with purpose?

"I'm not kissing Vidar." Her comment startled and sickened me.

"No, you're not."

The corners of her eyes tugged up. "I can't do it on purpose. I tried yesterday, and I blew up a dozen test dummies."

"I'd rather not be blown up."

"I'd rather not be the one doing the blowing." Magnus paused with a frown, and then chuckled lightly. "You know what I mean."

I did.

It amazed me that she had this kind of control after so little time. What she was doing had taken me centuries to figure out. I could offer a number of excuses like she had help and I didn't have a need to suppress what I was...

But less than a month was impressive regardless.

"I'll introduce you to Vindres," I said.

"And all I had to do was fuck you, to get a *yes* out of you," she teased.

We both knew that wasn't what we'd done. "Are you complaining?"

"It was worth it." She dropped to the mattress again, and snuggled into me.

Silence wrapped around us once again. This was

one of those rare moments where I was at peace, and I was going to treasure it for all I was worth.

"Why does he want me?" Magnus's question seemed to come from nowhere.

I could tease her. Ask if she meant Vindres, but her tone had grown serious. "Vidar?" I asked.

"Or does he? Am I just a stepping stone to someone else? Dahlia? If he took that data center—"

"He doesn't want Dahlia." I was certain of it. "He may want her out of the picture, because she can do a lot of the same things he can, but he wants you." I hadn't been certain until recently, but I should've seen it years ago.

"Why?"

I'd wondered that myself. Some of the students got special attention. Kirby, it was easy to figure out early on who she was and why Hel and Vidar would want to control her. Some of the other Nobles had their own unique pasts and lineage... Not that they'd ever achieve their potential.

And I knew why *I* was drawn to Magnus.

But I'd never unraveled why Vidar focused on her. "His attention to you pissed Hel off. She always assumed it was because of Dahlia. That he had some sort of soft spot for her because she was one of his, and that extended to you."

Magnus lifted her head from my chest. "How do you know that wasn't the case?"

"I felt it in my heart of hearts." I pulled her back to me.

"Has he always known I was a conduit?"

"Possibly." It was a huge surprise to me, but if it never came up between us, he never had to lie about it. "On the subject of Vidar, I paid a visit to an FU facility that should have been abandoned. He's reopening it, and has removed an ancient relic of Skuld's that was a part of the security. I don't know how that's related to what you've found, but whatever he's up to, it can't be good."

Magnus traced a lazy path over my chest, occasionally pausing to play with the short hairs. "When Kirby came back to TOM after Hel was dead... When things were falling apart..."

After Dahlia left. When I was planning my exit. "Yes?"

"It was really important to Vidar that Kirby make me a Valkyrie. She wouldn't have done it if I didn't want it, but he pushed me toward it."

"No." Pieces clicked in my mind. I remembered all of that. The things I wasn't there for, someone told me about. "He was pushing for her to use her powers on you." After a mission went bad, Kirby had healed Magnus, who turned around and was able to do the same to other soldiers for a few moments. That was what Vidar was looking for. "Kirby was proof of concept. Evidence that you were capable of what Vidar suspected."

"But why does he want me?" Magnus looped back to the beginning. "So power flows through me—He gets his from other places, and it's not like I'm going to give him more."

I didn't have an answer for her. "I knew another conduit and so did he. Not that long ago."

"As in last week or last century?"

I was entertained by her qualifier. "Closer to the latter." Sometimes the decades blurred together. "She was fascinating as a person. As a conduit? It was never important for me to dig into. She had a twin—an amplifier. I remember, put them together and one would absorb the magic and filter it and the other would enhance it."

"Did they fight together?" Magnus asked.

Back then the question would've been ludicrous. "That's not what we did—fighting. They put on some incredible light shows with it."

Magnus sighed and flattened her palm against my chest, over my heart. "I want to live long enough to say *fighting isn't what we did with our strength.*"

"You will."

"You promised no more lies."

"I'm not lying." I believed it. "Any doubt you feel is yours."

"Yeah, it is."

CHAPTER 17

MAGNUS

I was reluctant to pull away from the comfort of being wrapped in Bragi's arms. Had I really forgiven him enough that this felt safe? That I wanted to stay here?

I didn't know, but I did understand him more than I ever had before. "I need to go." With the words, I forced myself to sit up.

"Mhm." His grunt was unhappy.

I didn't have the full control of my empathy that I wanted, but I was close. Everyone was background noise unless I let them in or I slipped. "This was good. No, this was incredible. Thank you." Not only the sex—though that was the highlight of the evening—but the way more of my self-doubt had been bled away.

An invisible wall seemed to slide into place when I climbed from the bed. The extended moment was over, and this was business again.

I was tired of everything being business. Especially falling—

Nope.

I grabbed my bra and panties—which weren't suitable for wearing before they were washed. My leggings went in the nearest trash can. Oops.

Fortunately, my sweatshirt was long enough to cover everything, given my travel involved blinking from this room to the back entrance of NEON, and sneaking upstairs.

While I dressed, Bragi and I discussed timing for our *date* to visit Vindres.

"You'll need to drop the shield that hides you for a few hours." Bragi was even more reluctant to suggest it than I was to accept it. He has his own protections in place, and yours won't work there, so it's best not to push the issue. He's not empathic, but he senses certain things, the way Frey does."

"So desire and lust?" Not a big deal. I could stop fighting the pull of *fucking is fun* for a few hours.

"Exactly. And he's going to be fascinated by you. He'll want you to join him for the company."

That was always the hope—to be the unique gem in the midst of what the target already knew. I gave Bragi a look that said *I've got this.* "You act like I've never done this before."

He gave a huff of a chuckle. "You really were my best student." He both loved that about me and regretted it intensely. "I have a favor to ask, but I'll do this for you regardless."

"You need to work on your negotiation tactics," I teased.

"Perhaps. Ask Nico if he'll see me."

I didn't expect that, but I liked it. "I will. I promise. See you tomorrow night?"

Bragi nodded. "I look forward to it."

I blinked from his room to NEON, and slipped inside without encountering anyone, while wearing my makeshift dress. It was enticing to feel the cool air brush the exposed skin between my thighs, but I wasn't in the mood to run into most anyone while I wore so little.

When I walked into my apartment, I stopped short when three heads swirled in my direction to look at me. Nico was here, and his jealousy was so instant and white-hot that it knocked my control off-kilter.

That needed to be put back on track instantly, but not before I felt Dahlia's conflicted blend of glee and concern.

Fen wasn't happy that I was with Bragi, but he was otherwise unfazed. I was people doing people things.

"Hey." My voice was strained. "Did I miss the party invite? Wild time at Magnus's?"

The old comic I'd found in Skuld's house a while

back sat on the coffee table in front of them. The amulet sat next to the book.

"We're looking for hints about what this does." Fen pointed to the amulet.

He wasn't just indifferent, he was bored. He wanted to get to the hunting part of this.

"Any luck?" I could pretend this was fine. Nothing was out of place. This wasn't the first time I'd come home after a night of fucking.

The Bragi part of it was new.

Dahlia sighed. "No. It's part of this machine. But it's not whole and the only thing the book says about the machine is that it opens doors. Or breaks them. Or seals them. Or makes them pancakes. I don't fucking know. Why does language have to be so confusing?"

Nico was still staring at me.

"How'd it go?" Dahlia asked, as if there was more than one explanation for me coming home intact and content, with half of my clothes missing.

I shrugged. "Bragi's going to introduce me to Vindres tomorrow."

"Like that?" Fen looked surprised.

"Not *like that*," Nico didn't mean the same thing.

Dahlia was right—language was confusing.

She carefully closed the book and pocketed the amulet. "Fen and I are going to go."

"Can we do what she just did?" Fen jerked his head at me.

Nico's scowl deepened.

Dahlia batted her eyelashes at Fen. "Only if you make me beg."

He wrapped an arm around her waist and steered her toward the door.

She stopped next to me. "Apartment next door is free if you kick him out," she whispered. "My door is open if you need to talk."

"I'll be okay until tomorrow." I spoke as softly as she did. "Thank you."

Fen's growl was impatiently playful, and he yanked Dahlia from my apartment.

I gave Nico my full attention. Thank the gods I learned what I did tonight about control, or I'd be drowning in the mess of his feelings. Not that he was wrong for feeling them, but me doing so too would make this conversation more difficult.

I was so over difficult conversations.

"Was this *training*? Is that what he told you?" Nico asked.

Disgust slid through me at the suggestion. "No. It was because we both wanted it."

I want you too.

I wasn't sure if that was me or him feeling that way.

"What does this mean for us?" There was no accusation in Nico's question. No *how could you?*

"As far as I'm concerned, it doesn't change

anything between us. If it does, that's a question for you." I wasn't being cruel or dismissive. "I still feel the same way I did about you before I left earlier."

"How *do* you feel about me?"

Nico's question caught me off-guard, and I fumbled my thoughts. "I— You said it was okay if I didn't know."

His expression softened a hint. "I remember, and I still mean it. If I'm only here because you feel some sort of obligation—whatever that is—then I deserve to know."

"You're not." I told Bragi I needed to save Nico. To get his memory back. I needed to be the hero in *someone's* story. I still wanted that—to save him. To save everyone. But it wasn't the real reason I'd done so much to help Nico.

If I was going to demand honesty from Bragi, I owed myself the same.

"Then tell me," he said. "If your answer is *I'm still figuring it out*, that's still an answer. I watched him destroy himself when he became a member of the board. I watched him slide into a skin I didn't recognize. Seeing it all at once, as my memories realign themselves, it's easier to understand than it was while I lived it. But I don't know if I can forgive him for what he did to every single student he trained at TOM, and I certainly can't live through it a second time, watching you do something similar."

What Nico was saying made sense, but it also rubbed me wrong. "It's not on you to forgive him for what he did to the others. That's for each of us to decide. You can hate him for deciding to do those things. You can say you won't be with a person who could do that, but you also know—you do because you just said so—that wasn't him." Was I talking to Nico or myself?

"And that's not me, either. I've been living this for a few weeks—this swimming in emotional sludge—and I've done a damn good job of adapting. Less than a fucking month. I'm suddenly responsible for two other lives inside me because... fate? On top of that, apparently I'm half a key to destroying the world, I'm barely keeping my head above the grossness of *everyone's* feels, and the men I lo—ike are arguing with each other through me over something that happened before I was born."

I wanted to say more, but the words were carried on frustration, and I was tired of fighting.

Nico scrubbed his face and let out a noisy sigh. "You *are* carrying a heavy load, and I don't want to add to that. Vidar needs to be stopped. There's no question, and you don't have to do that alone. You don't have to do any of this alone, except that you're the only one who can answer my question."

Right. The question. The one I was avoiding because the truth terrified me. I didn't shove my frustration aside so much as ask it to move over and share the space in my brain. "I'm fucked up in the head. I learned so many things growing up that most people never have to deal with, and I missed those little things that almost everyone else experiences. It's hard for me to trust what I feel for anyone. I thought Vidar would help me save the world. I thought my fellow soldiers were as committed to the cause as I was. I thought..."

Bragi's name died on my tongue. *I thought he cared but he lied.* I understood why now. He *did* care. "It's hard for me to believe what my heart tells me about people. I've been drawn to you from the start. But of course I was. You saved me. You were kind to me. I thought I had nothing, and you gave me everything. And then you did it all again, and died because of it.

"How am I supposed to trust my heart when it says *don't let him go*? I want you. I need you. I..." There was that word again. If I said it, I was fucked. But if I didn't... "I love you. And it's the kind of feeling that tells me I'd let Vidar have whatever he wanted, as long as I got to keep you and my family. There is nothing more terrifying to me than realizing I'm capable of that."

This was where I should feel like a weight had been lifted from my shoulders, wasn't it? Then why did I feel a heavy stone in my gut that was threatening to drag me to Hel?

Because saying the words aloud made them real,

and gods help me, I didn't want it to be.

Nico tilted my chin up, and affection zinged through me. Genuine. Pure.

"I know you would do everything in your power, including destroying yourself, to keep that from being a choice," he said. "Which is why I won't let it come down to that. You don't see how much is amazing about you. The way you enjoy life. The fact that you still see good in the world, despite what you've been through. I won't let the world steal that part of you. Ever. Because I love you too."

"What now?" If I had my choice, we'd be done with these conversations, we'd be done with the wondering. We'd live happily ever after with no more questions ever.

Except *how does Bragi fit into all of this?*

Then again, if I had my choice, Vidar would be dead, and the biggest worry in my life would be morning sickness.

I'd much rather have morning sickness.

Nico traced a thumb along my bottom lip and followed the touch with the softest, sweetest kiss ever.

The light touch did nothing to mask the desire that hummed underneath.

"I think that next, we shower to unwind, and then I tuck you in, with me next to you, to make sure you get some sleep."

The suggestion made me smile, and the under-lying thrum of Nico's need made my pulse race.

"I think I like that idea." I slipped my hand into his and tugged him toward the bathroom.

CHAPTER 18
MAGNUS

"When we go in there, we're just a couple visiting the club," Bragi said. "You're my date. You heard about the debauchery and wanted to see it for yourself. You're dripping with lust and excitement and not much else. The conversation has to be one-hundred percent natural. No direct questions about the data center. He brings the topics up."

I thought it was sweet he was worried about me this way. Would the attitude have pissed me off a short while ago? Most likely. "I was trained by the best. I've got this."

"I know." His sigh was heavy.

I held out a hand. "Do you?"

"I've been playing parts like this since before your family had a name." He grasped my fingers.

I let some of my own nervousness flow through

the connection, to bleed it off and to let him know I couldn't do this without him.

His emotional mask slid into place, a layer of lust and possession on top of that, and he gave me a sharp tug.

The movement caught me off-guard, and I gasped as I stumbled toward him. He gripped the back of my neck and crushed his mouth to mine. The desire that overflowed in the kiss made my toes curl and teased reminders of last night to the surface.

There was no asking him to reign the want in tonight. I wanted to lose myself in the promise of all the things he wanted to do to me.

"Ready?" Bragi's voice was gravel when he pulled away.

I was breathless. "Let's go be naughty."

As expected, the location Bragi had me take us to was nondescript from the outside. A blank slate, similar to NEON. As we walked through a simple steel door, the air shifted around me. We were on a different plane.

And the lobby was dark velvet and mahogany and smoothness. Where NEON was classic meets modern, this was all a timeless sort of extravagance.

The doorman was nearly a foot taller than me, with shoulders as broad as my legs were long. He greeted Bragi with a tight but congenial, "Good evening, sir. Welcome back."

"Thank you." Bragi gave him a warm smile, and radiated confidence.

This was the god I'd been drawn to before I knew what kind of world I really lived in.

And I needed to stop analyzing how we felt, and get into my role. Instinct told me shy but curious was my best bet, and my instinct was rarely wrong in these cases.

The bouncer looked me over with a raised eyebrow, then moved aside to let us in. The moment we stepped through the door, I felt what Bragi had warned me about. The lust and debauchery was potent enough to choke on, and some of it blurred lines I couldn't afford to consider right now.

Not everyone wanted to be here.

I'd been exposed to worse. I'd never *felt* it, but I was as unsurprised as I was sickened.

Bragi rested his hand at the small of my back, and his touch on my exposed skin let me focus on him and ground myself.

The main club spread out in front of us, with a series of plush couches that sank too deep, and steps that led into short pits filled with pillows. Nothing overt was happening out here. People were dressed in gowns and suits, and chatting and drinking.

The physical was happening on the other side of a door at the far end of the room, but that didn't mean the people out here weren't indulging. Several of them were feeding off those same feelings heating my thoughts and simultaneously making my skin crawl.

I let the arousal show, which was easier with the recent memories of incredible sex. The touches. The sounds. The...

"Bragi." The man who approached us was beautiful in an unearthly way. Elegant and imposing. Powerful but subdued.

"Vindres." Bragi smiled warmly, but didn't offer a hand. "How many times have you remodeled since I was here last?"

If Bragi had spent time here, and Nico knew who Vindres was, had the two of them come here?

Hot.

"I've lost count." Vindres turned to me. "And who are you, my dear?" He grasped my fingers and kissed the back of my knuckles.

His lips were feather soft against my skin, but the sensation that raked through me was a step away from an orgasm.

Not the kind elicited from a long build up and slow love making. This was the kind of climax that came from being pressed against a wall and fingered in a frantic grind to get off in under a minute.

"I'm Gemma." My voice was meek, and I didn't try to hide any of my desire. When I was younger, I'd always wanted to be Gemma.

"Gemma." The way he rolled the letters off his tongue was like a deep, throaty kiss. "I'm Vindres, and this is my associate, Sylith." He nodded at the woman next to him.

"It's a pleasure." I couldn't help but stare at her. She had a similar air to her, and both gave me the impression I was dinner.

Shy had definitely been the demeanor to adopt.

Vindres pulled me closer to him, and Bragi wrapped his arm around my waist to tug me back. Bragi's touch was pure possession.

"Are you not for sharing, my dear?" Vidres asked.

"No." Bragi bit off the word.

Vindres never looked at him, instead focused on me. "I asked Gemma."

Uh-uh. Because consent was such a big thing here.

Not.

This was disturbingly comfortable though. Like putting on an old pair of jeans that had too many holes to be practical, but still felt familiar. I could do this without my newly discovered empathy.

Which was fortunate, because if I didn't keep myself closed off, I'd choke on what this man was radiating. "Maybe at some point," I answered Vindres's question in a soft voice. "I don't know if I could though. Be shared."

"I suspect you could." Vindres dropped my hand. "But you're always welcome to simply watch."

Sylith leaned in to whisper in his ear, and he

gave me another glance, this time with more curiosity.

"Do your Valkyrie sisters know you're here?" He asked.

It would be okay to be surprised. Expected, even. "How did you...?"

"I dated a Valkyrie once." Sylith's voice was a purr, sliding under my skin. "Ages ago, before Odin—" The twist of her lips was rage rather than desire, but the look vanished again in an instant. "You have a scent to you."

I wrinkled my nose. "I smell?"

"In the best possible way. Do your Valkyrie sisters know you're here?" If Vindres was fazed by the fact that I was one of a race that had been extinct until recently, it didn't show.

I shook my head. "I don't know if they'd understand."

Which was bullshit. They'd get it better than most, considering that Min and Kirby were regular guests at Frey's orgies. But I wasn't Magnus tonight.

"No judgment here, Gemma. No judgment, no pressure. Would the two of you like to join us at my table?" Vindres gestured to a nearby round couch. The free-floating glass in front of it wasn't so much a table as it was a tray, but I doubted it got used for much.

The invitation felt too easy, but this wasn't about me specifically. It was about the fact that Bragi had come back into this place after decades, with a barely-immortal god on his arm who was looking to be *taught*.

I glanced at Bragi for approval, never breaking from the part I was playing.

"It's up to you, Baby Girl," Bragi said.

The teasing, the nickname, was meant to lighten my mood. I'd get him back for it at some point. "I'd like that," I said to Vindres.

Bragi agreed as well. "I'd say we can catch up but..." He laughed.

But we all know that's not what happens here. That was what he didn't say.

Vindres, Sylith, Bragi, and I crossed the short distance to the couch, which sat a few steps higher than every other seat in the room, and Bragi pulled me into his lap when we sat.

Vindres waved a waiter over. "We have a witch behind the bar who makes a variety of drinks that let us get intoxicated. Tell me what flavors each of you would like."

I shook my head. "None for me. I'd rather stay alert tonight."

"Smart girl." Sylith's tone was hard to read. Was she deriding me, or was that actual respect?

Time for the interrogation to begin. Over-thinking it was bad. I'd let the words flow, and this would be fine.

I cast my gaze around the club. "Everyone here is so pretty. Aren't they?" I looked at Bragi.

"I suppose." He shrugged.

I pouted at his lack of enthusiasm.

The longer we talked to Vindres and Sylith, the more their features became distinct. Incubi and succubi tended to reflect the desires of the people they were talking to. His features were still hard for me to name.

But she had dark, iridescent hair, pulled into a high bun and secured with chopsticks, to show off a long neck and smooth, pale skin. Her eyes were the same striking color as her hair, and if I looked into them long enough, I might tumble in.

"Who's your favorite?" Sylith asked me.

I ducked my head and fiddled with the seam on one of my gloves. "I don't know." I kept my voice quiet enough that they had to give me their full attention to hear me, but not so soft as to mumble. "But I could never wear your dress the way you do."

"I'm sure you could." Sylith moved, so she was on one side of us and Vindres was on the other. "Not everyone can pull off The Tailor's work the way you do."

"Everyone can pull of The Tailor's work." Bragi's huff was inflated bravado and irritation. He wanted them to know he didn't appreciate them hitting on his date. "But Gemma would wear that dress in a way that would make you embarrassed if you ever thought you could pull it off, Sylith."

It was an indirect compliment, but also over the top. Comparing me to a succubus? As if. But this was still just a dick measuring contest, even if it took a different form. Who could get Gemma to open up? Who would have my attention at the end of the night?

"Perhaps." Sylith tugged a strand of my hair loose and twirled it around her finger. She hovered her lips near my ear. "We could find a quiet room, where you could help me out of my dress, and we can find out how incredible you look in it." She glided her mouth down my jaw, never making contact, and stopped just short of kissing me. "If you'd like."

I whimpered.

"*Sylith*." Vindres bit off her name. "Gemma made it clear when she arrived that she wasn't ready for that yet."

Uh-huh. I didn't buy for a minute that mattered in most cases. Still, Gemma managed to act grateful while still looking interested in Sylith's offer. "Maybe next time?" I squeaked.

Sylith scowled and moved to sit next to Vindres again.

In another time and place, I'd love to know her story. There was no way she was subservient to him because she wanted to be.

"If you'd like," Vindres said.

"How did the two of you meet?" Sylith asked.

"Poetry reading." My answer overlapped Bragi's.

Vindres rolled his eyes. "Are you still—" He smirked and shook his head.

Playing that tired game? The rest of his thought was as clear as if he'd spoken it. My empathy wasn't telling me that, my being attuned to the situation was.

"Why quit when it works?" Bragi was cool and dismissive.

I gave him a doe-eyed look. "What does he mean?"

Bragi drew a finger along my bottom lip. "Nothing, Baby. He thinks poetry is silly."

Okay. Sure.

If this was real Bragi, I'd be furious by now. Instead, I was pleased with how well the two of us fell into these roles based on what was needed. There was a synchronicity here that I'd really only had with Dahlia in the past.

But Dahlia, as much as I adored her, only knew one part—stream of consciousness babble meant to keep people off-guard.

"I love your poems." I let out a breathy sigh. "The one about the petals spreading wide and pink and glistening in the dew. How do you think of such beautiful, complex words?" That was me getting him back for calling me Baby Girl.

"That wasn't one of mine," Bragi said.

Sylith let out a tiny snort.

Good.

"No? Are you sure?" I fluttered my eyelashes.

"Metaphor has its place, but it's not always needed." Bragi lifted my chin to look me in the eye. "I was the one who told you I wanted to bury my face between your creamy thighs and dine on your nectar until dawn."

I giggled. "Oh, yeah."

"Magnus. Is that you?" A woman's voice interrupted, and my heart dropped into my stomach.

Not only that someone here knew me, but I recognized her. She should be dead. *Ice Queen*. Not her real name. Her Noble handle. She was one of the Nobles Loki had sacrificed when the TOM campus was destroyed.

I managed to hide my reaction. To not jerk my head in the direction of the call, to respond to my name or confirm it was her.

"Magnus?" Ice Queen was more insistent this time, and she stopped in front of us. "It is you, isn't it? Oh, gods. Bragi?"

It was her. I knew without looking. I felt it. My grasp on control slipped. As fractures formed in my mind, the debauchery around us slithered into my thoughts.

"I thought you were dead," Bragi said coolly.

"Me too." Ice Queen wasn't playing a part. She

was here to fuck and be fucked. I felt it, because I was starting to feel everyone. "Apparently I'm an elf. Did you know?"

Bragi shook his head. "That wasn't my job."

"Who are you, lovely?" Vindres asked her.

"Saga. But you can call me Queenie."

Vindres wasn't impressed. "I see."

"*Magnus.*" Holy fuck, would she leave it alone?

Bragi nudged me. "She thinks she's talking to you."

I finally gave her my attention. "I'm sorry, who?"

"You, dumb ass."

Yeah, that was Ice Queen. I fixed her with a confused look. "I'm Gemma."

"She's not who you think," Bragi said.

I gave him a hurt look. "Who's Magnus? Isn't that a boy's name?"

"No one. Don't worry about it." He was instantly dismissive again.

"She looks just like you, Gemma," Ice Queen focused on Bragi. "You couldn't have her, so you found her twin? Gross."

"This is a private table." Any hint of curiosity or patience vanished from Vindres's demeanor. "You can find what you're looking for somewhere else in the club." He pushed out enough influence to make Ice Queen walk away.

I used the few second distraction, and Bragi's fingers digging into my thigh, to repair the cracks in my focus and shut out the feelings in the club out again.

Vindres and Sylith were still lingering on Ice Queen's presence, though. They were suspicious. Wondering...

"Who was that?" I pushed the accusation into my question as I slid from Bragi's lap.

"A former student. No one." Bragi reached for me.

I scowled and crossed my arms. "Uh-huh. Who's Magnus?"

The tiniest growl escaped from his throat. "Another student. One who was obsessed with me."

If I were keeping score—which I was because that was the perfect level of distraction—we'd be at Bragi Two, Magnus One. I owed him.

"She implied you were the one who was obsessed." Pretending to be jealous of myself was a new and interesting experience.

"If someone turns you down, do you tell your girlfriends that, or do you tell them you didn't care and he couldn't get over you?" Bragi asked.

Gemma would never admit most things about boys or sex to her friends, so I let my expression slide to a pout. "Then I don't look like her?"

"You both have red hair, but I promise you're nothing like Magnus."

That was sweeter than he wanted it to sound.

Maybe I wouldn't get him back for the obsession comment after all.

Our audience was getting bored, though. We were no longer a fascinating young woman with an unpredictable god. Instead we were a couple fighting in a sex club, and Vindres and Sylith saw that all the time.

Time to put some bait on the hook. I sighed heavily. "I should've stayed home and worked on my thesis."

That caught Sylith's attention—suddenly I was more than a vapid hanger-on who wasn't comfortable speaking for myself. "You're a doctorate student? What are you studying?"

"Social Engineering." My comment would yank Vindres back into the conversation. He'd see this as a chance to prove to me I didn't know anything about how people were manipulated, compared to what he was capable of. He'd use it as a chance to remind me of my place.

"What's your thesis about?" Vindres asked.

"The Ramifications of the Sociological and Psychological Effects of Modern Social Avenues—" I cut myself off with a laugh. "It's a mouthful. Basically, how social media shapes us compared to other historical social gathering places."

Vindres was proud of the control he exercised on his part of the internet, and his knowledge was what made him the perfect person to help Vidar. He was about to *teach* me everything he could. "Do you spend a lot of time online?" he asked.

"Kind of. I'm so bad at it. Which is horrible, I know, but I'm like the most Boomer Millennial ever when it comes to technology."

"I have some expertise there." Vindres's tone was still smooth, but it had shifted away from seduction. "I could help you get set up if it would help with your studies."

Bragi's body stiffened, and he clenched his jaw. "She's fi—"

Vindres raised his brow. *Let her speak for herself.*

"Maybe." I was nervous. Unsure. And about to change the subject, so he'd fight hard to come back to it. "Are the people in back really doing... things?"

"You'll have to be more specific." Sylith's purr was back.

Fucking each other until the sheets are so covered in genetic filth that someone could play Jurassic Park with them, but making gods instead of dinosaurs. "Like... kinky stuff?"

"All flavors of fucking, yes." Vindres didn't want to talk about the sex anymore. He wanted to go back to whipping out his mental dick. "I can provide you a unique perspective on your thesis, if you're interested."

Hooked. "I have to cite my sources." I sounded skeptical. "I don't think I can do that with you."

"I assure you, you can do anything you want with me."

Reel him in. "Online just seems so unsafe. Like, people get their information stolen and hacked and stuff."

"It's not an issue if you know what you're doing—which I do. Very few—mortal or immortal—are aware that there are data centers with magic woven in." Vindres was a hair's width away from lecturing me. "They have shielding and the ability to handle, redirect, and manage any level of attack. *Any.* They can withstand levels of power that most don't realize exist."

"I have no idea what you just said, but it sounds really cool." I knew exactly what he'd said, and it sounded like a list of reasons Vidar would take a specific series of servers. Especially those that had hosted magical books and other similar bits of information.

As the conversation continued, I kept veering away, and Vindres steered back to the top of how much he knew about online security.

His ego was so big that this would've been a textbook extraction if it weren't for Ice Queen's interruption. And even that had worked in our favor in the end.

Bragi squeezed my thigh, and I trailed the toe of my shoe over his calf. Both were subtle, meant only for us. But the way he nuzzled my neck was all about the display. "We should get going, Baby Girl." His voice was rough, and he glided his hands up my stomach.

"But we're learning so much here." I sighed at his touch.

"I could teach you more." He growled as he bit my shoulder.

Vindres gestured toward the door leading to the back rooms. "You're welcome to stay here, if you'd like."

"No." Bragi slipped his hand under my skirt, through the slit up one leg. There was no attempt to hide that he was reaching between my thighs.

I sighed contentedly at his touch. "Okay. We'll go."

The goodbyes we said were hurried, as Gemma was horny and eager to get home and get her orgasms.

Ah, to be as naive and eager as Gemma.

We were halfway to the exit, when Sylith stepped in our path. The seduction was gone from her posture, and her face was hard. She pulled a chopstick—correction, thin blade—from her hair, and pressed the tip to my throat. "I don't know who you are, Abomination, but you're not welcome here again."

Abomination? *Fuck.*

"I'm not—"

"You're very good." Sylith's admiration was begrudging. "But not as good as you think you are."

It only took a thought for me to summon a Valkyrie dagger, and I knocked her hand away from my throat as I fell into a defensive posture.

Sylith lunged at me, and I jumped back, then slashed in counter.

"*Sylith*." Vindres's bark echoed through the room. "*Enough*."

She didn't pull her attention from me. "But she's—"

"I said *enough*. These are our guests."

What the fuck was going on?

Bragi grabbed my arm. "Go. Now."

Right. *You have to walk out of here first.*

No time. Even though my brain was right, I pushed *leave* into my thoughts, and we blinked out of the club.

I'd figure out how later.

NEON was the safest place, until we know how badly we'd just fucked up. Bragi wasn't allowed inside, though. Dahlia and Frey's wards would...

I didn't know. Push him into limbo if we tried to enter?

Where was I going to take him?

CHAPTER 19

NICO

Dahlia and I were in Magnus's place, studying every page of the comic for some hint as to what the piece from Artura would do.

Rather, that was the pretense.

I was checking my watch every two minutes, realizing no time had passed at all, and wondering if Magnus was all right.

I was loath to admit part of me was worried about Bragi as well. Walking into Vindres's place after so long, with none of his own power was an idiotic thing for him to do.

"They'll be fine." Dahlia had said the same thing more than a dozen times this evening. "They know what they're doing."

I didn't. The idea of the type of doubletalk

required of them made my mind and heart hurt. It always had. "I know."

"Just—" Dahlia's phone chimed, and she grabbed it from where it sat on the coffee table.

I caught a glimpse of Magnus's name and picture before Dahlia checked the screen.

"She's downstairs," she said, and vanished from the room.

I couldn't teleport, but I could fly. I sprinted from the apartment, and through the nearest stairwell door, already a bird by the time I left from the landing. Soaring down seemed to take an eternity, though it was probably only a matter of seconds before I reached the main floor.

Doors didn't work well with wings, so I had to assume a human shape again to leave the apartment complex and enter the club.

I saw Dahlia near the rear entrance, and Magnus across from her. For some reason, they still stood in the foyer. Magnus looked safe, but I needed confirmation.

"Are you okay..." I trailed off when I saw the dagger clenched in her hand, and that Bragi was with her.

"What happened?" Dahlia asked.

Magnus's mouth was twisted in frustration. "There was this succubus. She called me an abomination and attacked me."

She did what? "Where is she?" I asked.

"Down, boy." Dahlia rested a hand on my arm. "Did you...?"

I didn't appreciate her trying to reign me in like a dog, but if Magnus was safe, I didn't need to go after her attacker.

"Get exactly what we wanted? Yes." Magnus seemed to know what Dahlia was asking.

I was grateful she was intact and had been successful. There was another outstanding question, though. "Why is he here?"

"We needed to escape. I don't know where else is safe," Magnus said.

Bragi stepped away from her. "I understand I'm not welcome. I'll figure my own way out from here."

Magnus grabbed his hand, stopping him. "No. He was as much a part of this as me. Took the same risks. Played as big a part. Got me in the front door. We wouldn't have anything if it weren't for Bragi."

She was right.

It was difficult for me to do, but I said, "Thank you, Bragi."

He gave me a terse nod.

"So... can he come in?" Magnus asked.

Dahlia frowned. Propriety kept my mouth shut —this wasn't my domain—but I wouldn't stay silent for long.

"Magnus trusts you, and I'm not stupid. I know what you've done for her," Dahlia said.

A corner of Bragi's mouth tugged up, before neutrality slid into place. "You were always my second favorite."

"Bullshit. No one mattered to you besides her, and I'm fine with that." Dahlia grabbed both of them and tugged them the rest of the way into the building. "Temporary reprieve."

"I will do everything in my power to ensure you don't regret it," Bragi said.

Dahlia pursed her lips. "I know you will."

What did I miss?

"Let's go catch up."

At Dahlia's words, I grabbed Magnus's arm before she could vanish, and then the four of us were in Magnus's apartment.

"Are we going to talk about him being here?" I pointed at Bragi.

Magnus shook her head. "We just did."

"We're going to talk about what they discovered," Dahlia said. "Spill."

Magnus bent at the waist, which offered a stunning view of her ass, her legs, and her flexibility. She undid the straps on her shoes, and stepped out of the heels. "I'm changing first."

"Are you fucking kidding me?" Dahlia's disbelief was abrupt.

I couldn't help but agree with the sentiment.

Magnus shot her a pursed-lip look.

"Spill while you change," Dahlia said. "Anyone in

the room who hasn't seen you naked can raise their hand now. No one? Fine."

Magnus stuck her tongue out. It was a childish but endearing gesture in the midst of everything else going on. She strolled into her bedroom, but she did leave the door open a few inches.

"The servers Vidar took are magically shielded." Her voice was muffled, but carried out to us. "They were created to hold up to a lot of power trying to break them."

"Or flow into them and enhance them?" Dahlia asked.

Bragi was staring at the comic book on the coffee table. "Can anyone besides you do that, Dahlia?"

She shrugged. "Probably. I'm not unique."

"You're the only dragon born in centuries who's become a dragon." To me, that was unique.

"You are pretty weird," Magnus called.

Dahlia looked amused. "Takes one to know one, freak."

Magnus emerged from her room, in casual clothing far more appropriate to who she was. She also wore half a smile. "I'm not ashamed of that."

"What is this?" Bragi pointed at the book.

"We found it in an old house of Skuld's," Dahlia said. "It's kind of like a comic book prophecy. Every-thing in it has already happened, though."

"Is that me?" Bragi was looking at the scene I'd originally been drawn to. "Vidar and Skye?"

Magnus joined him. "Who's Skye?"

"Former student. Used to be obsessed with me," Bragi teased.

I didn't understand the joke, though. "No she wasn't."

Magnus snorted and smacked him playfully. "Who was she really?"

Their familiarity nagged me. When did they form this level of comfort with each other? "She was an inventor and a conduit," I said.

"How did you…?" Bragi trailed off as he looked at me.

I hated to admit I'd been reading his journals still. That felt like letting him know part of me still cared. This wasn't the time to hold back. "She's in your journals."

To his credit, his only reaction was a quick twist of his mouth. "This never happened, though. Skye had that machine, however she never got it to work. Her sister—twin—Bridget, was an amplifier, and it took both of them to power it. But they never found the remaining pieces. Skye insisted they needed a key and a few other parts."

Then why did the picture show otherwise? Dahlia had been convinced this had all come to pass.

"A few other parts," Dahlia muttered, and pulled the amulet from her pocket. "Fuck me. What does the machine do?"

"Skye thought it would take them to other

realms," Bragi said. "She was going to explore the universe."

No. Something tickled the back of my mind.

Dahlia dropped onto the couch, where she'd been before Magnus texted her. "You didn't think to tell her you could offer that service without a big fancy machine?"

Bragi shook his head. "Not the way that I do or that you do or that anyone we know does. These were supposed to be gates to realms we can't reach. Worlds that are supposedly forgotten."

"If they're forgotten, how do we know they exist?" Magnus asked.

"Because some of us remember." Oh, no. I *did* remember. "These aren't gates that should be opened." I was talking to myself as much as the others. Tucked among the memories that had surged back were a handful I hadn't seen in a long time. Centuries. They were old and foreign enough, even though they were my past, that I struggled to make sense of them. "When people mess with those gates, there's a lot of death."

Magnus frowned. "There's already been a lot of death."

"Not like this." Had I blocked out the past or had it been hidden from me? "This level of death is of apocalyptic proportions. Ragnarök levels."

The silence that settled in the room was deafening.

"That's not what Vidar is doing." Uncertainty rang in Dahlia's voice. "He's worked too hard to stop the prophecies."

He hadn't, though. "He's worked to make sure he was strong enough to withstand whatever was coming for him." I'd watched it for more than a century. From the outside, yes, but I still had a seat to the show.

"But why would he...?" Magnus sank onto the arm of the couch, next to Dahlia.

"You heard him in NOLA. He wants the world to be what it used to be." The realization in Dahlia's voice was peppered with doubt, as if she hated that she was putting the pieces together. "Ragnarök is rebirth. Those who survive see a new world."

"He doesn't have all the pieces, though. Even if he's building that machine, he doesn't have that." Magnus nodded at the piece in Dahlia's hand. "He doesn't have an amplifier. Does he?"

Bragi looked as concerned as all of us. "Not that I'm aware. He holds a lot of things close, though."

"In other words, we still destroy him, regardless of what he's planning," Magnus said.

"And we need to do it now, if Vindres knows who you are," Dahlia added. "We're out of time."

It didn't matter. "We can't do anything if we can't figure out how to destroy him." I hated to be the bearer of bad news. "Unless we have that information, it doesn't matter how urgent our need is."

The lack of argument that met me was as disheartening as the new revelations themselves. What were we supposed to do?

CHAPTER 20
BRAGI

The last time I was here, in this place, I was one apartment over and Fen was dying. Shot by magical god-killing bullets.

So much had happened since then, and I wasn't sure how comfortable I was here. Especially because Fen and joined us, and he kept watching me, as if waiting for a reason to evict me.

I was surprised Dahlia let me in so easily.

None of that seemed significant compared to the revelation Nico just dropped. Was Vidar truly trying to start Ragnarök?

Why? What would he accomplish? If he had any allies left, this would destroy them.

My phone rang, and I frowned. "It's Anubis."

"Answer it." It seemed it *was* possible for Magnus to be more on edge.

Not that I disagreed with her. I answered.

"I have some information for you." Anubis got straight to the point.

I was grateful for that. The evening had been too choked with fakeness and formality. "When can I come visit, and may I still bring my friend?" When I checked in with him a day or two ago, I'd mentioned Magnus wanted to be present for our conversations.

"I would prefer you did bring her, yes. Are you free now?"

It had already been a long night. We were stuck without answers, though. "We are."

"Are you going to visit him?" Nico's interruption was out of character. "I'm joining you."

"A moment, please," I said to Anubis, and put the phone on *Mute*. "I'm not taking the entire fucking building," I said to Nico.

Fen held up a hand. "We're not going. We're not even asking."

"We're not?" Dahlia asked.

He shook his head. "I'll introduce you to Anubis one day. You'll like him. That will be a social call when this is all over, and the more of us who go, the more it muddies the waters. Magnus is capable."

"Yeah, she is." Dahlia looked satisfied with the answer.

Good. I didn't care to risk the hospitality Anubis had extended by turning this into a family field trip. I returned to the call. "Apologies. Nicodemus would also like to join me."

"Absolutely. I'd like to see him again." Anubis's agreement was pleasant.

As we headed out, Dahlia gave Magnus's hand a squeeze. "Bring back good intel?"

Magnus nodded. "Of course. It'll be the best."

There was a hint of doubt in her voice, and I suspected we all felt the same, but hope and spite were the things keeping us going.

The elevator ride down to the main floor was silent and awkward, with Magnus standing between Nico and me, and him casting the occasional glance in my direction.

The fact that he was willing to share a lift with me felt like a good next step.

We reached the main floor, and the moment we stepped out of NEON, Magnus took our hands, and we were in front of Anubis's home.

When he answered the door, his smile didn't reach his eyes, and his tone wasn't as warm as when I called.

Magnus eyed him suspiciously.

"He's a friend," I said.

Her *hmm* was difficult to interpret. What did she feel?

He stepped aside to let us in.

The moment Magnus stepped into the foyer, she stopped. It looked as though she was pushing against an invisible wall. "What is this?" Anger spilled from her question. She leaned to the left and right, but didn't fall.

I whirled on Anubis. "What's going on?"

"Abomination." Sylith stepped into the room from the far doorway.

Nico was already flying toward her, flame enveloping him.

"Stop." Anubis's voice stayed calm, and he looked at Sylith. "You were to let me handle this."

"If either of you hurt Magnus, I will scorch you again and again." Nico's words were heavy and rolled through me.

Sylith didn't flinch. "If you do, she will die."

"No." Anubis off the word. "No death. Not tonight."

"Explain yourself." I hated that the only thing I could do was talk. This was the most impotent I'd felt since losing my power. It didn't matter, though. If this was a betrayal, and Magnus or Nico got hurt, I'd find a way to make someone pay.

"Let me *go*." Magnus stumbled forward. In a flash, she had summoned a dagger and was flying past Nico, to pin Sylith to the wall.

Sylith held a blade to Magnus's stomach. "Maybe you are more than a vapid child," Sylith said. "You still need to die."

"You're definitely still a bitch." Magnus's hand was steady and her gaze never wavered from Sylith's face.

"*Enough.*" Anubis's roar shook the room. Magnus and Sylith were pushed apart by an invisible force. He had put them both in magical boxes.

Magnus gave a threatening chuckle. "It didn't hold me the first time."

"No, but it will hold you long enough to listen, and it will hold Sylith. Are you working with Vidar?"

Magnus's face contorted with rage, and the flames around Nico grew.

The two were an impressive sight. *Creation* I loved them.

"So, one, *super* eww." In the midst of combat, Magnus was still herself.

That was reassuring. "You know we're not," I said.

"How dare you even suggest it." Nico seemed to be taking the question the hardest.

"Then why did you come to Vindres's club, asking questions about Vidar's project?" Sylith asked.

Magnus barely spared her a glance. "We didn't."

"I told you that you aren't as good as you think."

Magnus made a *pft* sound. "I'm the best, bitch."

"Abomination." Why did Sylith keep calling her that?

Nico reached for her, but the same box that restrained her, kept him from hurting her.

There was at least some level of miscommunication going on, and given how stubborn Magnus was, we could talk in circles all night if someone didn't change the direction of the conversation. "Why does she keep calling Magnus an abomination?" I looked at Sylith. "Why are you using that word?"

"Why doesn't Vidar trust Vindres?" Sylith countered.

Fuck.

"Vidar doesn't trust anyone but Vidar," Nico said. "Why would Bragi know his motives?"

"He's one of the few remaining members of the board." For the first time since we arrived, some of Sylith's confidence wavered.

I shouldn't be surprised to hear that Vidar was picking and choosing who he told about my walking away. "I left."

"You don't like him," Magnus said. "Vidar, I mean."

Sylith spat, and the liquid ran ineffectively down the side of an invisible wall in front of her. "I would crush him under my heel and feed him to the dogs if I could."

It was a nice sentiment.

"Now that's my kind of bitchiness." Magnus's posture relaxed, and her dagger vanished.

Nico was still tense and flaming. "Then why do you work for him?"

"I work for *Vindres*, because I owe him everything. He works with Vidar because he's been sold on the lie of a better world."

That checked out.

"What did Vindres do for you?" Magnus asked.

Sylith fixed her with a glare. "He saved me from vapid little girls."

So we were back to that.

Magnus rolled her eyes. "Sticks and stones, bitch."

"Answer their question, Sylith," Anubis said. "Tell them what you told me."

"You shouldn't exist, but you do, *Magnus*." The way Sylith ground out the syllables, it was as if she hoped to crumble the name simply by speaking it.

Magnus just scoffed. "I've been telling myself that for a long time. I'm a survivor, bitch."

The fact that she remained herself through all of this, sassy and intentionally antagonistic, was so very much the woman I loved.

"You're the woman with two hearts," Sylith said. "The child who shouldn't be."

Shit. I knew those words. They belonged to one of the prophecies no one ever deciphered. It was hard to pin that one to any single individual, because it could apply to so many potentials.

Sylith turned to Nico, then me. "You truly don't know. Neither of you. No one around you sees it?"

I recognized the phrase, but it could mean a lot of things. I shook my head *no*.

"Sees what?" Magnus asked.

"You don't just have one aura."

Magnus didn't look impressed. "No shit. I'm pregnant. Half the world can see that, apparently, and I don't even have a baby bump yet."

"You do." Sylith sneered. "And yes, each of the children has their own aura, but I mean *you*. Your auras are braided and intertwined. They look like one, but there are two."

"She's just vibrant." As he spoke, Nico turned his head this way and that, attention on Magnus.

"This is dragging on too long," Anubis said. "The Valkyrie's soul is a mix of two. Magnus, you're both conduit and amplifier. I don't understand why Vidar created you, then let you go."

Oh. Fuck me.

"Vidar didn't create me. I mean, in the way any adult who tortures a child molds them in to a fucked up adult, but as far as I know, he didn't give me any power, and he most certainly did not *let me go*."

"He's been fighting to get her back." And I finally understood why.

The lingering sensation of *fight and kill* in the room was evaporating, but a new tension had floated in. How long had Vidar known this about Magnus? Because I had to assume he did. Since she became a Valkyrie? Longer?

"Maeve told me..." Magnus trailed off. "When my mother was pregnant with me, they thought it was twins. That she was carrying two girls. A couple of months into the pregnancy, Maeve decided she'd made a mistake."

Nico looked like himself again. "You never told me that."

"It's been a long couple of weeks." There was a weight Magnus's words that pulled them to the floor.

The conversation from just a couple of hours ago rushed back. What Nico had to say about Skye's machine and opening doors. About Skye and her sister.

"Vidar doesn't need a separate amplifier." I had to say it, even though we were probably all thinking it. "He just needs Magnus."

"To what end?" Anubis asked.

Nico frowned. "The world's end."

Anubis sighed. "If I let you both go, will you behave?"

Magnus looked at Sylith, who shrugged. "I suspect we've all been played in many ways. I'll stop trying to kill the girl," Sylith said.

"Sure. Yeah. Me too," Magnus said.

Visually, nothing happened, until Sylith leaned against the wall casually, and crossed her arms.

Magnus copied her posture. I didn't know if it was to stay comfortable, or to mock the succubus. A bit of both, perhaps.

"Vidar is trying to end the world? Are you certain?" Sylith asked.

Could we trust her with this information? She was loyal to Vindres, not Vidar, but that was only one stop to the final source. I looked at Magnus, hoping she could read the question in my eyes. Then *does your empathy say we can trust her?*

Magnus pursed her lips. "Does the empathy lie?"

"If the person you're talking to believes what they're saying, but it's not true, then technically, yes," I said.

Magnus glanced sideways at Sylith. "Then she believes what she's saying."

"Sit, please." Anubis gestured to the couches and chairs decorating the living room. "Let's be civilized and direct." The last bit of his request was pointed, and he glared at Sylith.

"I like that plan. I'm Magnus by the way. It's nice to meet you." She extended her hand.

Anubis shook it. "I'm Anubis. It's a curiosity to meet you."

Magnus moved to sit at the edge of a loveseat. "I get that a lot."

"You're not Gemma, then." Sylith took a seat across from Magnus.

Magnus rose to offer her hand. "I wished for a long time I was. Truce?"

Sylith accepted the offering. "Unless you betray my trust."

"That's fair." Magnus sat again, and the rest of us did as well, with Nico taking the spot closest to her.

"If Magnus is both conduit and amplifier, that explains why she's had issues with control," Nico said.

The clench of Magnus's jaw said she didn't appreciate the phrasing, but I suspected it was accurate.

Anubis raised his brows. "What sort of issues?"

"I try to let other people's power flow through me and..." Magnus scowled. "It gets too big, and I blow things up."

That was even less reassuring than the last time she mentioned it to me. "How is it possible, though, for Magnus to be both?" Occurrences of either were rare enough, but to have those two powers in the same person was unheard of.

"I can only offer a theory," Anubis said. "In rare cases—as in I've seen it twice in my lifetime—when there should have been twins, one child is born with the power of both."

Like Nico, Anubis was older than most gods by at least a couple thousand years. I'd always known Magnus was special. This didn't change who she was, but it was proof to those who didn't believe it.

"We think Vidar has a machine that will—"

"Find gates and open them," Sylith cut Magnus off.

How did she know that? "How do you know that?"

"That will find gates and use them to start Ragnarök," Nico corrected her.

Sylith paled; an impressive feat considering how light her skin already was. "I know because Bridget was my lover."

Bridget was Skye's sister. The amplifier. To refer to her that way in front of Sylith would be callous.

Fate sure did like to fuck with coincidences.

"Vidar killed her." Sylith stared at Magnus. "In case you're wondering why I hate him, and why I'd kill you if you were working with him."

No. That wasn't right. "He didn't kill Bridget. She left. She…"

Magnus gave me a look of pity. "Is that what he told you?"

"That's what he told himself." Another lie I'd bought into because Vidar was so twisted and self-involved, he believed that *death* was the same as *she left*.

Sylith dropped her face into her hand. She looked the same as she had in the club, but the cool facade was gone. She and Magnus probably had more in common than either of them realized.

"Vidar pushed Bridget too hard trying to make that machine work, and it broke her." Sylith's words were muffled by her hand. "I swore I'd destroy him, no matter how long it took."

"I was right," Magnus said. "You were the prettiest bitch in the club."

Sylith's smile was sad. "You're much more stunning as yourself."

Perhaps they did see the similarities. It seemed they were friends now.

"What do we do next?" Nico asked.

Easy. "We keep Magnus away from Vidar. Far away." As if we needed another reason.

Magnus pursed her lips. Every protest brimmed in the accusing glare she cast at me. "Sure. Yeah. Okay. Back to reality, how do I work, Sylith? Do you know how Bridget did what she did?"

"The way any of us *works*. She just was."

Magnus huffed and sank into her seat.

"Is Magnus being an amplifier how she brought my memories back?" Nico asked.

Anubis seemed to consider this. "If the memories were still part of you, but sealed away somehow, it could be. Magnus's magic would let them flow through her, then amplify them and send them back to you."

If that was how she'd helped Nico, "Could you do the same for me, Magnus?" I asked.

"Did you miss the part about me blowing things up when I try to do this on purpose? I mean, I can feel your magic. It's all I feel most of the time, but that just makes me think pushing this back into you is a bad idea."

"You feel the baby, not the god," Sylith said. "Can you actually feel *Bragi*?"

Magnus opened her mouth and then grunted. This time when she looked at me, her expression was soft. Studious. She furrowed her brow. "I see threads of power. I didn't realize it before, but I think that's what keeps you healed. I don't see in you what I feel inside me. You're... You're like a void."

There was a metaphor in there for the last century of my life. "Then whatever took my power is different than what locked away Nico's memories." I was disappointed, but not surprised.

"If Vidar is recreating that machine, and it is what you say, why haven't you destroyed it yet?" Sylith asked.

Because you called us to ambush us before we made it that far. That wasn't the real reason, though.

"We don't know where it is," Magnus said. "We do know that the server that Vindres helped him take is magically shielded. Unless that was bullshit this evening. We also have parts that Vidar needs, and that means he doesn't have them."

"You mean the amulet?" I asked.

Magnus frowned. "That Dahlia retrieved from Artura. That could probably only be obtained by Artura gifting it. That Johnny tried to take... *Fuck.*"

Sylith sighed.

We were still playing our parts in Vidar's plan. *Idiots.*

Sylith stood. "I need to get back. I told Vindres I would make sure Magnus—Gemma—wasn't a threat, and now I can tell him that's not the case. He's my priority. If you fuck this up, if something happens to Vindres, you best steer clear of me for eternity."

"That's fair," Magnus said.

"And... let me meet the kids when you have them?"

Magnus almost smiled. "Okay."

With that, Sylith left.

That was intense.

"Why aren't we having Magnus try to give Bragi his power back?" Nico's question surprised me, mostly because it came from him.

"Do you want that?" I asked.

He hesitated. "I want as many allies as we can get in this fight."

It wasn't the answer I hoped for, but I'd take it. *Ally* was better than *enemy*. "Are you willing to try, Magnus?"

"I'm not willing to blow you up."

"I can insulate you," Anubis said.

Her laugh was bitter. "No more shields. I broke through your *insulation*. I broke through everything."

"I'm a living, breathing meter." Anubis leaned in to place a hand on Magnus's knee. "Unlike whatever else you've tried, I can tell you if it's too much. I won't be there to block you, but rather to tell you to yank the cord before there's any exploding."

Magnus worried her bottom lip. "I... I want to help. This is a life I can't... What if I fuck up?"

I knelt in front of her, to look her in the eye. "When Kirby made you a Valkyrie—the first in centuries—you owned it. Almost instantly." Vidar had been furious that she took that power in and then walked away from him. "What you've done with this empathy? You've learned a kind of control it took me hundreds of years to master."

"I also failed at combat in school. I failed marksmanship. I failed most of my Noble training. I only earned the title because Vidar wanted something from me."

"No." I wasn't reassuring her for the sake of pretty words. I meant what I was about to say. "You didn't earn top marks, but you did as well as any of your colleagues. Fistfights and gunfights aren't your strength. Your strength is your heart."

She let out a choking laugh and gave me a withering look. "I can't believe you just said that. *God*, you're cheesy."

"I am. Curse of being a bard—I'm a cheesy asshole." I gripped the back of her neck and kissed her hard. "I don't want to be blown up either, but I trust that it won't happen."

She rested her hand on my wrist and let out a long, slow breath. "We should do this outside, so I don't blow a hole in the roof if I have to redirect."

"We'll go to the graveyard. I'm strongest there."

Anubis stood and gestured toward the rear of the house.

Magnus hesitated. "Umm...?"

She thought he meant for people.

He didn't.

"See it before you make assumptions." I rose and pulled her to her feet, then offered Nico a hand.

He stared at my palm for a moment as if it might morph into something wicked, then accepted, and let me tug him up as well.

While we walked toward the property behind Anubis's house, I tried to tell myself I'd be fine if this didn't work.

I meant what I said about not wanting to die, and about trusting Magnus to not hurt me.

That didn't mean I trusted that she had the power to help me. That wasn't an assessment of her ability, but rather what fate had in store for me.

Despite my efforts to suppress hope, it swelled inside. If she could give me my power back... I wanted that. I needed that.

We reached the edge of *the graveyard*, which was rows of cars. Some just bodies, others frames, or pieces. All components waiting for Anubis to give their potential another chance.

"So pretty." Awe flowed from Magnus's voice.

"Yes, they are," Anubis said.

We walked a little further into the car graveyard, and stopped.

"What now?" Magnus asked.

Anubis stayed a few meters away, watching us. "I'm keeping an eye on you. I assume now, you do whatever you did to Nico."

Nico joined Anubis.

Magnus took my hand and pulled me closer, to drape her arms around my neck. "I don't know if the words matter," she said. "But just in case..."

I could feel her heart hammering against her ribs. Against mine. She was warm and close and I wanted to hold her here forever.

Or at least for a few more hours.

"I wish you had your power back." She brushed her lips over mine.

The spark was electric, despite her soft touch. I felt the trickle and then a surge, as she deepened the kiss.

There were the emotions. Hers. Nico's—that jealousy mixed with curiosity and adoration was unmistakable. Anubis was curious as well. On alert. Watching and waiting.

I gripped the back of her neck and kissed her harder, nipping her lips. Mashing my tongue with hers. Devouring her moans and feeling everything she did.

This was a hundred times more intense than in the hotel. This was pure. Raw. This was *me*.

Anubis didn't see any issues with what we were

doing. He wasn't concerned about a power surge. He wasn't stopping us.

What Magnus was doing was working. *Had* worked. I felt everything. If I let her go, I could blink to the other side of the graveyard and back. I could soothe her. Nico.

I was whole.

Magnus broke away with a gasp, pink flushing her cheeks. "How was that?" Mischief shone in her eyes like sparkling emeralds.

"Fucking incredible." My voice came out thicker than I expected.

She took one step back, and then another, finally letting go of my hand.

It all evaporated. The instant she let go of me, a switch was flipped. I couldn't feel anyone else anymore. The charge was gone. "What happened?"

"What do you mean?" Magnus frowned.

Anubis studied me. "The power..."

"You absorbed it," Nico finished for him.

"You're like a void," Anubis said. "Everything she poured into you, you absorbed. It's gone."

Nico shook his head. Disbelief? Disappointment? "If energy could die, that would be what happened to you."

"I can try again." Magnus reached for me. "Give you more."

"I don't believe it will matter." Anubis sounded

resigned. "Whatever happened to you, you're not meant to have your power."

CHAPTER 21
NICO

A spark burned inside me that I thought died decades ago. I would go to extremes to keep Magnus safe and happy.

Once upon a time I would've done the same for Bragi, until we reached a point where he wouldn't let me. Until he was the one destroying himself, and I couldn't stop that.

That part of my past was fresh as I watched Magnus try to restore his power, and the disappointment he tucked deep down behind a stoic expression when she failed.

They both thanked Anubis for his help, and we left him so we could return to NEON.

There was a conversation we needed to have—Bragi and I. He'd asked for it, and I'd avoided it. I couldn't confront my own muddled feelings.

I hadn't sorted them completely, but I was

closer. As we walked in the back door, I stopped him with a hand on his arm. "May we talk?"

Bragi looked shocked.

Magnus didn't. "I'll be upstairs."

I headed toward a back room, a lounge of sorts, that I'd been introduced to in my time here. The space itself was a bit large and sprawling for two people, and I hadn't gotten used to the beanbags on the floor yet, but there were a pair of chairs to one side that would work to give us comfort and privacy.

Though, as we reached them, I couldn't sit.

It seemed neither could Bragi. "I have a lot I'd like to say, but I feel like you deserve to go first."

Perfect. I could tell him the same things I'd told him again and again. While he was sliding into darkness. When I walked away from him. When he called me to help Magnus.

In the past with our arguments, he could feel me. He could pluck emotions from me that I hadn't identified. At times, that was useful. It helped smooth things over between us, because he understood where I was coming from.

Other times, especially toward the end, it was infuriating. Yes, there was a part of me reluctant to push him away, but that didn't mean it had been the wrong decision.

Now, for the first time since I'd met him, we were on equal footing.

In a way, I wished we weren't. Then he could

pluck out whether or not I wanted to forgive him, and I wouldn't need to confront the truth. Or I could get angry at him for it.

"I feel like I've said it all before." That was my cop-out answer.

Bragi picked up a paper coaster from a nearby table, and worried the edge with his thumb. His gaze was fixed on the blue and purple NEON logo decorating one side. "I feel like if that were the case, we wouldn't be here."

I should have waited. Taken more time to order my thoughts.

If I did that, we'd never have this conversation. I was tired of resenting him and hating him and blaming him.

The only thing I could think to do was start somewhere, and follow the thread. "When you joined Vidar... No, later, after you'd been on the board for a while, after you became... not you, I didn't see the downward slide. Mortals rarely think as they're aging *my joints hurt a little more than yester-day. My eyesight is two percent worse.* They wake up one day and they're ninety instead of forty."

Bragi stopped picking at the coaster and gave me his attention, but he stayed quiet.

Where was I going with this?

"I woke up one day and you were no longer the man I loved. And that man, the one who had wooed me across decades, he wouldn't have done the things you did. He wouldn't have allowed the atrocities to occur that you did."

Bragi opened his mouth.

"Wait." I silenced him. "I'm in the fairly unique position of recently having had all of my memories shoved into my head at once. When that happens, until the mind sorts itself out, they all took place at the same time. It's all like *yesterday*. Which is an eye-opening and jarring way to look at the long, painful decline of someone else.

"Of myself." It hurt to say it out loud. To make the self-accusations real. "Because you didn't do anything, and in so many ways, you made it worse. I didn't do anything either, though."

He set the coaster aside and sank into a chair, staring at the ground. His sigh carried the weight of the world. "What were you going to do?"

"Stop you. Stop them. Save you." I took the seat next to him as reality sapped my strength.

He gave the tiniest shake of his head. "Have you figured out yet that Magnus does what she wants?"

"That's not the point, but yes."

"It is the point though," Bragi said. "You can't make her do what she doesn't want to, and you couldn't have done any better with me. I didn't want to be saved. I destroyed myself."

Destroyed. I'd thought so too, for the longest time. I'd assumed there was nothing left of the man I'd fallen for aside from a name and a face.

Seeing Magnus go through some of the same things he had—experiencing her creep toward madness while memories of his were fresh in my mind—made it easy to see details I'd chosen to ignore for a long time.

"You didn't destroy yourself, though." When I thought about what he'd done to bring Magnus back from the brink of death, to get my memories back when he could have just walked away and ignored me... That wasn't someone who had shattered. "You hurt yourself. You hurt me. You sank into a deep, deep pit. You're still here, though. Not as someone who wants to delight in the world's pain or ignore it, but as someone who wants to save the woman who can make the world brighter again."

"You're wrong there." A strength and frustration sparked in his words. "You can't save Magnus."

What? I could. I would. "I have to."

"Believe me, I understand. That's the instinct. To protect this precious thing at all costs. That was where I fucked up. I thought that was the only answer."

Where did I lose him in this conversation? "It is. Rather, it's not the only thing that has to be done, but it's certainly at the top of the list."

"No," Bragi said. "She doesn't need to be saved. She saved us, and in return we keep her safe."

I frowned at the language. "Those are the same thing."

"They're not, though."

I rolled the words in my head, digging for Bragi's meaning.

He let out another sigh. The room would be filled with them shortly, if they didn't evaporate. "I was *saving* her when I lied to her about Dahlia and Fen. When I locked her away in my house, so the world couldn't get to her. She was my prize. The trophy on my shelf meant to be looked at, but too stunning to ever mar with the real world."

Oh. That made a surprising amount of sense.

"And that's what you wish you'd done for me," Bragi said.

It was. Not at the time it happened, but now... "Yes."

"You can't. I can't. She can't."

However, we could protect each other from the world, while it raged on around us. We could destroy any storm that tried to obliterate our haven. "I do still wish I'd seen what you were going through while it happened. That I'd been more understanding, and not let myself slip into the same thing I accused you of."

"I gave up a long time ago on the idea of winning you back." The way Bragi shifted gears, not a sharp tangent, but sliding into the curve, made my brain scramble to catch up. "That doesn't mean I ever stopped wanting you. Even with her here, even with all the adoration I have for Magnus, there's a piece of me missing when you're not in my life."

Bragi leaned across the space between us, almost touching me, but dropping his hand at the last moment. "But I don't want you to be my savior any more than she wants me to be hers. My redemption is on me."

"That's all well and good." My thoughts made more sense now, and I was both grateful and resentful of that. "I understand. There are decades of hurt between us, regardless of the rest."

"I know. I can't talk those away and neither can you."

I shook my head. "Then what do we do about them?"

"I hope that you'll give me time to show who I am now, and you'll show me the same."

It was a reasonable request. It was a painful idea, but it might be worth it. "I never stopped loving you either," I said. "Until that hurt fades, though... We're not better."

"That's fair." The hitch in Bragi's voice implied it wasn't as much so as he said. "Perhaps... What have you been up to for the last century?"

"Reading. A lot of reading."

One corner of his mouth quirked up. "Any favorite new authors?"

"That depends. Have you been writing anything under a new pseudonym?"

"Not a lot of time for writing about saving the world while I was busy helping someone else crush it." Bitterness leaked into his laugh. "I do have a few ideas, though."

"The bookstore near my home doesn't have anything that was written after 1950." I could imagine the scandal on Mr. Wilson's face if someone were to show him the book from Magnus's shelf of the shirtless man with the pet wolf. "He has carts of *trashy* pulp, though. I've read about sea monsters, submarines, and time machines a dozen times over."

Bragi almost smiled. "That sounds incredible."

We fell into old conversations, and on the surface it was with ease. Underneath, I continued to consider his words. Would we reach a point where this was natural, and not a facade to mask old wounds?

Was I capable of that level of forgiveness for him or myself?

CHAPTER 22
MAGNUS

It was after two in the morning, and I was exhausted. Why didn't we spend more time sleeping?

I desperately wanted to be doing that now, instead of sitting in my living room, listening to my brain on a loop about everything we'd uncovered. Occasionally my mind would take a break to ask *What are Bragi and Nico talking about?*

My stomach growled and I glared at it.

Food might be a good idea. If nothing else, it was something new to think about.

I went through my fridge and cupboards twice, but nothing grabbed me. Why couldn't this be my biggest worry all the time?

Because I'd get bored so fast. What would I do if I wasn't fighting for my life or someone else's every few weeks?

My tummy growled an answer I couldn't understand, but was probably *eat all the chocolate in the world.*

I didn't want chocolate tonight. That meant I was sick, didn't it?

I wanted ice—not the crushed stuff that came out of my freezer, but the little pebble ice like they had at the sandwich shop across the street. And apple slices. With olives. Unpitted Kalamata olives. That all sounded incredible.

Grabbing my purse, I dropped my phone into the outside pocket, and slipped on my shoes.

No one would miss me if I was gone for five minutes. And if these happened to be the five minutes that Bragi and Nico decided to return, then I wouldn't have to wait anymore.

Besides, now that I had the idea in my head—ice, apples, and olives—nothing else would work to sate the craving. If I listened closely enough, I could almost convince myself the babies were asking for this. For all I knew, that was something god babies could do. I didn't want to be a bad mom before they were even born by denying their request.

The instant I stepped out of NEON, I had my own protective shield up, to hide me from prying eyes. I stepped off the curb, to cross the street.

My vision blurred and went dark, as if I'd blinked away tears, and I dropped my purse in surprise.

And I was standing in front of Vidar, in a massive gymnasium, instead of outside of NEON.

I reacted instantly, summoning my Valkyrie form and lunging at Vidar.

I slammed into an invisible wall, similar to the one I'd encountered at Anubis's. Fine. I knew how to shatter this, and I grasped at the power surging around me. They were magical walls, and I simply needed to tear them down.

Vidar stood less than five meters away, watching me with an impassive expression.

Suck a dick.

I grasped at the transparent walls and yanked. Then yanked some more. Then continued yanking. It didn't matter how much I ripped away from the closet-sized prison, it was like pushing water in a cup with a straw—the magic just kept slipping back into place.

The longer I dug, the more the pressure built inside, swelling until I couldn't contain it anymore. The energy ripped from me, tearing a scream from my throat as it escaped.

My prison stayed the same.

"Shame. I was hoping you'd have learned more control by now." Vidar finally spoke.

Half a dozen questions bubbled up inside, and I suppressed them in a way I hadn't been able to hold back the magic overload. *How did you grab me? Where are we? What the fuck is up with this box?* "Do you ever get tired of hearing yourself talk?" Oops, one got out.

Vidar smiled. "I don't. I enjoy it enough for both of us. Do you like the box? I designed it for you."

"You should've just sent flowers. Maybe your heart on a platter."

"Ah, I missed our talks. The prison draws its power from a battery of sorts, so it doesn't matter how much you take from it, it stays intact. When you can't hold anymore, your energy release recharges the device."

Don't ask. Don't ask. Don't ask. "How did you find me?"

"I thought you were still in Wyoming, honestly. Until you stepped onto the street outside NEON wearing Vindres's mark on your hand."

When the incubus kissed my knuckles? Was that what Vidar was talking about? Fuck fuckity fuck fuck. I was such an idiot.

"I was getting tired of waiting," Vidar said. "Isn't that funny? I've been trying to do this for more than a century, and once I had all the pieces within my reach, my patience grew short. Though, I suspect a portion of that had to do with the two of you. So very trying. You should be proud of that."

I was. There was a great deal of satisfaction in knowing that Dahlia and I annoyed him. The feeling was ruined by the fact that he expected it. He couldn't even let us have smugness.

"Nothing?" Vidar punctuated the word. "No snappy comebacks? No clever quips? How disappointing." He wasn't disappointed in any way.

The longer I sat here, the harder it was to block out the smug self-righteousness he radiated. He'd won, as far as he was concerned. The entire sensation made me want to puke on his shoes. Unless he expected that, as well.

"I'd hate to disappoint you." I let my voice stay flat, like I was reading from a prompter. "After all this time, your approval means the world to me. Please, tell me what you're doing, so I can learn from your genius." I hated to ask, even in a monotone, but I also needed to buy myself some time. To think. To wait for the others to figure out I was gone.

That could be minutes or take hours. Dahlia, Fen, and Frey were working. Bragi and Nico were talking.

Fuck.

The way Vidar's smile grew, showing all his teeth and self-importance, was more terrifying than I wanted to admit. Yes, his blah blah blah was annoying.

His power could crush all of us, and me alone? I didn't stand a chance.

"Was that so hard?" Vidar said. "To simply—"

I snorted. "You said *hard*." The interruption made him furious, the way I thought it would. I couldn't help myself.

He fixed me with a glower. "To simply hear me

out. To shut your fucking mouth for five fucking minutes and listen. "

Annoying Vidar made me feel better. Pissing him off to the point where he radiated a massive cloud of *I will torture you in every way imaginable...* That wasn't so great.

Wait. Was that a sliver of fear underneath everything else?

No.

"None of you have any idea what the world was like before," Vidar said. "Not even your precious phoenix remembers the beautiful, vibrant place this used to be."

"And you do?" The current plan was keep him talking, don't piss him off, and find the source of power for the box holding me.

"Skuld told so many stories. Tales that would have made Bragi weep with their elegance, if he didn't have so much ego."

Look who's talking, asshat. "That seems to run rampant among gods," I said.

"And it's been our downfall again and again. Convincing the board they could stop Ragnarök? Because each and every one of them thought they were too important to die? That was far simpler than it should've been. "

"But you don't want to stop it." I couldn't believe I was playing along.

Just as bad, when I followed the threads of

power keeping my prison intact, they led back to him. Or rather, the leather bracelet he wore, with a charm attached to it.

Tatiana's bracelet.

Vidar glanced at me, eyebrow raised. "You figured out that much. Well done. No, I want to make it happen now."

"Because you want to be king of the ashes?" That felt a little Game of Thrones to me, but I'd never been able to guess at Vidar's motivations.

The anger he fixed me with, the rage at my incomprehension, made me stumble.

"Because it's not about who dies," he said. "It's never been about who dies. It's about the rebirth that comes after."

Not the way Nico described things. How good could a *rebirth* be, if his memories were focused on the significant levels of death?

"Does that include you?" I tugged on the power flowing from him, through the charm, rather than scraping at the box. I pulled and pulled, like finding a loose thread on a sweater.

Vidar shook his head. "The prophecies were never about me. Skuld assured me. You and your friends destroyed that incredible, ancient mind, and she left me here alone to rebuild the world. She abandoned me, so I could build this place into the paradise she remembered."

Well, fuck me. He believed all of this. The passion that spilled from him...

Now I knew how Bragi had been drawn in to Vidar's vision. Vidar was entrenched in this idea of a better, more beautiful world.

He also missed Skuld so much, it ached.

I'd be touched if I weren't put off by the whole *let's kill whomever it takes* mentality.

The more I grasped power from the bracelet, the more it fed me. Yards and yards of energy. This time I was prepared. I coiled it inside. I wrapped it in a tight little ball, to keep it from growing larger than I could contain it.

But there was so much of it. Too much. It was heavy. It was sinking into my bones. It was—

I had to release it in a scream of power, where it flowed seamlessly into my prison, and dissipated.

Vidar raised an eyebrow. "I'd be disappointed if you weren't trying, but I'd prefer you didn't exhaust yourself before we got to the part you play in all of this."

"And I'd prefer I was at home, eating olives and apples, and you were dead. We can't always get what we want."

He sighed and shook his head. "How do you not see? You can feel how beautiful this new world would be. You can be a part of it. You exist outside of fate, because you're two lives instead of one. You can be anyone. You can do anything."

I loved the idea as much as I always had, but I didn't think for a moment that he was the one who could grant me that.

"So what's up with the server farm? Come to think of it, what was up with destroying Bragi's house?" I grasped for the prison's power again, as I asked my question.

He was pleased I'd asked. Impressed that I'd put the pieces together that I had. Assuming that if I kept asking questions, he could win me over.

"The server farm will find the gates. It has a level of processing power I don't. It was the biggest flaw in Skye's machine—it didn't have enough power, even with her and her sister. You do, though. You just keep generating it.

"I would have preferred you draw from Dahlia," he said. "But she was my biggest failure and putting the two of you in a room together... No, you'll draw from me. As for Bragi, he's not a threat. I don't give a fuck what he does. Fate's taken his power, and he can sit back and watch this all happen for all I care. I did want to destroy those fucking journals of his, though."

The ones Nico had been reading. The ones that talked about Skye and everyone else.

So many little pieces. "You know what the problem with an intricate plan is?" I asked, but wasn't going to wait for an answer. "If one little thing goes wrong, it all falls apart."

"Unless you loved a dragon who told you how it would all play out." He was talking about Skuld, and there was actual affection in his voice.

Twisted, convoluted, weird affection.

The problem with his response was he'd told me I wasn't a part of those visions. So had Artura and Dahlia. I didn't show up in any of them.

Okay, so his plan wasn't as perfect as he thought, but that didn't mean I knew what to do to stop it.

"This is your last chance." Vidar stepped closer to me. "Will you help me?"

"Is it that easy? I just get to pick yes or no?" I let the sarcasm drip into my enthusiasm.

"Of course you do. I'd always rather you picked."

"Then I'm gonna go with a nice steaming pile of go fuck yourself."

Vidar's eye twitched and his body tensed.

The prison around me vanished. *Poof* the restrictive energy was gone.

Did he—

An invisible force grasped my wrists and ankles and yanked them tight, pinning me to the ground and air. A fifth restraint wrapped around my neck, pressing into my windpipe enough to be uncomfortable, but not cut off my air.

"I'll still use you," Vidar said. "But this would have been less time consuming if you'd agreed."

But of course.

A knife appeared in his hand. The paper-thin

edge and sharp hook along the back were enough to make my gut churn.

"First things first." Vidar closed the distance between us.

I struggled with everything I had, fighting my restraints. Each jerk of my body sent pain through me, but I needed to get out of here. Panic was setting in.

"We need to get rid of this drain on your resources." He sliced the blade toward my lower belly.

Before I could whimper or cry in protest, or do anything, the blade stopped, centimeters from my skin. It sliced my shirt, but it didn't cut me.

That wasn't me.

Was that the prayer from Tatiana?

I didn't know or care, as long as the babies were safe.

He sighed and shook his head. "That's fine. I'll get to that problem another way."

He hovered both hands near my head, neither making contact, but both close enough to my cheeks that I felt the heat. A shock of fire scorched one side, and an icy chill evacuated the other.

Vidar was flooding me with power, and drawing out the amplified result. The sensation was like pushing a peg into a cardboard hole that wasn't quite big enough, except that I was the cardboard hole.

No. Fuck this. Bragi's training slipped into my thoughts, as much instinct as conscious recognition. I knew where my power ended and Vidar's began. I could feel where inside me he was drawing from.

And I could cut him off from it.

The flow through my face stopped, and Vidar frowned. He studied me for a moment, and tugged again.

I kept him out.

He sighed. "That's fine. I learned things from Bragi too. Keep in mind, I could do this quickly, but at this point, you're just pissing me off. You get to suffer the way I am."

The sincerity in his words made me ill, but I didn't know what he meant.

Until he plucked at the air in front of me, and I felt the snap deep in my soul. Like a magical bone fracturing, then re-healing.

This was what Bragi had done to me to restore my Valkyrie power.

But Vidar was cracking multiple threads at a time, like crushing every bone in my hand, then letting magic heal before he did it again.

And again.

And again.

I couldn't hold back the screams of pain, and tears squeezed out of the corners of my eyes.

CHAPTER 23
BRAGI

I felt better about things with Nico than I had in a long time.

It wasn't a high bar, and *I love you, but I don't know if I can be with you*, was nowhere near a promise.

He'd heard me out, though. We'd talked. We'd moved forward.

Creation, I'd missed him. I'd given up hope of ever having a civil conversation with him again. So this? I'd take it, especially if there was a chance for more, no matter how slim that chance was.

He and I returned to Magnus's apartment, and he knocked.

There was no answer.

"With a little luck, she's sleeping." Nico pulled a key from his pocket.

Jealousy pinged my heart at the sight. I wasn't

surprised he had a key to her apartment, but that didn't stop my envy.

We pushed inside, and a strange emptiness greeted us. It was nothing visual—everything was where we'd left it before Anubis called—but there was a chill in my soul.

Nico frowned. "Her purse is gone." He strode further into the space as he talked, heading for the bedroom. The door was ajar, and he opened it further. "She's not in here."

"Shower?" That wasn't the answer, but I had to ask.

He shook his head. "She must have gone out to get some food."

"That's not right. You can *feel* it's not right." Not that I should have any sort of sense of where Magnus was or wasn't, but my instinct was screaming with alarm bells. This was more than paranoia. "We need Dahlia."

Nico and I headed downstairs again.

This was a misunderstanding. We'd get to NEON and find Magnus in the club. Or just coming back from a food run. Or grabbing a delivery from the back door.

None of that was true, but I wanted to believe it.

We reached the club to find Dahlia in the middle of a performance.

This wouldn't wait. I cut a straight line toward her.

"Whoa." Fen stepped in my path with a growl.

Nico blocked him from stopping me, and I kept moving.

I stepped into the middle of the stage, in front of Dahlia, to a chorus of *boos*. She fixed me with a withering glare.

"Magnus is missing," I said as Nico said the same to Fen.

Dahlia's frustration vanished behind a frown. "Are you sure?" She closed her eyes without waiting for an answer, and a heartbeat later, they flew open again. "Show's over." She was already walking off the stage.

"Everyone out." Frey's voice carried through the main room as the house lights went on, and he appeared next to Fen and Nico.

The grumbles behind me didn't fade, as Dahlia and I joined the others, but I heard the sounds of people standing. Leaving.

"Where is she?" Dahlia was talking more to herself than to any of us. She brushed past our group, and clothes appeared on her, replacing the frilly nearly-nothing she'd worn on stage.

The T-shirt and jeans were part of her—her dragon ability to change her appearance into anything—rather than individual pieces.

I'd be impressed with how far she'd come later. Other things were more important now.

I stayed by her side, while Nico, Fen, and Frey followed us out onto the street.

Dahlia stopped at the edge of the curb and crouched to pick up something. The bag looked like it had been run over a few times, and wasn't holding as much as last time I saw Magnus carrying it.

"Magnus's purse," Nico muttered. He squinted into the night. "There are traces of Vidar here. Not like he was here, but his magic was."

Fuck.

"Where is she?" Nico demanded.

The creases in her forehead grew deeper. "I don't know. I can't feel her."

I knew. "I can tell you where. Take me with you."

"You are *not* negotiating her safety for your ego." Nico was furious.

"No. I'll tell you regardless. The facility in Barbados. Dahlia, if you focus on the island, you'll feel a beacon. It's faint. It's meant to look like a mistake."

"I feel it." She grabbed Fen and Nico.

I gripped her arm. "I'm going with you."

Fen growled. "Don't get in the way."

"Bring everyone home safe," Frey's voice lingered in our ears as we vanished.

It made sense that he would remain behind. He was only a combatant when he needed to be. I should have stayed with him, but I couldn't.

Dahlia landed us immediately outside the entrance to the old FU facility. As we stalked toward it, Nico blasted the door out of the way with a burst of flame that should have scorched everything in the vicinity, but only destroyed the heavy steel obstruction.

"*Stop.*" There were far more soldiers here than last time I'd visited. Several pointed weapons at us, and Fen shifted as we continued walking without pause.

"*We will shoot.*" Whoever was shouting was terrified.

Fen charged, and Nico surrounded us with flame.

Dahlia held up her hand and flicked her wrist.

Everyone but the four of us vanished.

"Where did they go?" Nico asked.

"I sent them home. They don't deserve to die today," Dahlia said.

Home was vague, but if I had to guess, I'd say she sent them to the now decimated TOM campus. That put them a few clicks outside a small town, they'd be familiar with the area, and any accidental discharge wouldn't strike innocent parties.

"Center of the building." I pointed down the appropriate hallway as we walked. No one else stopped us. Dahlia was efficient.

As we drew closer to our destination, Magnus's screams reached us. The agony in the sound tore my heart to shreds and cranked my fury to never before known heights.

Nico blasted another door out of the way, and

the noise grew in volume. We walked into a now fully lit gymnasium, with Magnus and Vidar in the middle.

She looked tired. Her face was drawn and tear-streaked, and something invisible held her upright. She'd aged centuries in the last few hours.

"*Damn it.*" He looked annoyed more than concerned. "I thought I had more time. Okay, you can all die fi—"

Vidar's words were cut off when Nico flung a ball of flame at him, engulfing the god.

Vidar stepped from the fire unfazed and smirking.

He was knocked back when Fen lunged, teeth bared and aimed at his throat.

Fen was tossed aside with a flick of Vidar's wrist. He landed on his feet, and a half-dragon Dahlia was already slicing a razor-edged wing at Vidar.

Vidar vanished and appeared behind her, planting a foot in her back and sending her stumbling.

She blinked out of sight and appeared next to Nico, her balance recovered.

The three moved like a well-oiled machine, but nothing they did so much as scratched Vidar.

I crept toward Magnus. Could I free her? I had to. She was the goal. We could take her, destroy this place, and regroup to figure out what to do about Vidar.

"The charm." Magnus's voice was barely a croak as I got closer.

An invisible fist hit me in the chest, sending me flying back and gasping for air. I caught myself and looked up to see Vidar smirking at me, before he turned his attention to the others.

"Vidar." Dahlia's call rang out. She stood several meters from him, the amulet from Artura in her hand.

He vanished from his spot.

She crushed it, and the pieces clattered to the floor just as he appeared next to her. "Fuck you," Dahlia spat.

Vidar snarled, and she teleported away before his attack hit her.

Nico would turn him around with fire, while Fen leaped from above, and Dahlia slid low, aiming for his legs.

Again and again, they would be cast aside. It didn't matter how well they worked together or how quickly they recovered, Vidar tossed them back.

Each time I got close to Magnus, he would knock me away without so much as a glance.

The longer they fought, the more wear and tear shone on Dahlia, Fen, and Nico. Torn clothing. Scratches. Burns. Injuries that didn't heal everywhere.

Vidar looked as fresh as when we'd walked in,

but his frustration was growing. "Why won't any of you *die*?" His question rattled the building.

"We learned it from watching you." Dahlia charged again.

Instead of knocking her aside, Vidar gripped her by the throat and raised her in the air.

She clawed at his arm, sharp dragon blades slicing again and again, but every slice on his skin healed before it finished appearing.

"Minato should have killed you," he said.

Fen's roar was terrifying, and he lunged, only to bounce off an invisible wall.

"She got what I needed in that very first dream," Vidar said. "But you just kept coming back for more. Over and over."

Nico swooped in as a bird, to peck at the back of Vidar's head, and Vidar dropped Dahlia to swat Nico aside.

Dahlia stabbed Vidar in the back.

He vanished and reappeared behind her and a few feet up. He planted his foot in her skull, and sent her flying.

They couldn't keep this up. Dahlia and the others would last a long time, but Vidar would last longer.

I was helpless. I couldn't even get to Magnus, to free her so she could help. So we could escape.

"Help," Magnus whimpered. "I have to help them." She sounded so weak.

Vidar couldn't have her. He couldn't have Nico. I wouldn't allow it.

You're like a void. Anubis's voice echoed in my head.

If energy could die, that would be what's happening to you. There was Nico.

Fuck it. I knew how to save them. Vidar was occupied with a three-way strike, and I crawled up to Magnus. I brushed her leg to draw her attention.

"You can't save everyone," I told her. "But I love you for trying, and you need to keep the good happening to good people."

"What are you doing?" Her question was soft. Desperate.

Vidar was looking at us again. "What *are* you doing, old friend?"

Saving the only people who ever mattered. I pushed to my feet. "I want to talk."

"You always do." Vidar laughed. Though his attention was on me, he managed to knock Dahlia, Fen, and Nico aside with each of their attacks.

I strolled toward Vidar. Behind me, I heard Magnus struggling against her restraints. She knew. She could feel it.

I'd accepted that this was where I died.

I reached Vidar. "You want to make her suffer? Let her watch while you kill me."

He smirked. "You've always thought so highly of yourself."

"Takes one to know one." Sometimes the new insults were the best.

He gripped my throat, the way he had Fen, but I wasn't capable of breaking free. Vidar lifted me in the air.

My feet kicked freely without purchase, and I grabbed his arm. This was exactly what I wanted. "Go ahead. Destroy me." I spoke through gritted teeth.

His power flowed into me.

And kept flowing, vanishing the moment it was part of me.

Mostly vanishing. I felt the residual building. Clinging to components of me. Eating away at my existence from the inside out, like a slow-acting acid.

Would I be overloaded before he ran out of power?

I didn't know, but every single ounce of magic he poured into me was more he didn't have to use on them.

I dug my fingers into his arm, actively trying to draw more from him than he was giving.

Vidar snarled. "You want to die quickly? Fine."

He pushed harder. Blackness licked at the edge of my vision, and my thoughts deteriora...

CHAPTER 24

MAGNUS

These restraints were like one of those stupid finger toys, that the harder I pulled, the tighter it got.

Except that relaxing didn't make them looser.

In school, Starkad taught us physics. Not that he was our science teacher, but there was a lot of subconscious math involved in hand-to-hand combat, especially with noticeable size and weight differences in opponents.

What I was watching with Vidar and Bragi was what Starkad would have referred to as unstoppable object meeting an unmovable force.

Or rather, that was how it started.

I could see Bragi being torn apart from the inside out, where Vidar just kept generating more power. Where the fuck was it coming from?

Bragi thought this was some sort of grand

gesture. It wasn't that he wanted to die, but he was that determined that Nico and I should live.

Fucking asshole.

I jerked against the invisible bonds, struggling harder than I ever had.

Bragi was dying. Nico was going to die again. Dahlia. Fen.

I couldn't watch that all play out a second time. It nearly destroyed me the first.

I felt Bragi's every single emotion slipping away in a cloud of agony. I felt the frustration of the others. Bleed into futility.

Vidar flung Dahlia back. She hit the wall hard enough that her consciousness slipped. Only for the briefest second. Long enough for her dragon to vanish, along with clothes that weren't there, leaving her in half her stage costume.

Wait.

Something tickled my mind.

It vanished when inspiration struck Bragi. He let go of Vidar's arm, and ripped the bracelet— Tatiana's charm—away from Vidar's wrist.

Yes.

Dahlia didn't bother putting on pretend clothes again, she was already flying in for another attack, along with the others.

No one knew I was free.

You have to tone down the power display near the sound system.

That was what Frey had told Dahlia just a few days ago, right before she blew out the club speakers nearest to her.

I felt all of them. Their power. Their strengths. Dragon. Wolf. Phoenix. Heart.

Destruction.

I pulled on all of it, the way I always had before, letting it grow inside me until I was ready to burst at the seams. They were all so powerful, it didn't take much. But I pushed myself harder than I ever had. I stuffed myself at the all-you-can-eat buffet, and went back for seconds and thirds and coffee and dessert.

If I were feeling better, I'd make a Captain Planet joke, just to piss off Vidar. Instead, I yelled, "*Stop.*"

My friends did.

Vidar just laughed and looked at me in disbelief. "Why?"

"I'll give you what you want." I took a step toward him.

"It's too late for that, lover." Vidar dropped an unconscious Bragi, and bent to reclaim the charm that was still clenched in Bragi's hand.

I blinked out of sight and landed next to Vidar, snatching the bracelet before he could.

He regarded me with a glare. "I can always make this worse, lover."

"I know." I gave him a sweet smile, and slipped

the bracelet onto my own wrist. "But if you want my power so badly, you can choke on it."

I grabbed his arm, the same way Bragi had. But my goal wasn't to draw his power out, it was to feed him more. I let the overload spill from me, but instead of releasing what I had and stopping, I kept pulling from the world around me. From the air. From my friends. From myself. I ate and ate and ate, and the various energies mixed in me, growing far beyond what they should be. Swelling until I thought I might burst.

And I kept pouring it into Vidar.

His smirk shifted to a frown, and then horror.

His face contorted, and he clawed at my arm.

I didn't even know where I was finding this power. The shielding on the stolen servers? The artifact he had from Skuld, was radiating toward me from somewhere in the building? The shattered amulet from Artura that lay in pieces around the gymnasium.

Vidar crackled. The magical joints inside him split and snapped.

I pushed more in. I crammed decades of terror and frustration into him. I doubted that would make a difference, but I didn't fucking want that pain anymore.

I scorched him until he screamed in terror and agony.

Unlike him, I wasn't here for the torture.

Not much of it anyway.

I ripped a final chunk of power from the air, magnified it, and crammed it into him in a single blow.

The explosion that tore him apart also incinerated every last bit of him, and knocked all of us back several meters.

The massive magical discharge rang in my ears.

"I think I broke something." I was surprised I could hear my own voice. It sounded foreign to me.

"You did." Dahlia's words were tentative. "You broke Vidar."

Did I really though? "Are you sure?"

Around me, everyone was climbing to their feet.

A black scorch mark radiated out from the center of the room.

"You definitely broke something." Next to me, Bragi stood.

He was okay.

He was more than okay.

He was... "You look different." I studied him.

Bragi blinked out of sight, and returned a heartbeat later, something clenched in his hand.

"You have your power back?" Nico asked.

"Seems that way." Bragi handed me an amulet that was a mirror image of the one Artura had given Dahlia. "That's how you know he's gone. No one but him would be able to hold this without his permission if he were still here, because Skuld gifted it to him."

I stared at it blankly in the palm of my hand. It couldn't be real. This couldn't be real.

"It is," Bragi said.

I finally looked up. "I didn't say anything."

He closed my fingers over the amulet. "You didn't have to."

Because he felt my disbelief. And my relief. And my fucking exhaustion.

Bragi pressed his lips to my forehead, and the feedback loop of comfort nearly swept everything else away.

Nearly.

I shoved him back with a grunt. "You're an asshole. You were going to die for that? How the fuck was that going to help?"

Dahlia joined me and looped her arm through mine. She stuck her tongue out at Bragi. "She's right, you know. Dumbass. Dying never helps anyone. Have you been paying attention?"

Bragi looked past us, to Fen and Nico.

Fen slipped an arm around Dahlia's waist. "It's best to just agree, unless you like to be argued to death with sarcasm and pop culture references. They tend to be right about this shit."

Nico grasped my hand and pulled me to him. He cupped my face between his hands, and crushed his mouth to mine. When he pulled away, he reached past me, to rest his hand over Bragi's, where it rested on my hip.

"They're right. That was an asinine move. I'm grateful you're all right," Nico said. "Can we go?"

"Yes," I said. "But only if someone promises me they're buying the apples and olives as soon as we get back." I was *so* hungry, and the babies still had a craving.

Dahlia took us back to their apartment, where Frey was waiting with long kisses for her and Fen, and a hug for me. "I'm glad you're safe," He said.

It was a simple sentiment, but the genuine worry underneath, the relief he felt at seeing all of us, warmed me. "Thank you." I was home. With my family.

Except—

"Where's Bragi?" I looked around the room.

Dahlia shrugged. "I thought he was with us."

There was a knock on the door, and Frey frowned and went to answer.

I could already feel who was there, and it made me smile.

Frey let Bragi in, who handed me a large cup of pebble ice, a bag of sliced apples, and a jar of olives. "I took a detour."

"How did you know?" I wasn't impressed because he brought me things I mentioned in passing. It was because he got the right kind of each. The tart, green apples I loved, and the brand of olives I was in the mood for.

His shrug made it look like it was no big deal, but he was smug. "I know you."

There was an overall mood of exhaustion in the room, and the way everyone was dragging meant it didn't take empathy to know that. We agreed Dahlia and Fen could tell Frey what happened, and we'd debrief tomorrow.

Because it could wait. Vidar was gone. Fucking gone. So were the other gods and threats that had chased us since we left TOM.

We didn't have anyone to hide from or hunt. "We're free." I didn't mean to say that out loud.

Dahlia's grin was bright. Tired, but shiny. "You're right."

Holy shit. It felt like there was so much more to say, but what else could encompass that realization so well?

"Go home." Dahlia pointed me toward the door. "Cuddle. Sleep. I'll bring you coffee in the morning."

Bragi glanced at the clock on the wall.

It *was* morning. Nearly seven.

"In the afternoon," he said.

"Deal." Dahlia pushed us into the hallway.

I let us into my place, and without any words, all three of us collapsed on the couch. The bedroom was too far away.

I leaned into Nico, and he wrapped an arm around me. He wasn't letting me go anytime soon.

Bragi fed me—all of us—apple slices and olives.

This was simple. Basic even. The kind of life I used to think didn't exist. True, this was only a snapshot, and it would be reckless to think it would be an ongoing reality, but for tonight...

Reality sank in as exhaustion chased away the last of the adrenaline. I wanted to laugh and cry and scream and cheer all at the same time.

"Are you all right?" Bragi studied me.

Because he could feel me again. He was whole again.

"He's gone." I couldn't make myself say Vidar's name. "I can' believe he's fucking gone. If this was a movie, he'd come out of the wall or some shit, and we'd have to kill him again and again."

Nico kissed the top of my head. "He's not Michael Meyers. You saw the proof with your own eyes—he's gone."

I pulled away from Nico enough to twist and shoot him a look of disbelief. "How the fuck do you know Halloween but not Star Wars?"

He pulled me into him again. "I guess I never had the right person to explain the importance of sand orphans to me before."

"I guess not." I accepted another olive from Bragi. "You're lucky I got to you, you know. Otherwise you could've gone another thousand years without knowing who Luke Skywalker is."

"I *am* lucky you got to me." Affection spilled from Nico. "While that may be one reason, it's nowhere near the top one. You're staying, Bragi."

That wasn't a question. It almost felt like a command.

Bragi gave a single nod. "Yes. With both of you. Always."

"Does that mean the two of you had a kiss and make up conversation?" The one I wanted so badly to hear, before Vidar took me. The one I'd forgotten about until now.

"We had the conversation," Bragi said. "As for the rest, we're closer than we have been in a long time."

"I was wrong." Nico spoke softly.

Bragi leaned in and turned one ear toward us. "What? I don't think I heard that."

"Don't be a dick," I said playfully.

Nico didn't mind. He was enjoying this. "I was wrong when I said I wasn't sure I could forgive you. I do, and I want you here."

Bragi let out a melodramatic sigh. "And all I had to do was be willing to sacrifice myself for the world."

"No," Nico said. "It certainly sped up the process, though."

The love flowed between them as much as it did into me. There was some hesitation on both of their parts, about how they fit together after all this time and all the hurt. They both wanted to be together, though.

And I wanted to stop analyzing every single fucking feeling for the night.

I tried to fight my yawn, but it tore open my jaw regardless.

Bragi gathered the food and stood. "I'll put this away."

Nico scooped me into his arms and stood in a single, smooth gesture.

I liked that, and I rested my head against his chest as he carried me into the bedroom.

Bragi undressed me. This wasn't sexual. It was all sweetness and nurturing. Then he and Nico stripped their clothes off as well.

As we climbed into bed, they wrapped themselves around me. Their strength and grips told me they were never letting me go.

Good.

Growing up, Hel and Vidar and the other gods worked hard to reinforce that the other students were the closest thing we'd ever have to a family. The point of the lesson was always *this is who you put your trust in, because you have no choice.*

I wasn't there anymore. It no longer existed.

The place we were in now, this apartment, had never quite felt like mine. It wasn't my room or my apartment, but rather a place I stayed that was safe and near family.

But laying between the men I loved, in this sanctuary that Frey and Fen built, that Dahlia and Frey kept safe... Anywhere that I could have that and them, was home.

Bragi had set the bracelet from Tatiana on my dresser, along with the ring made of Dahlia's claw. They rested next to a stuffed teddy bear and a stuffed mouse, both gifts from Dahlia because *I saw them and thought of you.* A crystal still hung around my neck, a gift from Nico originally, and then from Bragi.

Regardless of what life held for us, the people I loved were here for me. My family. Kirby. My Valkyrie sisters.

A wealth of support like most people would never know.

Bragi kissed my shoulder, and there was an unspoken whisper of comfort and agreement that passed between us.

Nico pressed his forehead to mine. "Get some sleep. You're safe now."

"I know. And I love you." I needed to say it, not out of frustration or indecision, but so he could hear how much I meant it.

"I love you too," Nico said. "For eternity."

I leaned into Bragi. "That goes for you, too. I love you," I said.

I felt his playful smirk, despite not being able to see him. "I know."

This was the most incredible thing ever, and I was never letting it go.

CHAPTER 25

NICO

It was odd to wake up without a cloud hanging over us. To think that Vidar—

I wasn't going to give him my thoughts any longer. He didn't deserve that mental energy from me.

Instead, I was focused on how incredible it felt to have Magnus in my arms, and Bragi so close. I liked both of those realities quite a bit.

"You feel too hard," Magnus mumbled, her voice drowsy.

The comment made me smile.

She squirmed, her entire body rubbing against me, and her ass grinding into my cock.

"Correction." She didn't sound nearly so sleepy now. "You feel the perfect amount of hard."

"*Creation*, I missed you," Bragi said.

And I had missed him. "You need to be careful," I warned Magnus. "If you keep this up, you'll start something."

"Hmm..." Her voice was seductive and tempting. "What if I want to start something."

"Then let me help." I moved quickly, flipping her on the bed so her back was to me.

She squealed, and I pulled her into me.

This wouldn't be sex born of frustration or needing to escape. This wasn't about grieving. Today we celebrated joy and love.

Bragi captured Magnus's hands, and pressed his body closer to hers, sandwiching her between him and me. None of us wore much, and I felt every bit of heat... every movement she made as she writhed between us and giggled.

Bragi captured her mouth in a noisy kiss, swallowing her laughter, while I slid my palms up her stomach. I glided my lips along her shoulder, to nip and tease.

Magnus relaxed against me with a sigh that bordered on a purr.

It was one of the sexiest sounds I'd ever heard.

I bent one leg at the knee to drape it over her legs, trapping her even more effectively between Bragi and me.

"Oh no, I'm trapped." Magnus's whimper was laced with laugher. "Whatever will I do?"

"You might have to enjoy yourself." Bragi managed to make the words sound like both threat and promise.

She let out a light huff. "I mean, that's not really my thing, but if you're going to *make* me have fun..."

"We are." I was looking forward to turning her on in so many ways. Today. Tomorrow. Again and again.

I glided my hands higher up her torso, to cup her breasts and knead. I trailed my fingers over her nipples with the lightest touch, to tantalize and tempt.

Magnus struggled against me, but her movements felt less like trying to get away, and more like trying to get me hard. Each moan and gasp that escaped her throat added to the sensations.

I increased the pressure I was applying, to roll her nipples between my fingers, and to pinch and tug. That earned me a louder gasp. A sharper groan. A barely-there whisper of *more*.

I was happy to oblige. I drew out the pleasure with one hand, but moved the other lower, needing to feel both of my loves.

I brushed Bragi's erection through his trousers, and he jerked against my touch. I cupped my hand to stroke his cock at the same pace I teased Magnus.

The sounds they made filled the room and my thoughts. Nothing mattered but pleasure. Theirs. Mine.

Magnus pressed her ass into my cock. Bragi adjusted his grip on her wrists, so that he could restrain her with one hand.

I expected him to stop me, but he moved his hand between Magnus's legs. While I couldn't see what he was doing, the jerk of fabric and her body, the sharp intake of breath she made, told me he'd moved aside her clothing to tease her pussy.

Now she was rocking. Back and forth. Riding Bragi's fingers while she pressed her breasts into my hands. The sounds she made were those of rising desire.

I could lose myself in those noises. In her heat. In the feeling of her body against mine.

Her groans grew shorter and more punctuated. Stuttered. Delicious.

When she came, she cried out and bucked between me and Bragi.

Fucking. Incredible.

Bragi released her and pulled away to suck his fingers clean of her juices.

I needed to taste her, and him. I sat up and leaned across Magnus, to glide my tongue up Bragi's fingers. Licking her flavor from him. Kissing him. Melting into him.

It had been so long since I could do this with Bragi. Since I could even think about it. *"Fuck,* I missed this," I muttered against his kiss.

"Me too. More than you can imagine."

"I doubt that." The touch, the taste, the connection made my heart ache in the best way, and made my cock even harder.

I suspected I could cut glass with the tip.

Magnus rolled onto her back. "I'm just going to lay here and enjoy the show. You two keep going."

"No you're not." Bragi had his attention on her again.

She pouted. "I can't watch?"

"You can't just lay there," Bragi said. "We're not done with you."

Magnus let out an exaggerated huff. "I guess if I *have* to keep getting fucked..."

"You do." I rolled to straddle her, and placed my hands on either side of her head. The way she stared up at me with wide eyes lit my soul on fire. I knelt between her legs, and nudged her opening with the head of my cock.

I needed to feel her. I plunged inside, and my groan sang with hers.

I hammered into her, hard and fast. She was so tight. So slick. So incredible.

She rolled her head to the side to look at Bragi, and reached for him as well.

"Tell me what you want," he prompted.

"Your cock. My mouth." Even now, she didn't hold back.

Another thing I adored about her.

Bragi knelt next to Magnus's head, fisting his

shaft, and pressing the head to her lips. She flicked out her tongue, licking and sucking him, while I fucked her with abandon.

I loved the sight. All of it.

And when Magnus came again, squeezing me tight, I loved the sensation.

Bragi's grunts, familiar and enticing after all this time, told me he was close to climax too. He covered Magnus's face and chest with his orgasm, and she flicked out her tongue, licking him clean.

The entire show, the sounds, the sensations, it all pushed me over the edge. I spilled into her, continuing to hammer until I was spent.

We all collapsed on each other, catching our breath.

I was reluctant to get up, but I eventually extracted myself from the pile, to get washcloths. Our clothes came off, and we cleaned up, before falling back into bed with each other, in a contented pile of bliss.

"We should get up." Magnus didn't sound like she meant it or wanted anything to do with the idea.

Bragi pinned her to the mattress with one arm over her stomach. "A woman in your condition needs lots of rest."

"Her condition?" I asked. "Savior of the world?"

Magnus laughed and shook her head. "No. Definitely no. And a woman in my condition—*uncaf-*

feinated and hungry—needs food and coffee. And then after that, probably more sex and sleep."

It was incredible to have them both here, like this. So many walls had fallen away. What lay between Bragi and me wouldn't vanish because of a single conversation—that didn't erase a century of hurt—but the pure selflessness of what he did yesterday against Vidar, that went a long time toward proving who he was.

The act made me want to keep growing and being better too.

Magnus's phone chimed, and she made a weak effort to climb from under Bragi's arm, instead falling into the bed again with a laughing *oof*.

"What if it's important?" she asked.

"Then they can wait." I wasn't ready for more *important*.

She pouted, and I leaned in to nip at her bottom lip. "What if it's about coffee?" she asked.

I assumed that was a joke. "Why would someone text you about coffee?"

Bragi grabbed her phone and handed it to her. "Haven't you been paying attention?"

"*Knock knock*," Magnus read from the screen. She untangled herself from us with zero effort. "Love you both, but not like I love coffee." She hopped to her feet and got halfway to the door, her bare ass providing a stunning view, before pausing.

"Shirt." I grabbed mine and tossed it to her.

She slipped it on, and did up a few buttons. "Love you more." She blew me a kiss, and walked out of the room.

I put on some trousers. The only thing Bragi had here were the slacks he'd worn to the club, so I tossed him a pair of gray sweats.

He didn't look impressed, but he pulled them on.

We headed into the living room to find Magnus closing her apartment door, and bringing a drink carrier with three coffees, and a paper bag, into her kitchen.

"Magic food. I'm impressed," Bragi said.

Magnus wrinkled her nose and set everything on the bar top. "Psychic sister. Told you that text was important." She handed us each a drink, and opened the bag to reveal an assortment of pastries.

I moved around her to get plates and utensils. "You do realize that pastries aren't actual breakfast." I was going to have to get groceries. Do some refining in the kitchen space. Get set up to cook.

"I do realize you should take that back." Magnus grabbed a plate from me, set a cherry Danish on it, and cut the sweet into three pieces, before taking one for herself.

I looked at Bragi with an unspoken plea to back me up.

He shrugged and took a drink of his coffee. "Nope. If you want to play house, you deal with the consequences."

I didn't mind. In fact, I enjoyed being a part of this. Watching Magnus move around easily with a smile on her face and my shirt hanging halfway down her thighs. Seeing Bragi slotted into this picture as if he'd always been missing, and now he was here.

Tasting fresh, black coffee that Dahlia dropped off because she probably knew we wouldn't be prepared to face the world yet.

This was incredible.

"I hate to bring up reality..." Bragi trailed off when Magnus looked at him with raised brows. "But if I'm staying here—"

"Which you are. You promised," Magnus said.

He nodded. "I did and I am. I need my suitcase. Some clothes."

"You look good in that." Magnus dragged her gaze over him.

"I do. I'm not wearing it for eternity, though."

The longer I stayed here, the more I realized where I'd lived before had barely been more than a way point. A place to shelter and not much more. Still, most of my things were there. "I wouldn't mind stopping by my house either."

Magnus stuffed the rest of her pastry portion in her mouth and washed it down with coffee. "Field trip."

"Indeed." That sounded lovely to me.

We finished eating, and took our time together

in the shower. At least some of that was figuring how to fit three people into the small space. The answer? Creatively.

We went to Bragi's hotel first, so he could dress and check out.

Then he took us to my house.

We arrived in the living room. A familiar space, but not a warm one.

Something occurred to me. "You knew where I was," I said to Bragi. "When Magnus came to you and was injured, when you called me to help her, you knew exactly where to find me."

"Of course I did. I lost me for the longest time, but I never lost track of you."

The sentiment warmed, but, "I did. I lost me, too."

"And now you're both found." Magnus floated off the floor a few inches to drape her arms over both our shoulders. "Grand tour time."

There wasn't much to show off. "My house isn't big."

"Neither's my apartment. I still gave you the tour."

"We're going to need something larger, given this arrangement is long term." Everything I said last night about sticking around forever was amplified by passion, but the sentiment remained. "There's certainly not a lot of room for raising a family."

"I have a hard time picturing us house shopping," Bragi said.

I was sure we'd figure it out. "We don't have to decide every answer to life today. I will give you a tour, though."

It didn't take long to show them around. After, I packed some more clothes, and grabbed some things from my desk.

When I opened one of the drawers, Magnus gasped. "Is that me?" she asked.

It was the woman Bragi and I both had visions of. Who he'd drawn into our lives. I pulled out the picture.

"No," Bragi said before I could answer. "That's a woman who never existed." His answer was enough like what I'd told Magnus before, that it made me smile.

"Okay, well, she looks like me, and it's kind of weird to have a picture of yourselves with someone who isn't real."

"I drew her in a moment of whimsy," Bragi said. "She's not you because you're very real. A creature my imagination was never strong enough to fathom."

We'd have far more whimsical moments in our reality, going forward. With a whisper of a thought, I produced enough flame to ignite the painting in my hand. The ashes floated to the floor.

"Oh." Magnus twisted her mouth. "What's that?

Don't burn that one up." She reached past me to grab another piece of paper from the drawer.

This one was ink, but no color. Another that Bragi drew. A stylized phoenix curled around a book while he read. The picture hadn't meant anything to when I didn't have my memories, especially since only a sketch of a book had been visible when it lay in the drawer. Seeing the full thing now brought back a surge of adoration.

Magnus hovered her fingers over the parchment. "Can we keep it?"

"It's not a puppy," Bragi said.

"Of course you can." It would be wonderful to frame it and find a place to hang it, as well.

Magnus carefully rolled up the image, and slipped her scrunchy around it to secure it.

The next week or so passed in an odd blur of chaos and nothingness. There was always something to do, but none of it was world-ending levels of serious.

Magnus and Dahlia spent a great deal of time trying to figure out how to return the server farm that Vidar had stolen. According to them, it should've been a simple matter of planting the machines back where they came from.

Apparently the magic shielding was preventing them from doing so. It took them almost three days, but I wasn't surprised when they figured it out.

We also visited Kirby and Min, to discuss how to

reach out to the remaining soldiers from TOM. Min knew of a group that helped with deprogramming—helping those raised by the cult of Vidar slide back into a mindset that would let them ease into a life that didn't involve hunting and killing at a god's whim.

Bragi magicked a door in Magnus's apartment that led to her cabin in Wyoming. He joked that it wasn't Narnia, but it was a lot quieter. He could escape to write, and just as important, Magnus could hide from the overload of the world, enhanced by having two powerful beings growing inside her.

Some nights I cooked for the three of us, and other nights we joined Dahlia, Fen, and Frey. We spent a lot of time in NEON. Magnus liked the dancers, and Bragi liked finding a corner where he could captivate an audience with stories.

For the most part, I was content to observe. This wasn't the same cutting myself off from the world that I'd done before. I wasn't sitting in the shadows and hiding. Rather, I was absorbing as much as I could, because every experience showed me something new, and because I would never grow tired of Magnus and Bragi and the company they kept and the lives they led.

Eons ago, I'd dreamed of being surrounded by friends and family and lovers this way, but I'd given up hope. Worse, I'd convinced myself I didn't need the closeness, because losing it was worse than never having it.

I was wrong.

This live with Magnus, with Bragi, with everyone whose lives we brushed against, was the more incredible than I ever could have imagined. I loved them both with all my heart. I wouldn't give up this feeling for anything. In fact, I would have been an idiot to let it go.

CHAPTER 26

BRAGI

We had dinner with Dahlia, Frey, and Fen that night. The tension around having me in the room with everyone had been intense the first few days. There was a faint mistrust now, whenever I was around, like a lingering fish smell days after cooking it, but that lay in the background.

The discomfort was more on my part than anyone's. Moments like this, when there was a group of us sitting around talking and laughing, it frequently struck me that I'd given this up for far too long.

And I was fortunate that the people I loved helped me find my way back.

Some nights the meals were casual, and others they were the finest dining. Tonight, Nico had insisted on cooking, so it was the latter.

"We've been talking," Frey said as we moved from soup to the main course. "The village that should be connected to NEON? Myself and several of the residents believe it's safe to reestablish the gate."

Nico was confused but curious. "A village?"

I'd heard about this, but hadn't ever seen it. It was one of the places Ronan hid people, though that wasn't its only purpose.

"It's a small place where those who need to escape both worlds can live," Frey said. "The are a few ways to enter and leave, in different parts of the world, but I had to sever the gate from NEON when Vidar was a threat, to keep them safe."

"It's not cut off from the world though," Dahlia said. "Rather, it can be. It's this cute little place. But people can come and go like it was any other town."

It did sound lovely.

"There's a house there that's been empty for a while." Frey was struggling with the best way to say whatever came next, because he expected pushback and wasn't going to accept a *no*. "It's big enough to grow in, for a family for instance."

Magnus was touched but embarrassed. "No. We can't." She wasn't going to wait for Nico or me to speak, or even for Frey to finish making the offer, because it was too much of a gift.

Nico's house was barely bigger than Magnus's apartment, and both strained to hold the three of us. Adding two more wouldn't make that better.

Magnus jumped. "Ow. Don't kick me." She glared at Dahlia.

Dahlia glared back. "Never turn down a gift from an immortal who's lived more than a century."

This wasn't lunch, though. It was a house. I felt Magnus's hesitation. Her pride. Her concern.

"This is different," was all she said.

Frey pursed his lips. Magnus had to be feeling the same thing I was—his frustration that she was being so stubborn.

But there were two sides to this coin, and she already felt guilty that she'd taken so much from them.

"The entire town is full of magic families who have lived there for decades or centuries. It's generational. Houses are passed down and around, not sold. This isn't a matter of me handing you a half million-dollar home. This isn't like the world out there." Frey gestured toward the walls. "This has been ours for a long time, because we didn't have anyone to pass it along to. You're family, Magnus. It should be yours."

She was torn, but I understood. This wasn't the kind of gift that was attached to conditions or expectations. For Frey and Fen, this was like passing along a set of China or an old painting.

"Thank you. We love it." I would take the brunt of Magnus's wrath for speaking on her behalf.

Though, I felt her relief at not having to delve into the topic further.

Frey smiled. "That's settled. I was thinking we'd recreate the gate after dinner."

Dahlia clapped. "It'll be so good to have it back." She nudged Magnus's hand with hers. "Hot springs."

"Yeah, okay." Magnus cracked a smile.

Despite her reluctance to accept what she saw as a massive gift, Magnus was pulled into a conversation with Dahlia about where the babies' room would be and how they would decorate it. It seemed they were both familiar with the house layout.

The conversation was so *normal* compared to what I was used to hearing from them. In a way I missed the weirdness and sass, but I was also happy to see this was an option for them now. For all of us.

After dinner, the six of us headed to a blank spot in the wall, at the end of one of the hallways leading out of NEON. With a touch from Frey, the illusion hiding a door vanished.

The air crackled with magic as he and Dahlia clasped their hands together, closed their eyes, and worked silently.

A moment later, Frey pronounced the work done, and opened the door.

Sure enough, on the other side was a small town that looked like it was frozen in time. It could have been taken from a modern painting of a quaint little village, or a historical record.

The house in question was a few blocks away from Main Street, and there was plenty of room to grow as a family. There was also a grandfather clock in the front hallway that would make a great replacement door to get to the cabin.

Moving in was easy, given that most of us were capable of blinking items from one place to another with no effort. By the following afternoon, Magnus, Nico, and I were settled in our new home.

A few days after we got settled, Magnus announced she was going to visit Tatiana and return her bracelet. She warned us she'd probably be gone most of he day.

She was hiding something from me about the visit, but it was something that made her giddy. I was curious to see what it was when she came back.

To be fair, I was hiding something too.

When she was gone, I grabbed Nico. "We may only have four or five hours, but we can get a lot done in that amount of time."

"A lot of what?" Nico asked.

"To get a start on the nursery." I'd been paying attention when Magnus and Dahlia discussed ideas, and I knew which ones resonated strongest with Magnus.

Though, there were some things I would wait to buy until she could be there, like most of the furniture.

Nico nodded. "Let's go."

The room itself was already empty, and the hardwood floor didn't need to be replaced. Covering it would be a good idea, though. It didn't matter if someone was impervious to the harm caused by temperatures—walking on cold floors still sucked in the winter.

Nico and I flitted around the world for an hour or so, picking up paint, a rug, and a rocking chair.

"That's the fastest I've ever seen you shop," Nico teased me.

I smiled at the jab as much as at the ease with which it came. "Trust me, it's killing me to not take more time. Tight schedule and all that."

We laid down plastic sheeting and taped everything up, then set to work painting. Dusty rose.

I also intended to paint murals on the walls, but the paint needed to be dry for that. I had already sketched out my ideas though, on large sheets of paper, and Nico helped me hang those from the ceiling, just a few inches from the wall.

Last was pulling up the drop cloths and laying out the rug. When we were done, Nico and I stepped outside the room to admire what we could see of our work.

"I cannot believe this is us," Nico said.

"Which part of it?"

"Fathers. Lovers. This life."

"I know what you mean." How long would it take until everything about this situation felt real?

As long as I held onto it regardless, there was time.

Nico slipped his hand into mine. "It's amazing."

I gave him a squeeze. "It really is."

Magnus returned a few hours later, beaming and brimming with excitement. She wanted to share her secret.

I wanted to share too, but our surprise could wait. "How did it go?"

"Perfect. Better than perfect." She shifted her weight from one foot to the other, and bit her bottom lip.

"You should tell us whatever you're dying to tell us." Even Nico could see her excitement.

Her grin grew broader, and she unbuttoned her shirt.

What kind of surprise was this? One of my favorite kinds? That wasn't the feeling she radiated, but...

She slipped the shirt off her shoulders, leaving her in a sports bra, but that wasn't what drew my eye.

Around her neck, on her shoulders and leading up to her collarbone, was an intricate design in black ink.

I joined her in the middle of the living room, for a closer look. "That's the art you found at Nico's."

"It's different though." Nico was on her other side, examining it.

"I had her add a few new elements," Magnus said.

There was a dragon on the cover of the book. A shield behind the phoenix. "It looks incredible."

"It's not done. I have to go back and get it colored in."

Nico hovered his fingers over the ink, not touching the design. "I thought you were done with magical filters."

"This one is different," Magnus said. "It collects the little wisps of energy that escape from me, because apparently I'm leaking power all the time, and the tattoo uses that magic to protect the people I love."

"It's brilliant and beautiful, like you." Nico kissed her shoulder.

A blush spread across Magnus's cheeks. "Now it's your turn. Tell me your secret."

"This way." We led her into the babies' room.

She paused in the doorway with a gasp. "What... I love it. The art. Is that chibi Chewbacca?"

"It is." I crossed the room to tug one of the giant sketches down, and reveal the walls. "I'll draw it in once the paint dries."

Magnus clapped. "It's perfect. It's wonderful. Thank you." She threw her arms around my neck and gave me a long kiss, before gifting Nico with the same. "I love it. I love both of you."

I would never get tired of hearing that.

For so long, I thought I'd lost any chance at happiness, and I deserved it.

This though... The things that waited for us and the love the future held... I couldn't wait to be a part of it with these two amazing beings.

EPILOGUE

FOUR MONTHS LATER

DAHLIA

Keeping secrets was impossible around Magnus these days. But I had one that I needed her to not ask about, and I'd enlisted Tatiana's help.

Tatiana had given me a charm that would shield any emotions around the fact that we were planning a baby shower for Magnus.

Frey was happy to host the event at NEON during the day. Tatiana and I decided no stupid games, and that we had to invite a bunch of people. Kirby and Brit. Sylith of course, and all of the other

Valkyries. Not that there were a lot, but they should all be there.

And I was currently on my way to invite Maeve.

I was so freaking excited I might wet myself.

Magnus had been seeing her for regular check-ups, since Maeve was her midwife, but Maeve had asked her to come alone each time, because it made it easier to see which magic belonged to Magnus and the children.

I was going to visit Maeve tonight, though. I had done everything by the book, according to Fen and Frey, because I didn't want to piss her off.

Okay, sure, I wasn't always the best at respecting the customs of ancient beings, but Maeve was different. So a couple of hours ago, I'd started driving. I'd parked at the edge of the magical circle. Found the lamp, and used it to light my way to her door.

Which I was knocking on now.

The woman who opened the door looked surprised to see me. "What can I do for you, dragon?"

I just needed to play it cool. Bow. Be polite. Defer to my elders.

Damn it.

"First of all, I apologize, but I have to get this out of the way. *I can't believe it's actually you.*" I squealed.

Maeve didn't do a great job of hiding her smile as she opened the door wider. "Come in, please."

"Growing up, all my favorite stories were about

you." Apparently I wasn't done gushing. "And then I found out you were still around, and—Sorry, that was rude. I don't want to be rude. You're so amazing, and with everything you've done for my sister... I can't believe I'm meeting you."

"Who's your sister?"

I forgot the important details again. *Oops.* I pulled my backpack from my shoulder, set it on the ground, and knelt next to it. "She's why I'm here. She's not my sister by blood." I took out a thermos of coffee, courtesy of Tatiana's family recipe, and left-over cannoli made by Nico, plus two of his fresh mince and cheese pies.

"You're Dahlia."

She knew me. Fangirl moment. "How did you guess?"

"I recognize the food. You didn't need to bring me an offering." She was so nice and pretty.

I should stop swooning. "I did need to, though. It's the polite thing to do, and I'm here to ask for something. Come to Magnus's baby shower? Please? If safety is a concern, it'll be in NEON, which is safe, you have my word."

Maeve chuckled. "What does Artura think of you? Or Urd?"

"We're not fans of each other. We're learning, though."

"It's been a long time since some of us have learned anything, it seems fate has given us good teachers. Come in the kitchen. Enjoy the meal with me."

I was being invited to dine with Maeve? Did I have to follow fae rules? She was an elf now, and it was food I brought. Did that apply?

Fuck.

The phone on her wall rang, and she excused herself to answer.

It was impossible to not eavesdrop, since I was only a few meters away.

"Now?" She said. "We'll be there shortly." She disconnected and turned to me again. "Magnus is going into labor." She grabbed a bag from a nearby closet, and a small satchel.

Magnus was having her babies? Now?

That was way more exciting than this.

MAGNUS

Whichever creator decided that giving birth to immortal children should be the same or worse than human childbirth—at least as painful and exhausting—must have been almost as big a dick as Vidar.

His name still made me ill, but I was working on getting over it.

Most of the time. Right now, I was exhausted

and didn't have a choice but to not do anything else. I was lying in bed, trying to shrug off having pushed two lives out of my body.

Maeve had taken Bragi and Nico to give the babies their first bath, and to let me rest.

The silence in here was incredible. Almost unbelievable. The tattoo from Tatiana had quickly bled off the excess magic of hosting two other lives, and it was quiet in my head for the first time in months. Not quiet except for a whisper. Not me having to focus to keep the external feelings out.

It was. Just. Quiet.

The silence was disconcerting and amazing.

I was only pregnant for six months Maeve warned me this might happen, and told me it was hard to gauge how long magical pregnancies would last. Sometimes they were a day long, and other times they went on for years.

If anyone could hear my prayer, I wanted to thank them that I fell on the shorter end of the spectrum, not the longer one.

There was a quiet knock, and I called, "come in."

Maeve stepped into the room, with Nico and Bragi following, each of the men carrying a baby.

The one Bragi held had a shock of bright red hair. So much hair for a newborn.

I'd asked both Maeve and Nico if I needed to worry about accidental fires from the baby with phoenix powers. They both assured me it was possible, but not likely.

Maeve helped me sit up and propped me up with pillows.

Bragi handed me the first child.

This was such a tiny, precious life. It didn't matter that I'd been thinking about this moment for months, it didn't feel real now that it was here. How was I supposed to care for these little souls?

Nico handed me the other one, and a sense of calm settled over me. We'd figure it out together.

This boy was pale, with bright green eyes.

"Don't babies usually have blue eyes?" I asked.

"Human babies, yes." Maeve pulled a satchel from her pocket. "This is my gift to you. To your children. To your family." She set it on the nightstand.

"What is it?" I asked.

"The salve you need for the stream. The food. And the cord that ties the bag will serve as the clothing. You can make any wish you want."

"Thank you." It was an incredible gift, and I wouldn't refuse it. But I wouldn't use it, either. I was done wishing for things or relying on magic's interpretation of what I needed o get done. "Thank you for everything."

Maeve kissed me on the cheek. "Blessings to you." She kissed each of the children on the forehead. "And to them. I'll check back tomorrow, and you know how to reach me if you need me. When you're ready, your friends can come in."

Maeve vanished from the room.

My emotions were all over the place. I wanted to laugh and cry and collapse. And the greatest thing about it was that they were *my* emotions.

I gave Nico a nod, and he opened the bedroom door.

Dahlia rushed into the room. Frey and Fen followed at a more sedate pace.

Dahlia pushed Bragi out of the way to get to me. She was cautious with the hug, and spend several minutes oohing and ahhing over how adorable the new arrivals were.

"Welcome to the world, Birdie and Bard," She said.

I laughed at the names. "You know that's not what we're calling them. The redhead is Enna and the green-eyed baby is Osheen."

Dahlia wrinkled her nose. "Birdie and Bard."

Even if I argued it, the nicknames would probably stick.

And I was fine with that. In fact, at this moment I loved the entire world. I was filled with warm fuzzies and love for everyone in my life. For life itself.

This was incredible, and I wouldn't trade it for anything.

～

THANK you for reading the stories of these wonderful characters. Magnus, Bragi, and Nico. Dahlia, Frey, and Fen.

If you'd like more stories in this Legacy world, fate has more in store for other new Valkyries and dragons, in the multi-author Valkyries Rising series, starting with VALKYRIE DESTINED. Her entire life, Azzie's been told she's destined for greatness. The price is to take the life of the man she's falling for. She refuses, but destiny doesn't like being denied.